ALL
Full Tilt Duet, Book II
IN

Emma Scott

Copyright © 2016 Emma Scott

All rights reserved

Cover art by Letitia Hasser, RBA Designs

Interior art by Melissa Panio-Petersen

Interior formatting by That Formatting Lady

No part of this eBook may be reproduced or transmitted in any form or by any means, electronic or mechanical, including photocopying, recording or by any information storage and retrieval system, without written permission from the author.

This is a work of fiction. Any names or characters, businesses or places, events or incidents, are fictitious or have been used in a fictitious manner. Any resemblance to actual persons, living or dead, or actual events is purely coincidental.

ACKNOWLEDGMENTS

I'd like to extend a huge thank you to the following people for their support, love, and for their solidarity for me in my endeavors. Each and every one of you had a hand in bringing this book to life.

Melissa Panio-Petersen, Angela Bonnie Shockley, Joy Kriebel-Sadowski, Ashley Drew, Jennifer Balogh, Noemie Heloin, Elaine Glynn, and Kathleen Ripley. It takes a village to raise a kid, they say. It also takes one to write a book, and you ladies are my tribe. Love you all.

To Robin Hill, for everything, everything. There are no words to thank you for what you've done for me. None. And I say this as a *writer* who should have plenty. With much love and gratitude.

To my husband, Bill, for your incredible support, for taking the kids to give me time to write, and for believing in me, always. I will love you forever.

To my readers, the bloggers, and my friends in this wonderful community, without whom I could not do this, nor would I want to. I give my characters a voice, but without you, they could never be heard. Thank you.

And to my editor, Suanne Laqueur. For you, so much. For keeping the compass north. For love and bravery. You are a universe, *it is certain.*

DEDICATION

For Desiree, who holds these characters in her heart and keeps them safe for me,
and
for Tom, the little brother of the family, and the rock I set my back to.

PLAYLIST

Way Down We Go, Kaleo
Like a River, Bishop
Unsteady, X Ambassadors
Love is a Losing Game, Amy Winehouse
Everything I Do, Bryan Adams
Arsonist's Lullaby, Hozier
Lil Darlin, ZZ Ward
Love in the Dark, Adele
What a Wonderful World, Louis Armstrong

ALL IN

Full Tilt Duet, Book II

Full tilt (n): 1. with maximum energy or force; at top speed.

PART I

PROLOGUE

Theo

"Theo, dear. He wants you."

Kacey's soft hand tightened in mine. I looked at my brother's girlfriend, who gave a wan, reassuring smile. Another squeeze of her hand, then I somehow found the will to stand up.

My mother smiled weakly, hanging on Dad's arm in the hall outside Jonah's hospital room. She looked so lost and broken. Frail. Dad looked grim but stoic, holding Mom up. But Jonah was the glue in our family. Without him, we were going to fall apart. It was only a matter of time.

It was time now to say goodbye to my brother. As I walked toward the door of his room, a carousel of images circled my head, each faded with time, as if they'd sat out in the bright sun too long. Jonah and me feeding a goat at the state fair. Jonah and me in swim lessons together. In our Little League uniforms. Walking high school hallways where Jonah was effortlessly popular and I was his wingman. Visiting Jonah at UNLV, then at Carnegie-Mellon. Swimming with Jonah in Venezuela.

Where he got sick… and I didn't.

I pushed the door shut and moved to where Jonah lay dying. A thin, pale version of the healthy guy in my mind's photo album.

"Theo…"

My brother. Struggling to breath. Struggling to hold on. While I was still strong—strong and ready to tear down the walls of this goddamn place, to set the whole fucking world on fire at the unfairness of it all.

Still not strong enough to walk over to his bed and say goodbye.

Jonah managed a weak smile. "That bad, huh?"

"You've looked worse," I said, finally moving into the room and taking a seat beside his bed.

"Bite me." His chuckle was a horrible-sounding wheeze. His hand twitched on the blankets. He didn't even have the strength to lift it. I reached to clasp it, wrapping my fingers around his.

Jonah's smile faded and his eyes—still sharp—met mine. "I'm worried…about Mom." His heart could only pump enough air for two or three words at a time, squeezing them out between shallow intakes of breath.

"I'll take care of her," I said.

"And Dad… He'll come around…about your shop. I…believe in you."

I doubted our father would ever support my work as a tattoo artist, but at that moment, Jonah's *I believe in you* was all I needed.

"Now," Jonah said, his gaze intent. "The favor…I want from you… Remember?"

I sat forward in the chair. "Name it."

"Kacey…"

My voice stuck in my throat. I coughed it free. "What about her?"

"You love her."

The words were weak and soft, yet each one struck my chest like a hammer. I couldn't speak, couldn't move, could hardly blink. I was on fire, a million different emotions boiling in my guts, stealing my air, choking my words.

Despite keeping everything buried, deep down where it could never see the light of day and betray my brother… He saw everything. He always had.

He smiled at my paralyzed expression. "I'm glad, T. I'm so…*relieved*…it's you."

I almost found my voice to tell him it wasn't me. I wasn't anything. What the hell did I know about love? Not a damn thing. And he was wrong anyway.

She'll never love me because she loves only you. Which is how it should be.

"The favor..." Jonah's gaze bored into mine with all the strength his failing body lacked. "Take care of Kacey. Please. She'll need you. She's strong. But if she falls, help her... Love her, Theo. This life is...short. Don't hold back. Okay?"

I nodded. Only because he needed me to. Not because I had any fucking clue how to do what he was asking of me.

Jonah eased a sigh of relief. He was beyond exhausted and had yet to see Kacey, to say goodbye to the love of his life. I couldn't waste their time.

It was time now.

I clenched my jaw hard against the tears but they came anyway.

Say it. It's now or never. You'll never have this chance again.

"I love you," I said through gritted teeth.

"Me too," Jonah said, his voice so weak and thin. "Love you, T. Always will."

The grief slammed into me, pressed me down. I buried my face in the crook of my arm, battling it back. I had to be strong. For Mom and Dad, and for Kacey. For Jonah who had given me a job to do.

"I'll get Kacey," I said, wiping my eyes.

I planted my feet and tried to rise, but could only get halfway out of the chair. Still clasping Jonah's hand, I leaned to put my forehead to his, to hold him close to me one last time.

My brother...

Jonah sighed my name.

"I'll take care of her," I said, my voice cracking. "I swear."

It was half the promise, but the half I could keep.

I'm not going to be able to walk out of here.

But I did. I left my brother's room and leaned against the wall outside his door, feeling like I was on a ship tossed at sea.

That was it. The last time I'll ever see him or talk to him...I'll never talk to my brother again. Never hear his voice, his words...

And his last words. *Love her...*

My eyes sought Kacey in the waiting area; something to grab on to. Something real. She'd fallen out of the goddamn sky like a bomb, blowing up our careful life, smashing routines and disrupting Jonah's plans. First I was scared she'd leave him, and when it was clear she wasn't going to, I was scared her staying would hurt Jonah too much. He'd have to say goodbye after only a handful of weeks together.

Kacey walked toward Jonah's room. Her stride graceful, her face wracked by grief, but burning with love at the same time.

She filled up my eyes as Jonah's dying wish echoed in my ear. I had one short, selfish, miserable second of hope…

Then I squashed it flat. Killed it.

Sorry, bro. She's yours, and she'll be yours to the end of time.

But I could take care of her. Black days were coming. Weeks, months. Possibly years. However long she needed me, I'd be there for her.

One month after the funeral, I got a call from my mother.

"Theo dear, there's no answer at Kacey's. I've been calling for two days now." Her voice crackled with panic over the phone. She couldn't take another hit. Neither could I.

I called Kacey. An automated message said her cellphone was no longer in service.

I called the Luxor, where she'd managed to get hired after quitting Caesar's. They said she hadn't been in for three days.

I went to her place and banged on the door. No answer. I banged harder and her elderly neighbor came out.

"She's gone, young man," the lady said, annoyed. "Didn't you see? Her car's not here."

"When did she leave?"

The woman narrowed her eyes at me, sizing me up. "Two nights ago. Like she was sneaking out, stealing her own things. Nervous."

My heart's pulse slowed to a heavy clang of dread. "She took stuff with her?"

"Boxes. Suitcases." The woman ran her hands down her flowered housedress. "And these strange glass bottles with cords coming out of them. Don't know what on earth—"

"Lamps," I said dully. "They were lamps made from old whiskey bottles."

"If you say so."

I rubbed the stubble along my jaw. The tension had seeped out of my body, the grief now seeping back in.

"She left a letter with me," the neighbor said. "Asked that I only give it to Beverly, Teddy, or Henry Fletcher." The woman peered at me. "Are you one of those?"

"I'm Theo Fletcher." I cleared my throat. "She calls me Teddy. Called. Calls."

"Hold on." The woman went into her place and came back out with a piece of paper folded in half. My eyes scanned over the words:

I can't stay here. I tried but it's too much. I love you all. I'm sorry.
Kacey

The note fell from my hand like a dead leaf, rocking through the air to land at my feet. The neighbor said something softly and retreated into her apartment. I stood alone on the walkway, staring at Kacey's door.

I'm sorry, Jonah, I thought, the words blasting louder and louder with every beat of my heart.

I had one job here. Not even. Half a job. And I'd failed.

CHAPTER 1

Theo

Six months after the funeral…

The alarm blared at six a.m. I snaked out my hand and shut it off. For a few seconds, I was good. Everything was all right. Then I remembered Jonah was gone and the rest of the day sledgehammered into my chest.

I sucked in a breath and stared at the ceiling until the first wave passed, then immediately threw off the covers. The best part of my day was those first three seconds. Then I had to immediately get up, get ahead of it. Keep moving, otherwise I'd lie in bed all day like an ass, pissing and moaning over what I couldn't change. Get up, shake it out of the covers and kick it under the bed.

A small voice inside whispered I'd better clean that shit out and fucking deal with it before I exploded.

I *was* dealing. I was getting up. Going to work. Doing my goddamn best.

My gym clothes were waiting at the foot of the bed where I'd set them the night before. I dressed, hit the kitchen for some water and a protein bar. The morning sun glinted off the glass paperweights on the windowsill, all Jonah's creations. One had a sea life scene inside. The sunlight cutting through the glass made it look alive. It was Kacey's favorite. She once told me she thought it looked quiet inside the glass. Peaceful. The watery composition made her feel safe when she woke up the first time on Jonah's couch.

I looked inside the sphere and felt suffocated. Trapped. Immobile, like the sea life.

In my truck on the way to the gym, I passed Jonah's old place, then Kacey's three blocks later. Both empty now. Except for Jonah's glass paperweights sitting on my windowsill and a handwritten note, everything belonging to them was in a storage unit at the north end of town.

Idling at a red light, my thoughts returned to her four scribbled lines, mulling over them like song lyrics. Followed by the chorus: *I failed Jonah…*

A honk from behind jolted me: the red light was green. I hit the gas, tires screeching, then eased off and forced myself to chill the fuck out before I got in a wreck.

At the gym, I lifted and pressed until my arm muscles were screaming and the sweat poured down my face. I did sit-ups until I thought I'd puke, then set a bar over my shoulders and did squats until my legs were shaking.

I worked out for two solid hours, trying to sweat out the feelings buried in my guts. It left me exhausted and wanting more sleep—I didn't get much these days—but rest wasn't part of my routine.

I showered, dressed in jeans and a T-shirt, and went back to my place to cook up some lunch. I sat at my kitchen counter, the *Small Business Management* textbook open. An enormous fried egg, bacon, and tomato sandwich on my left, my laptop on my right. I had midterms coming up and the payroll tax stuff was giving me grief.

Three hours of solid study made me feel a little better. About my tests anyway. I closed up my textbooks and laptop, and hid them away in a drawer in case Oscar and Dena dropped by. They always asked a million fucking questions about me going to back to UNLV for an MBA degree, and I didn't want to talk about it. It was stupid anyway. As if a dumb degree could make anything better.

My cell phone rang as I started to head out for work at Vegas Ink, my mother's number on the display. Right on time.

"Hey, Ma."

"Hello, darling. I'm sorry to bother you."

"You're not bothering me, Ma. You never are."

"I just wanted to see how you're doing."

She called every day. Rarely with any real purpose or news to impart, usually just to touch base with the only son she had left. When I saw her in person, she literally touched base: her hand floating toward me whenever I was in reach. I couldn't blame her—I did the same to Jonah every day after his CAV diagnosis.

"Dear?"

I jerked out of my thoughts. "Sorry, Ma. What was that?"

"I was asking if you'd heard from Kacey?"

"Still nothing. I'm sure she's fine," I added, like I would fucking know after I let her slip away.

You had one job here. Half a job.

"I wish she'd at least call," Mom said with false lightness, "I wonder where she's gone off to?"

I rubbed my hand over the dull ache in my chest. "I have to get to work, Ma. If I hear anything from Kacey, I'll let you know."

"All right, dear."

Realizing I was barely giving her sixty seconds of my time, I asked, "What are you and Dad up to?"

"Oh, nothing much," she said. God, if she didn't always sound like she was perpetually on the verge of tears. "We'd like to have you, Oscar, and Dena over for dinner Sunday."

"Sure, sounds good," I said, gritting my teeth. Once a month or so we rallied together, mostly because we felt we should. Our duty to old memories and better times.

It sucked.

The dinners were torture, filled with stilted, stiff conversation, haunted by Kacey's laughter and Jonah's voice. No matter how loud we tried to talk or laugh over it, their love affair lingered like the light from one of Jonah's glass lamps. Not even Oscar could lighten the mood. His gigantic personality had been tamped down and Dena's smile was heavy now.

My mother still cooked, but often she let pots boil over while she stared into space. She'd lost weight. So had Dad. His eyes followed my mother constantly, but rarely looked at me. He hardly spoke to me, either. We'd never been close, but Jonah always bridged our gap. Without him, an abyss lay between me and my father. A distance neither of us made an effort to close.

Goddammit, Jonah, come back and fix all this because I fucking can't.

"I'll let Oscar and Dena know," I told my mom. My glance flickered to the front door, the car keys jangling in my hand.

"How are your studies going?"

"Fine. Big tests coming up."

"I'm so proud of you, Theo. I think it's wonderful what you're doing. In another year, when you have your degree, just think of what doors will open for you."

"Thanks, Ma," I said, trying not to sound as irritated as I felt.

Mom's pride in me sounded good on the surface, but she wasn't entirely sold on me opening up a tattoo shop either. She was more supportive than Dad by a mile, but I didn't hold any illusions she was eager to see me spend the money Jonah willed me on a place with loud music and 'colorful characters', where I'd draw flaming skulls and roses all day long.

"Oh, Theo dear, would you mind stopping by the store this afternoon? I'm out of milk and eggs."

I clenched my jaw. I couldn't go after work or I'd never make it to class on time. I'd have to go now, swing by my parents' house, then go to work. Late.

"Dad's working again today?" I asked tightly.

"Yes." She sighed. "You know how he is lately."

"Yeah, I know." I rubbed my hands over my eyes. "I'll hit the store before work. Be there in thirty."

"Thank you, dear. You take such good care of me."

"I gotta go, Ma. I'll see you in a few."

"Wonderful, dear. And Theo?"

"Yeah?"

"If Kacey calls, tell her I'm not angry with her. Tell her… Tell her I'd just like to know she's okay."

"Sure, Ma."

I hung up and stared at the screen a long time, willing it to ring again, to light up with Kacey's number so I could hear her voice. I only wanted what my mother wanted: to know Kacey was okay.

Vegas Ink was busy that day. Our small waiting area had two chicks poring over a three-ringed binder of art, and another guy leaning against the wall. It was Edgar's day to pick music, so the buzz of tattoo machines was barely audible under pounding death metal music.

Vivian, our receptionist, gave me an arch look as I rushed in.

"You're late."

"Sorry, Viv," I said, checking over her book for the day's appointments. "Don't tell Gus."

"I never do, but he's heard the complaints, honey."

I shrugged. Nothing I could do about it. My mother, although perfectly capable of doing things on her own, had retreated into herself. Like a kid who'd been burned, she hardly stuck her hand out anymore. And Dad had thrown himself back into work as if he were a first-time city councilman instead of a thirty-year incumbent on the verge of retirement.

Someone had to take care of my mom. But sometimes, like today, I knew I had too many balls in the air. My arms were getting tired and sooner or later I was going to start dropping them. Gus, the owner of Vegas Ink, firing me for being late all the time would be the first to smash to the floor.

"These two are waiting for you." Vivian nodded her completely shaved head in the direction of the two young women. The expression on her heavily-pierced face was knowing. "New clients. Both asked for you, personal."

I shrugged. "Referral."

"Mmhm." Viv raked her eyes up and down my black t-shirt and jeans. "Word must've gotten out about your impressive body…of work."

I rolled my eyes as I closed the appointment ledger. I was booked straight through to six o'clock.

"Oh come on, it was a little funny," Viv said, leaning over the desk, toying with a pen in her ringed fingers. Tattoos covered every inch of skin up to her neck and creeped up the back of her skull. She gave one of my biceps a squeeze. "And true. Someone's been hitting the gym harder than usual. I'm not the only one who's noticed."

Viv rubbed her chin on her shoulder, putting her gaze in line with one of the shop's other artists, Zelda Rossi. The small woman was bent over a client, tattoo gun in hand. Long black hair fell like a curtain to shield her face. She raised her head as she wiped the blood welling up from her client's shoulder blade. Her large, green eyes—rimmed in black—met mine. A smile started to break over her face. She caught it under her teeth, stuck her tongue out, and went back to work.

Viv smirked. "Must be so tough to have so many women throwing themselves at you."

"Can't complain," I said with a smug grin. "Give me a minute then send my first appointment in."

"Sure thing, babydoll."

Vegas Ink was a small, cramped hole-in-the-wall. The bright red paint and black-and-white checkered floor only made it feel smaller. My place would be different. Darker colors, older furniture and art on the walls from funky, fringe artists like Edward Gorey and Ann Harper. A living room in a haunted house.

My place…

Jonah gave me the money to open a shop, and I was taking business classes to make sure I didn't fuck it up. Even so, the thought of actually pulling the trigger and buying a place made me sick to my stomach. If I failed, I'd have nothing left of Jonah. He sold his glass so I could have my dream, but what if it went under? What if no one showed up? I'd already lost Kacey. One broken promise. I couldn't take another fucking failure.

Edgar, a huge, hulking guy with a Tool concert shirt stretched over his bulk, looked up from his client and gave me a nod. "Hey, T. What's shakin', man?"

"Same old, same old," I said, preparing my gun and rags from the second drawer in the armoire. When my first client told me what she wanted, I'd set up the ink and choose the needles.

"You want to hang tonight? Me and some friends are going to see Killroy at the Pony Club."

I flinched, covered it up with a cough. "Nah, I'm busy."

"Hot date?" Edgar wagged his brow at me as his client used a hand mirror to inspect the new dragon curling around his calf.

"Yep," I said. Out the corner of my eye, I saw Zelda glance my way, then bend over her work again.

Edgar chuckled. "Don't tell me. It's the redhead you had in here last week. Rose and dagger, right ankle?"

"Maybe."

Edgar let out a whoop. "You're a whore, Fletcher. Don't ever change."

The two women from the waiting area approached my station. The blonde took a seat in the chair, her friend beside her to hold her hand. They were both hot, both flirted with me as if their lives depended on it. I did my best to reciprocate because Edgar was watching.

Twenty minutes later, the blonde got up from my chair with *Stay true to yourself* delicately scrawled across the inside of her wrist. She and her friend invited me to a party.

"Yeah, maybe I'll stop by," I said, and waited with mounting irritation as they giggled and insisted I get out my phone to take down their number and address. I pretended to punch the girl's number into a new contact with my thumb, then slipped my phone back into the back pocket of my jeans.

"Hope you can make it," the blonde tossed over her shoulder as the two left.

When they were gone, Edgar laughed and shook his head. "I thought you had a date tonight?"

I shrugged. "I'll take her with me to the party."

He laughed a great bellowing laugh. "You're my hero, T."

No, I'm a lying asshole.

Ages ago, I would've dialed that phone number the minute I got out of work, and probably gotten little sleep that night. Now, a smoking hot blonde and her friend were no more interesting than a weather report. But letting everyone think I went out with a different woman every night was better than the truth. That since I heard Kacey sing around a campfire all those months ago, I was a lost cause.

I finished out the day, and as we cleaned up our workspaces, Edgar jerked his chin at me.

"Enjoy your date with the redhead," he said. "Or the blonde. Or the redhead *and* the blonde. I want a full report tomorrow."

"You'll get it," I said, shrugging into my leather jacket. "If they don't wear me out."

Edgar laughed and Zelda flinched. I smiled at her with a small shake of my head, trying to signal this was all bullshit. I'd heard she had a crush on me since she started working here a year ago. It didn't suck to look at her, but I didn't date coworkers. Too messy if things go sour, and with me and women, they always did.

"Have a good night, Z," I said.

"You too, T," she replied. She looked up then, flashed me dry smile. "Slut."

Edgar and I laughed, and the second my back was turned, the smile started teetering on the edge of my face. When I stepped outside the tattoo shop, it dropped like a mask and shattered on the sidewalk.

At the Lee Business School at UNLV, I listened to the professor go on about payroll tax and employer ID numbers. I wasn't lost. I got it. The data made sense to me and I almost felt sort of proud. Like I was getting something *done.*

"I'll remind you again," Professor Hadden said from behind her lectern. "This midterm exam is worth forty-five percent of your final grade. You cannot—and will not—pass this class if you miss it or fail it. Arrange to consult with me if you feel either of those scenarios is a possibility."

My pace to the parking lot was a small victory lap. I wasn't going to miss or fail. No chance.

My phone chimed with a text from Oscar.

Want to meet up tonight? I don't miss you but Dena does.

I chuckled at the backhanded offer. It had been a long time since I'd hung out with my friends. They were Jonah's friends first and foremost—his best friends—and hanging out with them had the same quality as having dinner at my parents' place. Ghosts of other times hovered everywhere like shadows in the periphery.

I tapped back, **Can't. Have a date.**

Should've guessed, Oscar replied. **Try for next week?**

Sure.

How easy it'd become to lie. Lie to my coworkers, lie to my friends. It hardly bothered me anymore.

We'd all drifted apart after Jonah. He was the center of our goddamn universe and without him, we were starting to lose whatever pull it was that kept us in the same orbit. Oscar and Dena tried. My mom tried. But I couldn't muster the energy to smile and laugh and bullshit my way through small talk. It took too much effort to keep the grief in check. Grief of losing Jonah, then Kacey.

I drove my truck out of the university parking lot, down side streets running parallel to the Strip. Taking back roads to the Wynn Hotel and Casino. I parked and knocked on the service entrance door.

All the security guards knew me. Wilson was on duty tonight.

"Evening, Theo," he said, waving me in.

"Hey, Wilson."

I traversed the back passages and innards of the hotel, down a corridor of cement and bright fluorescent light. Eyes in the sky watched me, but their gaze was benevolent. Nobody would question me. Eme Takamura, the gallery curator, had seen to that.

Three right turns, one left, and I pushed open a heavy door, emerging near the elevators on the first floor. I slipped down the hallway across from the clanging casino that never closed.

Paulie was standing guard over the locked doors of the Galleria. He'd shooed away the last visitors hours ago.

"How's it going, T?" he asked, punching in a key code. The red light flashed to green.

"Can't complain," I said. "Thanks, man."

He smiled, his smooth dark skin and white mustache rising in a small, sad smile. He pushed open the door and held it for me. "Have a good night."

I nodded and stepped into the gallery.

After the funeral, I came here every night religiously. Then every other night. Lately I'd been holding steady at three or four times a week. When I had a shitty day, or when I missed Jonah too damn much, I came here.

Jonah's individual glass pieces were long gone, all sold and now living in a hundred different people's houses. The long end of the L-shaped gallery was now lined with sculptures, the work of some local up-and-coming. I didn't spare them a glance. I rounded the corner to the short leg of the L. Here Jonah's installation, a permanent fixture, rose up like a tidal wave on the far wall. The sun, always shining and vivid, beat down on waves and sea life that seemed ready to move at any moment.

I took my usual seat on the bench opposite, and leaned back against the wall. I crossed my arms over my chest and took in Jonah's glass. The installation was perfect. Flawless. Like Jonah had been in my mind's eye—the idol big brother who could do no wrong to his little brother who'd worshipped the ground he'd walked on.

I squeezed my eyes shut against the perfection. I knew if Jonah were here, he'd tell me it wasn't my fault. He'd say Kacey was an adult who could make her own decisions.

Sometimes I believed him. Sometimes the gallery was my sanctuary, the cathedral of glass where I found peace. The same serenity Kacey discovered in Jonah's glass paperweights.

Sometimes.

Tonight, there was no peace. I'd made my brother a promise and failed to keep it.

I forced myself to open my eyes and look at Jonah's masterpiece. The brilliant colors blurred in my unblinking gaze. The blue of the sea poured down from ceiling to spill over the floor. I could smell the salt, feel the cold water against my skin and the sting of salt water in my eyes like tears. An ocean of never-ending tears.

CHAPTER 2

Kacey

"This song is from my album, *Shattered Glass*. It's called 'The Lighthouse.' I hope you like it."

The audience at Le Chacal clapped and whistled their approval. Murmured conversations ended. A few clinks of ice in a glass and then the little jazz club went silent. Waiting.

Honestly, I didn't give a shit if the audience liked the song or not. It just sounded like something I should say. I believed in it more than *This song is from my album.*

My album. Big fucking deal. Me and my *album*. As if it were a tangible object—a packaged CD or even digital files—instead of twelve songs I scratched into a notebook and slapped against some music. I sold my songs onstage and called it an album. People paid a cover to get into the club, I got a cut. Four different clubs, four nights a week. And since I packed every house of those four clubs, it was good money. Good enough to keep to a routine. *I* had a routine now.

I adjusted my guitar and nearly knocked over the mic stand. The floor was spinning lazily beneath the stool I sat on, and the stage lights hurt. Big fuzzy blobs of light to sear my eyes. The audience beyond was a blur of faces. I closed my eyes. I didn't need to see anyway. My fingers found the frets, my right hand strummed the strings, and a song came out.

Routine.

My body knew what to do and it seemed no matter how drunk I was, it would always remember. Muscle memory, or maybe something more. Maybe when a song lives this deep in you, it becomes part of you. I hit every note and sang every word of 'The Lighthouse' with no more thought than I paid to breathing.

Frets. Strings. Strum. Song. Breathe. Four nights a week. Wednesday through Saturday.

"It's funny we have the same exact work schedule," he said. "Wednesday through Saturday nights."

"I requested those days." I said. "They're the best shifts."

Jonah smiled. "They are."

My chest constricted and tears burned behind my closed eyes. After six months, I should've been used to the way he snuck up on me. Little bits of conversation. Little slivers of memory.

Little moments.

Jonah.

I was crying now, but the audience loved it. They expected it. Tears were part of the act. *La Fille Submergée,* they called me. The Drowned Girl.

I cried just hard enough to enhance the song without disrupting it. At least, that's what some chick in the bathroom at Bon Bon—my Saturday night gig—once told me. I made the tears and the sharp intakes of breath part of *the experience.*

She had *an experience* listening to me sing.

What a fucking abomination, I'd wanted to tell her. *Jonah is dead and I'm turning it into an experience.*

I finished the song and applause drowned my murmured *thank you.* I slipped off the stool and carefully picked my way across the stage, more than ready for my post-show cocktail.

"You sounded good tonight, sweets," Big E said as I took my reserved seat at the corner. The bartender had a short-cropped reddish-blond beard and a perfectly shaved head. His real name was Mike Budny, but everyone call him Big Easy or Big E. He reminded me of Hugo, the Pony Club bodyguard in Vegas: big and intimidating on the outside, but total mush inside.

"When are you going to invite one of your friends to listen to you play?" he asked. "Or family?"

Every night I worked Le Chacal, Big E tried to pry some personal information out of me. He openly worried about me, and never gave up trying to dig up some kind of hint about my past.

"The third degree again?" I squinted up at him. The lighted shelf of liquor bottles behind him pierced my eyes. "I should call you Sherlock."

"You do call me Sherlock," he said quietly. "You just never remember."

I snorted a laugh and sipped my drink. "My family is busy," I said, my words tripping over themselves. "And you're my friend." I gave him a watery, playful smile. "You always listen to me play. What more do I need?"

"A lot, sweets," Big E replied somberly. "You need a lot. You need help."

Help.

For all his prying and not-so-subtle intervention, he'd never said that word before. Since I'd moved out of Vegas and cut myself off from everyone, I hadn't heard it before either.

I need help.

I sniffed and downed my whiskey, pushed the glass across the bar toward him. "If you want to help me, you'll give me one more."

"Last one," Big E said, pouring a finger of whiskey into my glass. "I'm not giving up on you, Kacey."

I raised my drink in a mock toast and took a sip. I clinked my teeth painfully on the edge of the glass, ruining the I've-got-my-shit-together-thank-you-very-much vibe I was trying to exude.

"Ow. Fuck."

"You okay?" asked a voice on my left. A young, good-looking guy with tatted arms and slicked-back hair had slid onto the barstool beside me. "That sounded painful."

"All teeth intact," I muttered, sipping my drink.

"Good thing," the guy said. "You have a beautiful smile."

I snorted wetly. "Is that so?"

"I don't know actually," the guy replied. "The Drowned Girl doesn't smile, but I'd like a shot at changing that." He flashed his own winning smile, and held out his hand. "I'm Jesse."

"Kacey." I shook his hand, then tried to take it back but he held it fast.

"Love your ink," he said, inspecting the creeping, thorny vines that crept up the loose sleeve of my off-the-shoulder blouse.

"Don't remember," I said, giving over a lie and withdrawing my hand.

Big E watched us as he cleaned a glass with a white rag. Guys hit on me on a semi-regular basis. They didn't have a snowball's chance in hell of going home with me, or even taking me out on a date, but I let them try. Listening to their bad pick-up lines, or even their genuine attempts to get to know me reminded me of another time. Another girl. The one who would've laughed and flirted and jumped into bed with a guy like Jesse.

The girl I'd been before Jonah.

Now, the hollowed-out wreck I'd become was repulsed by the idea of being touched by a man. But sometimes they bought me drinks. And since Big E had been acting especially ridiculous about my cocktail quota lately, I sat up a little straighter and gave Jesse my version of a smile—a weak quirk of the lips. I pretended to be interested in the ink that covered his nicely muscled forearms, and within minutes, I had a fresh drink in front of me and we were comparing tattoos. I was drunk as shit, and being very, very careless.

I showed Jesse the tiny black stars smattered over my middle and ring finger. "This was my first. I got it in San Diego. Pacific Beach." I flipped him the bird. "I chose that finger in particular. A big fuck you to my dad."

"Nice."

I traced the vines up my arm. "This one came from a place in San Diego too."

"So you *do* remember," Jesse laughed.

"Honey, you buy another round, and I'll remember anything you want me to."

I would've cringed to be on the receiving end of such sloppy, fake flirtation, but such is the beauty of being drunk—it's so much easier not to give a shit. The only beauty, actually. The one and only shining truth.

Jesse bought another round. I got drunker and we compared ink like soldiers comparing battle scars. He lifted his dark blue T-shirt to reveal a nicely sculpted chest and abs, though he could've been covered in moles and boils for all I cared. He turned in his seat to show me the coppery Saints football helmet inked on his right shoulder blade.

"This was my first," he said. "From Jake's up on Canal Street." His eyes drifted blearily to my bare right collarbone bare. "Show me another, Kacey," he said, in what he probably thought was a seductive voice. Hell, in another life, it would have sounded that way, and I'd have climbed onto his lap until Big E kicked us out for inappropriate PDA.

I played along and rubbed my chin on the bare skin of my shoulder. "I can't," I said. "Not without taking something off."

Jesse's blue eyes glazed over. "I can deal with that."

"Mmm," I said, closing my eyes against the spinning room. It wasn't cool to lead him on like this. *I should stop. I have nothing to give him.*

"I have nothing," I muttered, the words falling off the train of thought chugging sluggishly through my whiskey-soaked brain. "I was supposed to have one here." I nudged my bare shoulder with my chin again. "But I never picked one out. I left before I got my tattoo from Teddy."

His name made me flinch, and I kept talking to drown it in a sea of meaningless words. "I didn't know what I wanted so I left it blank. I left with nothing. I have nothing. Because I left. I was supposed to stay but I left."

The tears were welling in my eyes. Drowned Girl fame or not, crying in the middle of being hit-on is a big turn-off. Jesse rubbed his hand over his lips, none too sober himself and unsure how to proceed.

"Hey, it's okay. So…" His smile was obscenely bright. "You like football?"

Big E leaned his bulk over the bar, looking more like a bouncer at a motorcycle club than a bartender at a jazzy dive. "She's done, man," he told Jesse. "You get me?"

Jesse nodded and slipped off the barstool with a sour expression. He'd blown $20 plying me with top shelf whiskey, but he didn't argue with Big E. Not many people did.

The bartender turned his gaze to me, his features softening under his rust-colored beard. "Call you a cab, sweets?"

I nodded and whispered, "Thank you."

Big E got the bar-back to cover him, and half-carried me and my guitar through the dim confines of Le Chacal to the curb outside. Our own Thursday night routine.

The New Orleans night was cool and breezy, the neon sign of Le Chacal bright against its brick façade. I tried to muster a shred of dignity as we waited for the cab, but the sidewalk kept slipping out from under my feet. One more drink and I might black out. I wondered what would happen if I did? Would I end up in the back of Jonah's limo?

"Put me there, Big," I slurred. "Where he is. It's the only place I want to be."

"Teddy?"

"No." My shaking head stilled. "Maybe. I miss him too. I miss them all. But I left and…that's the end of the story."

Big E tightened his grip on my waist as the cab pulled to the curb. "You came here from Las Vegas, right? I think you said so once."

"So?"

Ignoring my question, he told the cabbie my address and helped me into the backseat. There was something about Big E's cool expression I didn't like. Even drunk out of my mind, I could sense he was up to something.

"What, are you going to tell Rufus about this? Lose me my gig?"

"Never," Big E said. He leaned his bulk into the open door. "But I told you, sweets. I'm not giving up on you."

He shut the door and banged the roof of the cab to tell the driver to head out. I slumped back in the seat, a vague sense of disquiet humming along my nerves, making me itchy.

The French Quarter was a murky blur on the other side of the taxi window, giving way to the darker rows of shotgun houses in my Seventh Ward neighborhood.

Vegas had been brown. Beige. Pale yellow and light blue. New Orleans wore the colors of time and vibrant history. Chipped paint in red and white. Green everywhere: the greenish-brown river, green bayou, green air thick with humidity. Green plants and bushes and weeping trees.

I stumbled up the short walk to my front door. It took three or four tries to get the key into the lock because the porch was dark.

Jonah's whiskey lights had long since burnt out.

Inside my tiny shotgun, I dropped onto the couch, my bag and my guitar hitting the ground with a *twang*. My head sank against the cushions and my eyes closed.

There is beauty everywhere, even in the things that scare you the most…

I came awake with a gasp. Sprawled on my couch. Not Jonah's. No ugly green and orange afghan on my shoulders, no glass art on the coffee table. The clock on the wall said I'd been out for twenty minutes. A sobering twenty minutes. Or maybe it was Jonah's words echoing in my ear.

Beauty in the things that scare you the most.

What scared me the most was letting the pain in. Or out, rather. It was already in me. It lived in me. I had to keep it down deep, drown it, so it didn't break me apart into tiny pieces.

ALL IN

I went to the kitchen to make my nightcap. A shotgun house is aptly named: in days of old, you could aim a shotgun from the front door and shoot it straight to the back door. Every room in my small house was lined up in a row: Living room, kitchen, bedroom and bathroom. A straight line to the back porch. A simple route, easy to stumble along. Important details in the home of a 24/7 drunk.

I opened a cabinet holding more bottles than food. My nightcap was vodka over ice with a splash—a tiny splash—of water. I carried the glass to my bedroom.

Like the rest of my place, the bedroom was filled with second-hand furniture. Pieces I'd picked up from yard sales when I'd first fled Vegas for New Orleans. It had a 'shabby chic' charm the home and garden shows were always crowing about, but mine was more shabby than chic.

I needed a couch to sit on—sometimes sleep on if I didn't make it to the bedroom—and so I bought a couch. In orange. I needed a chair so I bought a chair. It was blue. The area rug over the hardwood floors was multicolored. Hell, even the exterior of my house was painted in sea green with sky blue trim and a maroon door. Colors everywhere, like the rest of this city. Except for one place.

I shuffled into the bedroom and flicked the small lamp on my nightstand. My bedspread was white, the universe orb Jonah made me set at its exact center. A dark ball of shimmering black and blue and glowing stars. A black hole in the center of a white universe, sucking me in. The orb drank in the pale yellow lamplight. The planet in the center shimmered red and green.

"It was a good night tonight," I said, kicking off my shoes. I lost my balance but caught it again after only spilling a tiny bit of vodka on my wrist. "Four hundred bucks with tips. The place was packed. You should've seen it."

In the bathroom, I set my cocktail on the sink and used the toilet, then washed my hands. The reflection in the glass was a ghastly mess of smeared mascara, tangled hair and pale skin.

Jonah would hardly recognize you.

The small, weak thought spoke up from the place that hated what I'd become. A stubborn, self-preservationist instinct that tried to snap me out of my inebriation. It never worked.

"Jonah would recognize me *anywhere*," I snapped, and snatched my drink off the counter. I drained it as I went back into the bedroom.

Ice cubes clinked as I set the highball glass on the nightstand. The alcohol slipped coldly into my gut, sloshing around with everything else I'd consumed today and tonight, and all the days and nights of the last few months.

The room spun faster now. I'd hit the sweet spot where alcohol would drop me quickly into sleep, and where any dreams I had would be too slippery for me to grasp when I woke.

I made sure the flask in my drawer had enough to start my morning—or early afternoon, depending on how late I slept. It was easy to get bombed at a party or after a show. I would know—I used to do it after every concert with Rapid Confession. But there's a science to staying drunk all the time and still being able to function.

Sort of.

I *sort of* functioned. I held jobs that didn't require sobriety. I kept to my routine, part of which was downing a nightcap, checking the morning flask, and curling up next to the orb to tell Jonah about my day.

I lay down on the bed, my body feeling like it weighed a thousand pounds. I rested my aching head on the white duvet and curled my body around the orb. Knees up, arms curved, I pulled the universe snug against my chest, cradling it to my heart.

"Rufus, the owner…he says they want me at Le Chacal more than once a week. Word's gotten out. But I have a routine, right? Four different clubs, four nights. No getting too attached to any one venue." I closed my eyes for a moment as the shame swamped me. "But I can't do more. I can't keep going like this. It's killing me. I have to quit, don't I? But I don't know how."

Help me, Jonah.

"Big Easy…I told you about him, right?" I sniffed, wiped my nose on my sleeve. "He's the bartender at Le Chacal. Remember? I call him Sherlock sometimes, because he's always trying to find out about me. Asking about friends or family. He worries about me. He wants to know where I came from or who…who to call. He wants to call someone. I know he does. He thinks I need help."

I closed my eyes to hear the words aloud and tried to press them down with everything else.

"There's no one to call. It would only worry them. Or mess up their lives."

What a crock. Henry and Teddy and Beverly were probably

already worried.

I focused my bleary gaze to the orb. As always, I felt myself being sucked in, lost in the dark expanses of stardust and the glowing swirls of illumination ringing the lonely planet. I searched for Jonah there, held the orb tighter in my arms as the tears fell unheeded.

Unending.

"I'm so sorry," I whispered, my voice a watery croak. "I left. Your mom…and Teddy. I didn't want to. People shouldn't leave, I know that. I should know better than anyone. But I couldn't stay. And I'm so sorry. For leaving and for failing you. I *am* the drowned girl. I'm drowning, Jonah. I need you back. Please come back…"

My stomach clenched at the effort it took to hold back the grief, terrified of what would happen if I succumbed to it.

I wrapped myself tight around the orb, completing the last step of my routine. Every night I held the orb and begged Jonah to come back, tears leaking from my eyes as if from a dam that was ready to burst. I cried and begged until the booze dragged me down into the black depths far beneath the surface.

Every night, I called one final thought into the deep darkness: *Come back to me.*

And just before the dark consumed me, a whisper returned: *My angel, let me go…*

CHAPTER 3

Theo

Friday afternoon and Vegas Ink was as packed as the tiny place could get. Zelda, Edgar and I worked nonstop, the buzzing of our needles competing with pulsing electronica music—Friday was Zelda's turn to pick music.

Vivian manned the front desk, answering calls and setting up appointments for walk-ins that might or might not come back. Las Vegas was saturated with tattoo shops. Most of the turned away would probably go somewhere else.

"You got any plans this weekend, T?" Edgar asked when we were both between clients.

"Got a hot date?" Zelda asked from her station. The words were sharp but a hunch in her shoulders made the lie on my tongue hesitate. Behind her luminous green eyes, I could see a flicker of pain, strangely familiar to my own.

"Nothing major," I heard myself say. "Lot of studying to do."

"Come out racing on Sunday," Edgar said. He finished his Red Bull, crushed the can and lobbed it at the trash basket. "Me and some buddies are going to rent ATVs."

"Yeah, maybe."

"*Maybe*." Edgar snorted. "Come on, man,"

"I got three midterms next week," I said, crossing the black and white checkered floor toward the restroom behind the reception desk. I gave Zelda a nod as I went by.

Sorry, Z. I'm running on empty.

I had to wipe my hands on my jeans after washing them. "Viv, we're out of paper towels," I said as I emerged from the bathroom. She was on the phone and only raised her chin at me. I started to walk away, right at the moment the music on the sound system faded to a low pulse. Above the quiet beat, I heard Viv say, "Teddy? No, no one named Teddy here."

The name slugged me in the back. I whipped around, my heart pounding out of my chest, yelling, "No," as Vivian lowered the phone to its set. "Viv, don't…"

I raced forward and yanked the receiver out of her bewildered hands. I put it to my ear and said in a rush "Hello? Don't hang up."

My ears burned, poised to hear Kacey's voice—rich and clear, with a little gravel at the edges.

"Is this Teddy?"

It was a man's voice. Disappointment caved my chest in.

"Yeah, that's me," I said, turning away from Viv's raised brows. "Who's this?"

"Name's Mike Budny. Listen, this might be a long shot, but do you know a girl by the name of Kacey Dawson?"

I froze. *She's dead.*

"Yeah," I said. "Yeah, I know her. She was my brother's girlfriend."

"Thank *fuck*," the guy said. "I been making long-distance Hail Mary calls all day, looking for a tattoo artist in Vegas named Teddy. Do you have any *idea* how many tattoo shops Vegas has?"

I squeezed the phone. "You found me. What's going on?"

She's dead.

"Yeah, listen, do you know her family? Or a friend? Someone who can help her out?"

"Me," I said, like staking a claim. "I'm a friend. Where is she?"

"New Orleans. I'm a bartender at a club called Le Chacal. She sings here every Thursday night. You getting all this?"

"Yeah, yeah." I fumbled around Vivian's desk for a pen and paper, ignoring her frantic gesture at three other calls flashing on hold. "New Orleans. Chacal. Thursday nights." I scratched the words down stupidly, as if I'd forget where Kacey was now that I'd found her.

"How is she?" I asked at the same time the bartender said, "How soon can you get here?"

The panic in my chest ignited and tightened. "Fast. Tomorrow if I have to. Why? What's wrong? Is she okay?"

"No, man." The sigh he exhaled was somewhere between relief and resignation. "She's pretty fucking far from okay."

I hung up with Mike feeling like a runner at the start of the most important race of his life. Vivian was yammering at me, but I hardly heard her. My heart was pounding and my stomach twisted as I made a mental list of all the stuff I had to do to get to Kacey as fast as possible.

In New Orleans.

She went halfway across the country to drink herself to death.

"I gotta go," I said, snatching my black jacket off the coatrack. "Cancel the rest of my appointments."

Vivian stared. "Cancel your... Where are you *going*?"

I headed for the door. "Call Gus for me. Tell him I gotta leave town for a few days. Family emergency."

"A few days? Gus'll lose his shit. He'll fire you."

"Just call him, Viv, okay?" I pushed out the front door without waiting for a reply.

I raced to my truck and sped down the Vegas streets, equal parts frustration and relief. Cursing at every red light while wanting to cry like a baby because I'd found her.

The rest of my conversation with Mike Budny echoed in my head: *Drunk all the time... Keeps to herself, no friends... They call her the Drowned Girl, and man, it's true. She's fucking drowning.*

I had a second chance to make things right.

I hit another red light and slammed the heel of my hand on the steering wheel, then honked the horn. The sound howled in the desert air, then faded away to nothing.

Back home, I fired up my laptop to search for cheap flights. Tuition for UNLV had eaten a good chunk of the money Jonah left me, and I obsessively guarded the balance, thinking of my future shop. Round trip to New Orleans with no advance would eat up $700 of my savings, and required a return date.

I hesitated. I had the money, but no idea what would happen when I saw Kacey in New Orleans or how long I'd be there. Or if I'd come back alone.

"Don't get ahead of yourself," I muttered. I looked for one-way flights and found a redeye leaving tonight, arriving in New Orleans

11:00 tomorrow morning. A shitty option with a layover in Dallas/Ft. Worth, but it was the soonest they had. In fact, it departed in less than two hours. This was going to be tight, but if I waited even one day, I'd go fucking crazy.

I rushed to my bedroom, dragged a rolling suitcase out of my closet and started throwing clothes into it. I juggled my phone in the other hand, scrolling through contacts as I made a mental list of people to call before I skipped town. My parents. Oscar. I should call Gus personally so he wouldn't fire me.

I hit 'call' put the phone to my ear, and kept packing. The voice that answered stopped me cold.

Hey, you've reached Jonah Fletcher. Leave me a message and I'll call you back. Have a good one.

An automated message said the mailbox was full.

My parents had insisted on continuing Jonah's phone service so we could hear his voice. The mailbox was full of messages from old friends saying goodbye or telling him how much they missed him.

Instinct had made me hit Jonah's number. Around Jonah, I felt calmer, less stressed by my own emotions that ran so fucking hot all the time.

I stared at the phone in my hand.

My vision blurred, and I blinked furiously until it was clear again. I resumed packing with a vengeance.

I found her, bro, I told Jonah, tossing a pair of jeans into the suitcase and the force of my conviction had me talking out loud. "I found her, and I'm going to make sure she's safe. I won't fail again, I promise."

I gave my parents a white-washed version of the truth: a mutual friend had contacted me about Kacey. She wanted to see me. I was leaving tonight.

"Tonight?" my mother cried. "Why the urgency? Is she okay?"

"She's fine, Ma. Last-minute flights are super cheap," I lied.

"What about school?" my father asked from the line in the den. "Don't you have midterms next week?"

Fuck.

I hurled a T-shirt into my suitcase. If I missed those tests, I'd probably have to take—and pay for—the courses all over again. "Yeah," I said, thinking on my feet. "I'll email my professors, tell them it's an emergency. They'll let me reschedule."

"Are you certain?" Dad asked. "Last I remembered, college exams were serious business. You can't just skip them…"

He lectured on, and I muttered a bunch of bullshit assurances as I hit the bathroom and collected my shaving kit. Finally, he hung up his end with a disgusted snort.

"Tell Kacey we love her," my mother said. "Tell her I understand why she left. Okay?"

Maybe she understood, but I didn't. On the drive to McCarran airport, the edges of my worry morphed into anger: I wanted some fucking answers. But by the time I was at the gate, the fury had burned out, leaving the reality I'd be seeing Kacey again. Soon. Tomorrow.

The Drowned Girl.

I imagined her hair a tangled curtain over her face, her eyes streaming black mascara tears, a bottle of booze clutched in her hand instead of a guitar.

I slumped in my chair, putting my feet up on my suitcase and wondering what pushed her over the edge. She'd been a mess after Jonah's funeral, but we were all a wreck then. Walking around like zombies, dazed and shattered. We knew for months death was coming. Still, when it arrived, it was like a cruel surprise. You can prepare all you want for someday. Nothing prepares you for the *day of.*

The night Kacey and I drove to the desert to scatter Jonah's ashes, she looked ready to blow away. As the wind took Jonah's remains into the black sky, I reached for her hand and let the words fall out of my mouth: "Stay here."

I wanted her to stay in Vegas, and I gave her my hand to tell her I'd help her.

"Help *me*," I may as well have been saying.

Help me, and stay here.

Stay with me.

"I will," she said. And I believed her.

Yet I didn't see her much after that night. I was trying to cope with my grief but my true feelings for Kacey kept getting in the way. How do you console a woman over the loss of her man when you wished—with every particle of your body—she'd someday feel that deeply about you?

The fact that her man had been my brother made the tangle of fucked up-emotions snarl into something I didn't need or want.

I dropped by her apartment one night after work, and found her writing songs. On the couch with her guitar, a notebook open beside her.

"The words are *pouring* out, Teddy," she said.

But I should've heard how her voice trembled at the edges and how her eyes were shining and bright. Not for excitement or joy. But in the way you look when you're scared to death and that fear is lighting up your nerves like a switchboard.

Two weeks later, she was gone, leaving me with only a simple truth: I needed her. Maybe more than she needed me.

CHAPTER 4

Theo

New Orleans was a city as green and old as Vegas was brown. In April, the heat wasn't bad, but the air was filled with water.

The GPS on my rental car guided me to the French Quarter and the Le Chacal club. It was almost noon. Mike said he wouldn't be there until six, and he wouldn't give me Kacey's home address or any other personal information until he met me in person. I appreciated the caution, although it left me impatient as hell.

I checked into a small hotel on the fringes of the French Quarter and took a nap to recover from the sleepless night on a cramped airplane. I had a quick bite at a café, then took a walk up and down Canal Street, searching faces. Every blonde-haired woman I passed made my heart leap. None were Kacey.

Time crawled by until six, when I went back to Le Chacal. It was a small, dim club with a cartoon jackal in pink and green neon buzzing over the front entrance. A small stage area was on the left, a smattering of thin wooden chairs and tables facing it. The bar was tucked into the back right corner, where a huge guy with a rust-colored beard was getting ready for the night. Backlit shelves of glasses provided the most illumination. A jazzy song played from a sound-system and a few patrons were already there, talking and drinking in low voices.

I stepped up to the bar. "Mike Budny?"

The big guy sized me up. "Yeah?"

I offered my hand. "Theo Fletcher. Teddy."

He shook my hand, then planted both palms on the bar, his expression tight. "Call me Big E. Everyone else does."

"Sure."

"You weren't kidding about getting here quick," he said. "Still, I can't be giving out her personal info until I know the whole story. Are you the reason she split Vegas to drink herself into a stupor every night?"

"No," I said. "It was my brother, Jonah. Kacey was his girlfriend, and they were real close. But he…"

"Dumped her?"

Shit, one of the perks of shutting down my social life was I hadn't had to explain this situation to anyone in six months. My chest tightened as I said, "He died."

Big E nodded. "Sorry to hear that, man. But it explains a lot. I can hear it in her songs, you know?"

"I'll bet."

He rubbed his beard and sighed. "Beer?"

"Sure."

The bartender popped the tops off two bottles of something dark, handed one to me. He clinked it to mine, and we both drank. I took a long pull of the cold, bitter ale, as if I could wash the words *he died* out of my mouth.

"So what's your plan, Theo?"

"See her," I said. "Help her. Whatever she needs."

Big E kept nodding over his beer. His blasé attitude was starting to irritate me.

"Look man," I said. "All I care about—literally, the only thing I give a shit about in this world right now—is making sure she's okay. You called. I came. Now tell me where she is."

The big guy gave me one more appraising glance, finished off his beer and set the bottle down. "Saturday nights she plays the Bon Bon on Baronne Street. You might see flyers around. Set starts at nine."

"Thank you." I finished off my own beer and reached for my wallet.

"On me," Big E said, and offered his hand again. "I'm glad you're here, Theo."

I shook it hard. The guy was genuinely concerned and without his phone call, I'd be sitting in the Wynn Galleria, apologizing to Jonah for the thousandth time. "Thanks for calling me, man."

And for saving my fucking life.

Bon Bon was bigger than Le Chacal, and a lot more crowded. I got there early enough to grab a two-person corner booth which I jealously guarded. Twice, women asked to squeeze in with me, and twice I said the seat was taken. The label from my beer bottle was peeled off and torn to shreds by the time the lights finally dimmed. From the booth, I had a clear shot to the stage. A stool and a mic stand stood pooled in a circle of light, waiting.

The stereo music faded to silence and so did the conversations of fifty patrons or so. All eyes turned to the stage. Then she was there. No announcement, no introduction. She just appeared, her guitar already strapped around her, her long blonde hair falling like a tangled curtain to conceal most of her face.

Kacey. Damn, baby…

I froze, my eyes drinking her in, gulping down six months.

She looked thin, dressed in sleek black leather pants and a ratty, olive-colored sweater, oversized and hanging off one shoulder. The stage's lone spotlight glinted off her hair and skin.

She was drunk.

I knew it from the slow, careful way she took her seat on the stool, adjusted the mic, and strummed her guitar once or twice.

The place was hushed and seemed to hold its breath when finally she moved her mouth to the mic and said in her rich, somewhat weakened voice, "Hi, I'm Kacey and I'm going to sing a few songs for you tonight."

The crowd erupted into applause, breaking me out of my trance. Then Kaccy started singing and I was immediately plunged into another one.

That voice…

She sang about waking up surrounded by beauty and peace. Opening her eyes after a long nightmare of loud music, a party that never ended, and a costume she could never take off.

I sat still, my eyes either open to inhale her, or closed to better hear her words. The first song gave way to one about a lover's kiss that erased every other kiss that came before. The next was about a night spent under stars.

I was transported to the Grand Basin, a camping trip with friends, listening to Kacey sing around the fire. Something shifted in me that night. Some cataclysmic alteration of who I was as a man. It was that night that she ruined me. Or saved me. I didn't know which.

Song after song, I relived Kacey's time with Jonah. Specifics hidden in the lyrics, leaving the emotion exposed in sharp detail. By the time Jonah's health was declining in a song called "One Million Moments," I was clutching my beer bottle hard, half hoping it would shatter, cut me open and break the spell of pain. Stop the tide of feeling from rising to the surface.

God, she's so fucking beautiful.

Drunk and disheveled, reeking of misery and defeat, and she was beautiful to me. I wanted to bulldoze through the chair and tables in front of the stage and grab her, carry her out of this place and the people who applauded the grief she gave them in songs. I wanted to put my hands on her, confirm this was real; that I wasn't dreaming of sitting in a New Orleans jazz club, listening to Kacey Dawson sing.

"This is my last song," she said. "It's called 'The Lighthouse.'"

Kacey strummed a long intro of sad harmonies. Over the course of the song, they degenerated into purposefully discordant notes evoking a ship breaking apart, plank by plank. Through the melody, Kacey's tears fell, her voice hitched and faltered but never quit. Her breaths were stolen, like someone gasping for air, but they didn't disrupt the song. They *were* the song, as much as any lyric or chord.

The last note hung in the air, then dissipated. The crowd sat hushed for half a second before breaking out into subdued applause that grew in intensity, until the small, dark club was suffused with sound.

I watched, transfixed, as Kacey brushed the hair off her face, smearing the mascara that stained her cheeks. "Thank you," she murmured into the mic. "Goodnight."

She slipped off her stool and disappeared behind the black curtain. As the crowd around me returned to normal conversation, I sat in my booth, feeling her voice and music reverberate through me. When the sound system came on with some jazz number, I jerked out of my thoughts, and frantically scanned the club for Kacey.

Shit, I'd fucking lost her all over again. She probably slipped out the back while I was mooning like an idiot. I relinquished my seat and wound my way through the crowd, searching faces.

I spotted her at the last stool on the bar. She sipped a cocktail as a man at her elbow scribbled something on a cocktail napkin and slid it across the bar to her. She picked it up with a game smile and nodded. As the guy left the bar, his smile was hopeful.

I realized my hands were clenched into fists. Kacey told me once that during her time with her old band, she'd take roadies or fans to her bed at night. Was she back in that habit too?

Kacey stared after her admirer, waited until he was out of sight, then tore the napkin into long shreds.

Good.

I let go my fists and my breath, and moved toward the bar as Kacey slid off her stool and picked up her guitar. She stumbled, nearly fell. Another guy steadied her, and she flashed him a grateful smile. He leaned to say something in her ear. She shook her head and squeezed through the crowd of people, many of whom grabbed her arm or hand or even reached to hug her.

I followed, my pulse pounding faster with each step that closed the distance between us. She pushed out the front door and stepped into the street. Her hair—not pale white anymore but brassy blonde—glowed like a flame under the street light, then the door sliced her off.

Fuck.

I pushed through the crowd, now closing in on me like a zipper, and shoved open the door. I looked right and left, up both sides of the street that were lit with ornate, old-fashioned-looking street lamps.

Gone. Again.

"Fuck me."

I chose a direction and started off down the sidewalk, thinking it was impossible Kacey could've gotten far when she was drunk and lugging a guitar case. Unless she hopped into a waiting cab…

I passed an alley between Bon Bon and a bustling café. Stopped. Backtracked.

She had her back to me, trying to light a cigarette, her guitar case on the ground. I approached slowly, not wanting to freak her out. My pulse jumped in my throat. She was so close. Only five more steps and I could touch her.

I swallowed hard. "Kacey."

Her thin body jerked, and she slowly turned. Her cigarette and lighter fell out of her hands. Through a veil of stringy blonde hair, she stared at me.

"Teddy?"

Her large, beautiful eyes filled with hope. Her dark brows came together and her mouth tried to smile and collapse into tears at the same time. Relief. She was relieved to see me…and for a split second, the misery that had wrapped itself around me for the last six months loosened.

Then her features hardened. Instead of looking like she was going to fly into my arms, her expression turned murderous, her luminous blue eyes icy.

"You shouldn't be here, Theodore." She picked up her guitar case and pushed past me. "Go home."

CHAPTER 5

Kacey

My low-heeled boots clopped on the sidewalk as fast I could manage. My guitar case banged my knees, trying to trip me up. I wanted to throw it down, turn around and run to Theo, fly at him and dive into his arms.

You came. You're here. You found me.

The city was New Orleans but my drunken eyes only saw Vegas in the days after Jonah's death. The grief coming out of the past, roiling in my guts, making me more nauseous than liquor. Making me need his arms holding me. Need his chest to cry against as I begged forgiveness.

I'm sorry. You're horrified to see me like this. I know. Jonah would be too.

That's when shame hit my veins like a shot of whiskey, and a panic chaser sent me running in the exact opposite direction I wanted to go.

I heard heavy footsteps behind me, a breathless call. "Kacey, wait."

His hand closed on my upper arm and yanked me to a stop. I yanked back, knowing I couldn't outrun him, knowing I was kidding myself but I fought him anyway.

"What are you doing here? How did you find me?"

"Mike called me," he said. "Mike Budny."

"Big E," I muttered. As sloppy a drunk as I was, I'd been obsessively secretive about my past, keeping all details on lockdown. My booze-soaked brain tried to recall what I might've told Big E that led him to Theo.

"He's worried about you," Theo said, letting go of me and crossing his arms over his broad chest. He wore a black T-shirt and jeans, and the eyes boring into me were whiskey-colored, fiery under the streetlights. "Now I'm worried, too."

"Well, I'm tired and I want to go home, so can you make this quick?"

His light brown eyes widened in disbelief. "That's all you have to say to me? After six months?"

"What more do you want me to say? I'm sorry?" I blew a lock of ratty hair out of my eyes. "Fine, I'm sorry. Happy?"

"Not remotely."

"What do you want, Theo?"

"To talk," he said. He scrubbed his hands through his short dark hair. "Jesus, Kacey, it's been six months."

"To talk." I pretended to think it over, while my mind was a shocked blank. "Sorry, Teddy, but I got nothing to say."

"Sorry isn't good enough."

We stared each other down, and somewhere behind the alcohol, I knew I wasn't going to win this standoff.

"Fine," I said, handing him my guitar. "Let's talk."

"Where?"

"Somewhere neutral."

"Like?"

If he was shocked when I gave him my home address in the Seventh Ward neighborhood, he didn't show it. He punched it into his phone's GPS and Siri helpfully chirped directions at him.

"Now I'll have to move," I muttered.

"What?"

"Nothing."

We pulled up to my street with its rows of shotgun houses. Theo parked his car in the carport behind the Toyota I'd bought used in Vegas. On my frantic drive to Louisiana, the universe sat on a pillow in a box on the passenger seat, seatbelted in. I never drove the thing anymore. My house was only ten blocks from the French Quarter.

Not to mention driving when one was blitzed 24/7 was highly irresponsible.

God knows I'm responsible, I sneered at myself.

My porch lights—the beautiful whiskey-bottle lamps Jonah had made for me—were burnt out. Had that just happened, or had I not noticed until now? My cheeks burned as I struggled to get the damn key to find the lock. Inside, I strode toward the kitchen to make a nightcap, leaving Theo to shut the door and pick up my dropped purse.

I poured vodka over ice. "You want one? Or a beer?"

He shook his head. He stood with his arms crossed, his dark-eyed gaze unwavering. I sipped my drink, self-conscience of every movement. "You wanted to talk, right?"

"I didn't fly all this way to listen to bullshit."

My eyes flared wider. "Bullshit? I haven't said a word."

"Yeah, no kidding."

"You're the one stalking me."

"People are worried about you, Kace," he said, his voice softening slightly.

"Oh, it's a guilt trip then. Do you get frequent flyer miles for those?"

Theo didn't laugh and his eyes didn't leave me. My cheeks burned. I slammed my drink on the tiled kitchen counter.

"Look, I don't need you coming here and...*humiliating* me."

That seemed to throw him a little. His shoulders hitched. "Humiliate you? How?"

"By *being* here. By seeing me like this. Why do you think I left? To hurt Beverly or Henry? Or you? No, I left Vegas because he was *everywhere*, Teddy. Jonah was everywhere and I couldn't take it."

"What, you think he's invisible to me?"

"I'm telling you why *I* left."

"You mean bailed." His handsome face was stoic but his voice was filled with pain.

"Fine. Bailed. Snuck off in the night and left a note. I could've stayed but for what? So you all could watch me fall apart?" I shook my head, raised my vodka to my lips and took a long swallow. "It's better this way. It's fucking awful but it's also better. In the long run. For everyone."

"It's killing you."

I snorted into my glass. "I can handle it."

"Bullshit."

"Is that why you're here? An intervention? Get me into rehab?"

"No."

I looked up, studied this man in my living room, his arms still crossed and his feet planted apart. Like a bouncer. Or even Hugo, Rapid Confession's bodyguard, who'd scooped me drunk off a stage and put me in the back of Jonah's limo, changing my life. Too many memories. Too many coincidences circling back to memories.

"So." I drummed my fingers on the counter to hide how they were twitching. "You're going to throw my booze away? Force me to quit?"

"No." His tone stayed even and hard, while mine edged toward panic. I slapped my hand on the counter. "So what, then? You wanted to talk. Talk."

"I'm waiting."

"For what?"

One of his shoulders rose and fell, that was all. He looked so strong and solid and heavy; a boulder of muscle that had planted itself in my living room with no intention of moving.

"You're waiting." I ran my hands through my hair, and clasped them behind my neck, trying to stop the room's spinning. "Well, you can't *wait* here. Get out."

Theo didn't move.

"Did you hear me?" I said. "You can't stay."

Not a blink. Not a breath. He looked paused. Like a robot with the switch flipped to off.

My arms dropped and I planted my hands on my hips. "Are you deaf, Teddy? I said get out."

He drew a deep inhale then. With the exhale, his booted feet seemed to imbed deeper into the floor.

I lanced my finger at the door. "Get. Out."

Silence.

Frustration mounted in me, tinged with something else. A bone-deep certainty this was it. My one chance at salvation.

Help me...

"Goddammit, get out of my house," I cried. "Leave me *alone.*"

When he didn't budge, I seized my cell phone. It was a burner phone, the kind you buy at a convenience store. It had nothing in it except contact numbers for the clubs I sang in. I'd thrown my other one away into the Nevada desert months ago.

"I'll call the cops," I said, brandishing the cell in front of me like a gun. "I'll have you arrested for trespassing. Is that what you want?"

He didn't move. I felt something start to crack in me. The eggshell-thin barrier I'd erected against the grief. A levee against the river of soul-deep pain.

"I swear to God, Teddy, I'll call the police," I said, my voice trembling.

A muscle in Theo's jaw twitched but his gaze was unbreakable.

My breath started hitching, getting no deeper than my throat, and my hands were shaking so badly, I nearly dropped the phone. I threw it at Theo instead.

"*Get out.*"

He inclined his head slightly, didn't even flinch as the phone sailed to the right of his ear and smashed against the wall.

"I mean it, Teddy. Get the *fuck* out!"

I grabbed a couch cushion and hurled it at him. It landed at his feet. The second cushion hit him square in the chest and bounced off. I was screaming now, as I dug through my purse for objects to throw at him. My wallet, a compact, a wad of tissues. Everything missed or fluttered to the floor. Finally, with a hysterical cry, I swung the purse itself, like a shot-put. It careened across the room, the force swinging me halfway around. I lost my balance and fell to my knees. The impact against the hardwood crackled through me, and I hunched over, hugging myself to keep from breaking apart.

He won't leave.

"I'm sorry," I cried, my face aching with the strain of holding back the river. "I'm so sorry, Teddy, but go. Please go. I don't want you to see me like this…"

He won't leave.

He won't ever leave. He's strong and healthy and well and he won't leave…

I heard the creak of floorboards, felt them shift under my kneecaps. Theo's booted foot appeared in the murky blur of my vision. When he spoke, his voice was a mountain.

"I'm staying here." He knelt beside me and picked up my head. His large hands held my face, brushed the hair from my eyes and made me look at him. His hard gaze implored me to give in. Let go. But the terror of jumping in the river and confronting my grief wouldn't let me. I needed to drink. I needed to *stay* drunk, or I'd die.

I'd drown.

I opened my mouth to tell him that, and the words came out all wrong.

"I need help." I whispered. The words were cool in my mouth. My skin felt feverish, my tears were scalding as they streamed down my cheeks to his fingers that held me. Everything hurt. Except the words.

"Help me," I said, swallowing it like cool, clear water in the desert. "Please. Help me."

Theo's hands spread wide on my face. His eyes shone. "I will," he said. "I'm here and I'll help you."

I searched his eyes, desperate to believe him, clutching his black t-shirt and twisting it in my hands. He was telling the truth. There was nothing about Theo that wasn't solid and honest and fiercely loyal. I'd seen the same conviction in his eyes when he'd held Jonah's hand through that awful biopsy. And now he was offering the same to me.

But I couldn't quit the booze. I couldn't survive it. I collapsed against him, sobbing hard but not turning myself inside out. Not yet. The urge to drink was furious and malevolent. It had sunk its teeth deep into me, and wouldn't be purged so easily. But I'd begun. I clung to Theo and he held me tight, the solidity of his presence bolstering me, as if he were lending me some of his strength. After a few minutes, he shifted off his knees to sit on the floor. I wiped my eyes on his sleeve.

"I've been drunk every day for six months."

I felt him nod against the crown of my head.

"It's going to hurt bad, isn't it?"

The nod grew bigger. "Maybe you should see someone. A doctor…"

"No." I hauled myself off the floor. Theo rose too, steadying me when I wobbled. "I looked it up a month ago, when I had a bad night and thought about quitting. Hospital rehab programs give you drugs to cope with withdrawal. Drugs that make you feel nothing."

I looked up at him, clutching his forearms, still needing his strength.

"I have to feel everything, don't I? Feeling is the whole damn point. Because it's not just the booze I'm getting out of my system."

He nodded. "You can do this, Kace."

"It's going to suck for you too," I said. "If you're sticking around to watch."

"I can take it."

"What about your job?"

"It's fine."

"I can't ask you to—"

"It's *fine*, Kace," he said. "I've got it covered."

His hard tone and stony expression left no room for argument. I hugged my sides and rocked back on my heels. "If you're sure."

His face softened. "I'm sure. And it's late. You should probably try to get some rest."

"What about you?"

"Once you're sleeping, I'll get my stuff from the hotel. Crash on your couch."

In my bedroom, I kicked off my boots, peeled off my leather pants and sweater, and exchanged them for baggy sweatpants and a plain T-shirt. I crawled onto the bed and curled up around the universe orb, my eyes already starting to droop.

Theo came to the doorway. He stared at the glass a moment, then cleared his throat. "You have a stash in here?" he asked.

"The drawer in the nightstand," I murmured. Sleep was already coming for me. Behind closed eyes, I heard the drawer open and close. My morning flask of brandy confiscated. A pang of fear and doubt shook my shoulder, begged me to get up and save the stash. But I was sinking too fast.

"Thank you, Teddy," I said. "I know it's so much to ask. Too much."

He pulled the covers higher. I smelled the clean scent of his cologne. "It's not too much," he said.

"Liar."

He grunted what might have been a laugh. "Goodnight, Kace."

For one short second, his hand rested on my shoulder. I wanted to take it and hold on all night, but the dark kept me limp and motionless.

Still, I knew Theo was there. I wasn't alone anymore

And that was enough.

That was everything.

I woke in the morning with my stomach twisted in painful knots and a craving in my blood, roaring like a hurricane.

I found Theo asleep on the couch. He wore gray flannel pants and a white wife-beater revealing the inked muscles of his arms. I wandered into the kitchen with the idea I'd make coffee. Like normal people did.

The trash had been taken out and a fresh, empty bag lined the can. I knew then I could check every cabinet, drawer and hiding spot in the entire house and I wouldn't find one drop of liquor.

I stood in my kitchen, my mouth dry as the Vegas desert, my heart pounding. I didn't want coffee. I wanted my morning brandy. Or a Bloody Mary. I wanted something hard to drink the way a starving lion wanted red meat.

I tried to muster my courage. No going back now. I had to do this. For Beverly and Henry. For Oscar and Dena. For Teddy, who was giving up so much to stay here with me. Far more than he let on.

For Jonah, I thought. *For you, my sweet love. I'll do this for you.*

And though I felt utterly worthless, and the task in front of me seemed impossible, I dared to add myself to the roster.

For me, too. To live.

"Teddy?" I called to him in a tiny voice. He came awake at once, sitting up and glancing around until he saw me. Standing in the middle of the kitchen, clutching my elbows. My skin already felt itchy.

"It's okay, Kace," he said, rubbing the sleep from his eyes and nodding. "I'm right here."

CHAPTER 6

Theo

It didn't take long for the addiction to torture her.

She had no real food in the house. After leaving my hotel the night before, I'd bought a bunch of healthy foods and bottles of water at a 24-hour grocery store. Mid-morning of the first day, I found *Dirty Dancing* on a cable channel and coaxed Kacey to the couch to watch. She had a thing for 80's movies. She sipped water as the movie played, but didn't eat. Her leg bounced and she constantly wrung her hands together.

By afternoon, watching movies was abandoned. She paced her small living room, her face dampened with sweat, her eyes wild.

By early evening, she alternated cursing me out with begging for a drink. Soon, dry-heaving was added to the rotation. Rage. Plead. Retch.

I stayed out of her way. I gritted my teeth through her tearful begging. I held her hair until she regained the strength to start the cycle again.

Rage. Plead. Retch.

Occasionally she fell into short, exhausted sleeps that gave me ten or fifteen minutes to catch my breath. They didn't give her anything. She woke up more angry, more desperate, more wretched. *Thirstier.*

By midnight, she was in free-falling anxiety. There were short fits of uncontrollable tears as she paced—she never stopped pacing, pulling at her hair and glancing around with frantic eyes, as if she'd lost something precious.

I watched helplessly, unable to do more than block the front door and coax her to drink water. Sometimes she clawed and hit me. Sometimes she curled limp into my arms, her body trembling as if she were freezing to death.

It was a long night. The second day dawned and we were already exhausted. Withdrawal, however, was just getting warmed up.

Day Two nearly killed her. And it nearly broke me, too. By afternoon, I wanted to call it quits. Resign and take her to a professional.

"No, Teddy," she begged. Her face was blotchy red from crying, her clothes drenched in sweat, her voice hoarse from screaming at me. "Don't give me to strangers. Please...I can do this. I can. I *will*."

What could I say? If she could, I could. I held her close until she pushed away to pace more, to vomit the water I'd managed to get her to drink into the kitchen sink.

I didn't think it could get any worse. Then delusional tremors—the DTs—started.

Kacey's hands shook as if she'd been doused in ice water, and it scared me to the bone.

I answered a knock on the door in the late morning to an African-American woman in jeans, an orange shirt and wielding a baseball bat. She jumped back when I opened the door, and readied her bat for a swing. Turned out she was a nurse who lived next door. She heard Kacey's screaming and thought something criminal was happening.

I let her in and she helped me check Kacey's vitals. Her pulse was fast, but not too fast. She wasn't hallucinating. She wasn't convulsing beyond tremors. The nurse—Yvonne—okay'd me to keep her home unless it all escalated, and I felt a little calmer after she left. The ordeal still tore at my goddamn heart, but I was less terrified.

We spent the second night on the living room floor. It must've been eighty degrees in that small house with no air conditioning, yet Kacey bundled herself in blankets, crying at how cold she was. She didn't sleep more than a handful of minutes.

I didn't sleep at all.

Day Three.

Kacey burst out of her blanket cocoon and sat up, ramrod straight, as if she'd remembered what she'd lost and knew where to find it. She kicked her legs free. Her T-shirt stuck to her skin with sweat, all down her back to darken the waistband of her sweatpants.

When she glanced at me, her eyes had a clarity I hadn't seen in days. The terrible fever had finally broken and hope rose in me. This fucking nightmare was almost over.

"How do you feel?" I asked.

"Hot," she said in a croak. "It's so hot in here."

She scrambled off the floor and hurried to the bathroom, stripping off her shirt. Her tattoos were dark blotches against her pale skin. I followed.

"What, you don't trust me alone?" she said, turning on the shower then stripping off her sweatpants, leaving her in nothing but her underwear.

"No." I averted my eyes from her almost-naked body, and busied myself getting a clean towel from underneath the sink.

Kacey stepped under the stream of water and shivered.

"Cold," she murmured through clenched teeth. "It's like rain. Cold rain."

The water fell over her tangled hair and pale, goosefleshed skin. Her face crumpled, and her hands clutched her chest between her bare breasts, over her heart.

Here it comes, I thought. The worst. The lowest. The most excruciating. The demon king of pain. What I was too fucking scared to face myself.

"The rain," Kacey whispered, the water dripping off her lips and chin. "Up at the Basin. I danced for him in the cold rain. I danced for him…"

She slowly slid down the tiles, collapsing to the shower floor. Pulling her knees to her chest, she rocked back and forth under the water. Great howling wails filled the small stall.

I stood frozen a moment, my chest tightened, my own grief trying to well up in an echo of hers.

I shut off the water, took a towel and bent into the shower to wrap it around her before lifting her up. She felt like nothing in my arms, yet she clung to me hard as I carried her into the bedroom and laid her down on the bed. I lifted Jonah's glass orb out of the way and set it on its stand on a near-empty bookshelf.

I'm not going to let you down, bro, I vowed as I set it down, and curled up next to Kacey. I wrapped my arms around her and she clung to me.

She cried forever. Hours, maybe. I lost track of time, but just held her, stroked her wet, tangled hair, and rocked her gently.

"Is it over?" she said.

"Almost. You can sleep."

I tucked her blankets tighter around her, watching as her breathing deepened. Her chest rose and fell in long, even waves. Even though her face was splotchy red and her closed eyes puffy, the tense edges of her expression had relaxed.

I exhaled from my bones, eased off the bed and left her to sleep. Leaving the bedroom door ajar, I staggered down the arrow-straight hallway to the couch. I could hardly keep my eyes open. Every muscle howled in protest as I sank into the ratty cushions.

"Holy *shit*," I muttered, and then I was gone, but only for a few hours.

I shot awake in the deepest part of the night. Creeping into the bedroom, I found Kacey still sleeping on, deeply and peacefully, and I knew then that she'd be okay. She'd fought the hardest battle and come out the other side.

I lay back on the couch, covered my eyes with the arm, and let out another breath, this one loose and shaky.

That was a close call, bro, I told Jonah. *But she made it. She fucking made it. You'd be so proud of her.*

My thoughts began to scatter like beads of oil over water as sleep took me again.

Proud of Kacey. She loves you so much.

Loves you…

CHAPTER 7

Kacey

I woke up feeling as if I'd been running for miles and miles—and months and months—chased by a monster that wanted to drown me. And now it was over. I'd won.

I lay on my back, my bones sinking into the mattress. Had it always felt this soft? A deep sigh gusted out of me, and I closed my eyes against the too-bright light filling the window of my bedroom. The last few days—three? Four?—were like some awful, twisted nightmare. I remembered it in bits and pieces, sweat-soaked and agonizing. My body felt wrung out, squeezed dry, and I suspected that if I tried to talk, my voice would be hoarse from screaming.

Teddy...

I'd screamed at Teddy. He had run from the monster with me, catching me when I stumbled, and helping me keep my feet. I fell down a hundred times, but without him, I don't know that I would've gotten back up again. And last night, I'd been on the verge of shattering into a million pieces until I felt Theo's arms around me, holding me together. I remembered the sound of his strong heart beating in my ear, and how afraid I was until he said, "I'm here." And then I could sleep.

I climbed out of bed, my arms and legs full of lead, my head thudding in time with my pulse. In the living room, Theo lay on the couch, eyes closed. He was too big for my ratty old couch—one arm and one leg were dangling—but he lay deep asleep despite the shaft of sunlight slanting across him.

It felt a little intrusive, watching him sleep, but I couldn't help it. I'd been alone for so long, and Theo had materialized out of thin air on Baronne Street all those nights ago. Profound gratitude that he was there, lying on my too-small couch, brought tears to my eyes. I brushed them away and felt the puffy skin. My hair fell around my shoulders in a rat's nest and I stunk. Badly.

I retreated to my small bathroom. A small cry caught in my throat at the reflection in the mirror. I looked as if I'd been punched in both eyes and now had mild shiners. I touched the mess of my hair and wondered if I might have to cut it off.

"But it's over," I told my pathetic reflection. The fluorescent light caught the glint in my eyes that was dimmed but not snuffed. "You did it, and it's over."

Not quite. A small voice warned that I'd have to fight against the urge to drink for the rest of my life, but for the first time in a long time, I thought I had a chance.

I shuddered as the shower loosened my stiff, aching limbs. My skin felt paper thin, my muscles weak. Dried off, I put on a fresh pair of sweatpants and the oldest, softest T-shirt I owned. I dragged a brush through my hair until my arm protested, then gave myself one last look in the bathroom mirror.

Dark circles, sallow skin, bloodshot eyes.

A definite improvement.

Theo was still asleep as I slipped past the living room to the kitchen. A glance at the stove clock said it was after eleven a.m. I began making coffee as quietly as I could, but as I flicked on the faucet, he stirred and sat up, scratching his face and blinking.

"Morning," he said.

"Morning." My voice felt like sandpaper against my throat.

Theo watched me closely. "How're you feeling?"

I forced my own small smile. "Like a truck hit me, threw it in reverse and backed over me to finish the job."

As he stood up and stretched, I reached in a cabinet for a canister of coffee, while my mind reached into the blurry mess of the last few days, trying to sort the memories out. My hands shook as I struggled to separate one coffee filter from the stack.

"Here, let me." Theo got up and joined me in the kitchen.

"I'm weak as hell," I said, my cheeks burning with shame. "I wore myself out taking the shower and wrestling with my hair."

"But you did it."

I looked up at him. He practically filled my entire kitchen and yet I still couldn't believe he was here. Solid and real, not a figment of my alcohol-drowned imagination.

"Sit," he said, his large hand gentle on my shoulder. "I got this."

I shuffled out of the kitchen and fell into the easy chair facing the couch. My body hugged around a pillow while Theo moved around my kitchen like he lived here.

"At the risk of sounding like an idiot, when did you arrive in New Orleans?"

"Five days ago," Theo said.

I shook my head, incredulous. "Five days and they're all a blur." I looked over at him. "How did you know where to find me?"

"The bartender from Le Chacal called me," Theo said, pouring water into the coffeemaker. "Mike. Big E. He overheard you talking tattoos with some guy and you kept repeating the name Teddy."

"And you dropped everything and flew halfway across the country."

The first scent of brewing coffee curled around the air. I hugged the pillow tighter as Theo came to sit on the couch.

"I'm sorry," I whispered.

"Don't," he said, waving his hand.

"I have to," I said, wiping my eyes on the back of my hand. "I have so much to be sorry for. Need to start somewhere."

"Start later," Theo said. "Right now, you should try to eat something. I wasn't able to get more than a few cups of water in you all this time, which is why you feel weak. Is there a place around here you like?"

"Rooney's Cafe. It's a diner about a three-block walk from here. I stumbled in a couple of times when the booze made me crave greasy food."

"I'll get us something from there," he said, heading back to the kitchen. "You mind if I take a quick shower first?"

"No. Go ahead."

I heard the watery bubble of coffee being poured into a cup, then Theo pressed the mug into my hand. I sipped and immediately set it down. Too hot. Too strong. Too much. Everything was too much, as if my body were made of rice paper, inside and out.

Theo emerged from the shower ten minutes later looking darkly handsome in a blue T-shirt, jeans and boots. "What do you want to eat?"

I tried to think of the least offensive food, something easy to chew and swallow. "Oatmeal would be great, thanks."

He started for the door, then stopped. "You got a house phone?

For emergencies?"

"No, just my cell…" My voice trailed off as a vague memory swam up at me. I sank into the chair under its weight. "Oh my God."

"You *had* a cell," Theo said with a wry twist to his lips.

"Teddy, I'm so sorry…"

He cut me off again. "I'll leave you my phone."

"What for?"

"I don't know. In case you feel really sick." He shrugged, grinned. "Or maybe play some Fruit Ninja."

I smiled. "You think of everything."

In the quiet house, I took tiny sips of coffee and played one game of Solitaire before opening Theo's contacts. The sheer amount of women's names—mostly just first names—made me roll my eyes with a small laugh, but the laugh died out when my random scrolling landed on Dena. Then Oscar. The Fletcher's home number. Tania, Jonah's assistant. Eme, the curator at the Galleria.

And Jonah.

My thumb shook as it hovered over the call button. Would I hear his old voicemail message? Or did the Fletchers have it disconnected?

Don't. You're barely hanging on after last night. You got nothing in your stomach. You don't have a hand to hold. Don't do this; you're not strong enough yet.

I hit call and slowly put the phone to my ear.

Hey, you've reached Jonah Fletcher…

My heart ripped in two as I remembered why I'd thrown away my old cell all those months ago.

Leave me a message and I'll call you back.

He sounded so healthy. No hitching breaths, no fatigue turning his voice to a whisper. I could leave a message and he'd call back in five minutes. He could walk through the front door, bickering with Theo, carrying take-out from Rooney's.

Have a good one.

I was still crying when Theo came back, bringing the scent of hash browns and eggs with him.

He didn't ask any questions, only set up the takeout on my splintered wooden coffee table: a small container of oatmeal for me and what looked to be like one of everything on the menu for himself.

"I called Jonah," I said, putting his cell on the table. "His number, I mean. The voicemail message set me off again. Serves me right for snooping. I'm sorry about that."

Theo's thick dark brows furrowed. "No big deal."

"I just…want to stay honest," I said. "From now on. It's not much, but…I'm sorry—"

"Hey."

His tone was sharp and I looked up miserably.

"I do it too," he said, his voice now low and soft. "I call him all the time. Just to hear his voice."

"I couldn't help it," I said, wiping my eyes. "I had to throw my old phone away because I was calling him dozens of times a day."

Theo nodded. "I still talk about him in present tense."

Those simple words did more to lift my spirits than anything else; almost more than Theo holding me together over the last few days. I wanted to confess everything to him: why I left Vegas, why I was drinking myself to oblivion, but he was tearing into the food.

"Fuck, I'm hungry," he said, digging around the bags.

"I'm sure you are," I said. "I don't have much to eat around here. I was on a liquid diet." I glanced up at him. "You had your work cut out for you."

Theo shrugged. "What friends do," he said, digging into a huge portion of biscuits and gravy.

"Yeah, they fly halfway across the country to wrestle a screaming, puking banshee for three—"

"Eat," he said, jerking his chin at my oatmeal.

I laughed a little—a rusty sound. "If you insist."

I picked at my oatmeal. My body felt like it had been turned inside out, then put back right-side in, but with everything in the wrong place. I put the smallest amount of oatmeal on my tongue. It tasted like warm paste with cinnamon. I forced myself to eat half a dozen bites, then set it down to watch Theo devour the feast in front of him. I rested my cheek in my hand, half-concealing my smile as he put away the biscuits and started in on a side of hash browns.

Theo must've felt my eyes on him. "What?"

"It's good to see you again," I said. "I'm sorry the circumstances are—"

He pointed the fork at me. "Stop. Apologizing."

"It feels like I have a lot to apologize for." I plucked at my paper napkin. "How's Beverly?"

"She's okay. As good as can be expected."

"Is she upset with me?"

"She was worried about you. We all were."

"I should've called her. I should've said something but…" I started to offer an excuse but swallowed it down, like bitter bile. "I owe *her* an apology, to say the least."

"I called her yesterday. Told her you were under the weather but getting better."

"Thank you."

He shrugged, wiped his mouth on a napkin, and took a sip of coffee.

"What about your dad?" I asked, toying with my oatmeal.

"He's thrown himself into his work. He was semi-retired, but he's been spending more time at the city hall trying to make himself useful. Fill the hours, I guess."

"And how do you do it?"

"Do what?"

"Fill the hours."

"Work, mostly. The shop's been really busy lately."

I dropped my spoon. "But now you're here with me."

Theo tossed down his napkin and looked at me with hard eyes. "Yeah, I am. And I'd do it again in a heartbeat so stop stressing over it." He smiled a little to soften his words. "You needed help, so I helped. Not a big deal."

It was a huge fucking deal but I let it drop. "Jesus, I don't even know what day of the week it is. *I* might be missing work too."

"It's Wednesday," Theo said. "And I think you need to take some time off."

"I think you're right. Can I borrow your phone?"

I called Rufus, the owner of Le Chacal and told him I was too sick to play the next night. Sudden laryngitis. Thanks to my hoarse voice, he sounded only mildly irritated at the last-minute cancellation.

"And Rufus?" I said, before we hung up.

"Yeah?"

"Tell Big E I said thank you. He'll know what for."

I called the other clubs, telling them I was sick and would let them know when I was able to come back.

If I come back, I thought.

I handed Theo's phone back to him. "When do you need to get back to Vegas?"

"I was thinking I'd fly back Sunday night," Theo said, cleaning up the remnants of our food. "Sound okay?"

I nodded. "Of course."

Honestly, the thought of being alone scared the shit out of me. I'd only been fully sober—and not ravaged by withdrawals—for half a day. Theo was here for two more, so I decided to allow myself those two days to figure my shit out. I was too tired, too mentally and physically exhausted to do anything yet anyway.

"Tomorrow I might be up to showing you around New Orleans," I said. "Right now, I'm so tired. Do you want to watch a movie?"

"Sure. I don't know if you remember, but *Dirty Dancing* is making the rounds on cable. That's 80's right?"

I smiled. "A classic. I'd love to give it another try."

He turned on my small flat screen and found the movie On Demand.

"I didn't even know I had cable," I said.

"That means you've been paying your bills," Theo said.

"Yeah, I guess I have," I said.

Theo sat on the couch, arms along both sides of the back, legs spread out. I curled tight in the chair but it wasn't comfortable, and that old longing to touch and be touched was fierce in me. My body felt small and fragile, and needing the protective embrace of another human being. I cursed myself for being so pathetic. Theo had seen me at my worst—hysterical and sick, naked and puking—and had held me through it all. I felt hesitant to ask for more. Or maybe it felt hard to ask now *because* I was sober.

I asked anyway.

"Teddy?"

"Yeah?"

"Do you mind if I sit with you?"

He looked over at me. Something gentle passed over his eyes, then melted down his features, softening all the hard edges.

"If you want."

He scooted to one side and I curled up beside him. Not touching him, but nearly. I could feel the warmth of his body, and smell the clean scent of his skin. Right around the time Baby and Johnny were practicing the lift in the lake, my head began to droop and my eyes kept falling shut.

"Come here." Theo put his arm around me. He sank lower into the cushions, making a pillow of his chest. His hand reached to pull the blanket from the back of the couch and drape it over my legs.

"Sleep," he said.

I sighed, melted against him and drifted away on the lake.

CHAPTER 8

Theo

The next morning, she emerged from her room looking a million times better than she had all week. Her color was back, her hair brushed. It wasn't bleached anymore—she said she'd been letting the natural color grow out, a kind of honey blonde.

"I was too wasted to keep up with the peroxide," she said, she put down her onion bagel to examine a lock of hair. "I haven't seen this color since I was fourteen. Kind of blah."

Kind of fucking gorgeous, I thought. The strange color of her eyes—light blue iris ringed in darker blue—was more vibrant against the brass-gold of her hair.

I shrugged over my coffee cup. "Looks good."

Kacey smiled and chatted on. "How are Oscar and Dena?" she asked.

"Engaged."

She sat up straighter. "Really? He finally popped the question?"

"Yep."

"How did he propose?"

"He took her to Great Basin a few months ago. Not exactly a surprise, but it's his favorite place."

"It's a great place." Her eyes seemed to retreat, pulling inward. The gaze of someone falling back in time. "I think I blocked that entire camping trip to Great Basin from my mind. I had to. It was too perfect. The first time Jonah and I…" She glanced up through tears and sniffed a laugh. "Well, you know."

I kept my face expressionless. "Yeah, I know."

"It was the kicker though," she said. "The memory that finally pulled me out of the withdrawals. I wonder why."

"It was a powerful memory. Like you said, you'd blocked the entire trip out. Yesterday morning you let it back in. Proverbial floodgates."

She laughed a little. "Literally and figuratively. I look like I lost a boxing match."

"But better now," he said.

"It still hurts. Really fucking badly. But it's a different kind of hurt. It's cleaner, somehow. Like I can cry if I need to, but I can stop if I need to, too. I didn't have that before. It's why I drank, I guess. To keep numb. So I wouldn't have to always be fighting back the pain. That was too exhausting."

A short silence dropped between us.

"Do you want to get out of here?" she asked suddenly. "I've lived in this city for six months and still haven't *seen* it."

"If you're up for it?"

"I think so. I feel better. And it doesn't seem right you came all this way to just sit in the house."

"I wouldn't mind getting out."

"Great." Kacey slipped off the chair, still moving a little slowly, as if she were breakable. "I'll get ready."

We drove into the French Quarter and parked near Jefferson Square. Her arm linked in mine, Kacey pointed out various landmarks—the St. Louis Cathedral, a museum, an art gallery. Every other minute my eyes were drawn to her. She'd put on dark jeans and an oversize, dark gray sweater that left one shoulder bare—she seemed to like that style. Her hair fell like brushed brass and she'd put on some kind of perfume that made it hard to think.

She was beautiful. Walking arm-in-arm with her, it was easy to pretend her bloodshot eyes, thin face and the hoarseness in her voice were because she was getting over an illness. Just a bug that had knocked her out a little while. All was fine now. We were out for a walk. We were…

Together?

Rein it in, I told myself. *Before you do something stupid.*

It was hard to be subdued in this setting. New Orleans was alive in a different way than Vegas felt alive. My city was wide open and filled with lights. New Orleans held you tight in the past. City center was a maze of old buildings with wrought iron lattices and French fleur de lis. We walked past clubs and cafés, restaurants and bars. A bar on every block. A watering hole on every corner.

"Basically the worst part of town for recovering alcoholics to wander around in," Kacey observed.

"You want to leave?" I asked.

She chewed her bottom lip for a moment. "No. I want to go there."

I followed her pointing finger to a tiny shop with beads and colored lights strung along the window. On the glass was a hand in white paint with an eye in the palm. Above the palm, red neon said *Palm & Tarot Readings*. Below, it read, *Love, Fate, Destiny*.

I frowned. "A psychic?"

"Just to check it out," she said. "I used to love Tarot cards when I was a teenager. And there's something about New Orleans. The Cajun history, the voodoo traditions." She jerked her shoulders up. "I think it's neat."

It was the first time she sounded a shade above sad since I'd been here. That was enough reason to let her tug me into the tiny shop.

A bell jingled above the door as we stepped inside and the scent of incense hit me hard. The dimly-lit entry looked like the front foyer of a house, with a heavy, purple curtain with gold fringe separating the shop from the residence. A small, round table with four chairs stood to the right of the front door. An even smaller table displayed trays of beads, rough-cut crystals, and pieces of wood carved with runes. Old books lined the shelves, and between the shelves hung with dream catchers, straw voodoo dolls, and colorful drawings of sugar skulls—large, laughing faces, some wearing top hats and smoking, some wearing wedding dresses with straw hair and sewn lips.

Palm readings and psychic powers sounded like bullshit to me, but I liked the vibe of the place anyway.

"Isn't this cool?" Kacey said, letting go of my arm to trail her fingers over the purple crystals in their slot on the tray.

The heavy curtain was drawn aside and the owner of the shop stepped out. I'd half-expected a woman in a turban with a crystal ball under her arm. Or maybe that googly-eyed professor from the *Harry Potter* movies.

This woman was neither a cliché gypsy nor a crazy-haired weirdo.

She looked in her mid-forties, with long cornrows that ended in colorful beads that clacked with every movement. Her clothes were billowy silk but modern. Thick gold hoops dangled from her ears.

"Welcome," she said in a smooth voice. "My name is Olivia. You have come for a reading?"

"We're just looking," Kacey said. "You have a beautiful shop."

Olivia smiled and swept across the room to the small table. "That is kind of you to say. But that is not why you stepped inside, no?"

It was an effort not to roll my eyes. I knew the opener of a sales pitch when I heard one.

"Come. Sit." Olivia gestured to the two empty chairs at her table and pulled out a deck of oversized cards from a pocket in her robes. "You are curious, yes? Maybe a little intrigued?"

"Not really," I said at the exact same time Kacey said, "Yes, a little."

Kacey and Olivia laughed, and the fortuneteller tapped long, red-painted nails on the stack of cards. "A full reading is $20. Three card-draw is $10. One card is only $5. A small taste of what I offer."

"The one-card reading doesn't sound too bad," Kacey said.

"$5.00 each. That is cheap, yes, for guidance and wisdom from the Other Side."

The way Olivia's voice wrapped reverently around *the Other Side* told me it was a real place to her. I felt Kacey's hand slip into mine, then she was tugging me toward the table. "One card, Teddy. It'll be fun."

Feeling like an idiot, I sat beside Kacey at the too-small table while Olivia shuffled her deck. The backs were black with gold edging. Once shuffled to her liking, she fanned them out on the table.

"These cards tell the future?" I asked dubiously.

"A full reading tells us where you have been, where you are, and where you're going," Olivia said. "One card gives us a snapshot of the present. By understanding where you are now, you are able to see more clearly what lies ahead. Clarity is the goal. Wipe away the fog of uncertainty…sometimes that is all it takes to bring a little relief to a troubled soul."

She said these last words to Kacey, and Kacey nodded hopefully.

"So," Olivia said, beaming. "Who is going first?"

"He is," Kacey said.

"I'm not going at all," I said. "This is your deal."

Olivia laughed heartily as Kacey jostled my arm.

"Come on, Teddy. What have you got to lose?"

I looked over at Kacey, at her eyes punching bright and blue through the dim shop. I huffed a sigh of defeat. "Fine, okay."

Those damn eyes.

Olivia trailed her fingers over the card. "Choose one, and lay it down in front of you."

Figuring most people picked cards from the middle—and Olivia probably counted on that—I chose from the far right of the deck. I flipped over a card, revealing a sketch of a man hanging upside by one foot from the limbs of a T-shaped tree.

"The Hanged Man," Olivia said, scooping the cards back into a neat stack, leaving my card on the table in front of me. "This does not surprise me."

I suppressed another eye roll. Beside me, Kacey leaned forward in her seat. "What does it mean?"

"The Hanged Man represents ultimate surrender."

I blinked. "What?"

Kacey elbowed me in the side. "Ultimate surrender, Teddy. Sounds kinky."

Now I *did* roll my eyes and Olivia laughed heartily. "The ultimate surrender of the Hanged Man," she continued after a moment, "is the surrender of self for others. Personal sacrifices made for the greater good. Putting self-interests aside, or giving up goals in favor of that which he perceives to be higher causes." She fixed me with a strong gaze. "You put the needs and wants of others first, always, and without complaint. Yes?"

I sat back in the old wooden chair, not sure how the hell I was supposed to answer.

"Yes," Kacey said. "*Yes*. That's Teddy, one hundred percent." She looked at me, her eyes soft and warm. "You've always been that way."

I shifted in my seat and turned to Olivia. "So where does the guidance part come in?"

"The Hanged Man looks content," she said. "Note the calm expression on his face. Yet, he is tethered to this tree. Suspended. A *life* suspended." She settled back in her chair. "You content yourself with the belief what you're doing is best for those around you. Yet your own dreams and goals suffer for it. You must choose a path. Finalize a decision that has been looming before you. Take action for your own sake, not for the sake of others, or remain forever suspended."

Kacey nodded as if she knew exactly what Olivia meant, and they both looked to me, expectantly.

"Yeah, okay," I muttered, just to get the reading over with. Hell, who isn't facing major decisions in their life? Who doesn't want to feel like they're selfless and always put others first? Olivia probably had a generalization memorized for every card, with a little ego-boost thrown in.

Granted, the Hanged Man's meaning hit a little closer to home than I wanted to admit. Fine, I admitted it. Didn't make me a believer.

As if she'd read my thoughts, Olivia returned the Hanged Man to the deck and began to shuffle again, her expression smug and satisfied. She fanned the cards over the table in front of Kacey. "Choose your card, sweetheart."

Kacey bit her lip, her eyes scanning the cards, and finally chose one toward the middle of the deck and flipped it over. She sat back with a small gasp. My hands clenched into fists under the table as my heart skipped a beat.

On the card was a sketch of a skeleton using a scythe like a broom, sweeping up gold crowns and jewels. XIII was inscribed at the top. At the bottom...

"Death," Kacey whispered.

Olivia watched her closely. "It is not the card you think it is, my dear."

"No?" Kacey's eyes were fixed on the sketch, her voice small. "Seems like it's exactly the card I think it is."

I leaned into her. "We don't have to stay."

"No, it's fine." She looked at Olivia. "What does it mean?"

"The card of Death is a harbinger of change," the psychic said. "It is the closing of one door, and the opening of another. Transition. You feel cast adrift, no? Trapped in an in-between state that has left you unsure of how to proceed. You cannot go back, and yet..."

"I can't go forward," Kacey murmured. "It's true. I'm stuck."

"No, my dear," Olivia said. "You can't let go, but that is not the same as stuck. When you hold tightly to something behind you, you cannot move forward. The answer is to unclench your heart from the past. Close the door. Open a new chapter. Only then can you be free of the pain that haunts you."

The psychic paused for effect, and goddamn if I wasn't hanging on every word.

"Acceptance, child," Olivia continued. "That is the key. Accept that which has ended and let go so you can move on. So you may grow. So you may thrive. The light in your eyes—in your heart—has dimmed, but it is not put out. Let it roar once again."

A moment of breath-held silence. Then Kacey exhaled and sat back, her eyes shining. "Thank you."

We left the shop after I slipped Olivia $20. Five bucks for each card, another ten as a tip for how Kacey hugged the woman, declaring how *relieved* she felt.

"Wasn't that amazing?" Kacey said, her arm tucked in mine. "I mean, you can chalk it all up to coincidence, but I felt some real truth there." She looked up at me. "Did you?"

"A little," I said slowly. I'd felt hope as well as truth. Hope that the new chapter in Kacey's life might include me in a meaningful way.

So much for putting self-interests aside.

"The big decision you've been putting off must mean the tattoo shop, right?"

I shrugged. "I guess."

"How come you haven't bought your own place yet, Teddy?"

I could've told her I was in the process of getting a business degree, but that would only make her feel like shit if she knew I'd missed my exams to be here.

I shrugged again. "Haven't found the right place yet."

Kacey frowned, then shivered a little, even though the night was warm. "I'm getting a little tired. I'd like to go home."

By the time we reached Kacey's house, I was regretting tipping Olivia or even stepping foot inside that psychic shop. Instead of lying down for a nap, Kacey curled up on the chair in the living room. Hugging the pillow tight and staring at nothing.

I sat on the couch and reached over to tap her knee. "You okay?"

She shook her head. "Not really."

"Look, these so-called psychics—"

"She was exactly right," Kacey said.

"About what?"

She looked up at me, her eyes drowning in tears. "I can't let go of Jonah."

I sat back, nodded. "Yeah, I hear you."

"Sometimes, when I'd come home drunk," she said. "I'd fall into bed, and just before I passed out, I swear I could hear his voice. Telling me to let go. And I'd wake up feeling so guilty. Like maybe Jonah can't live in the stars until I let him go." She plucked at a stray thread on her pillow, the tears dropping onto the orange fabric. "I always brush it off as a dream. I'm not ready to let him go, and it doesn't feel like a choice anyway. It feels…impossible."

I wished I knew how to talk to her, to make her feel better. But I was struck mute, my own grief trying to rise up and swamp me.

"And how can I ever let go when there was still so much I didn't do?" she demanded with sudden fire "Because I could have done more. I *should* have done more. I should've married him. Did he want that? A wedding? Or I could have had his baby. So he could know that a part of him would go on forever."

"Kacey—"

"I could've done it," she said fiercely. "How can I let go when I didn't do enough?"

"Bullshit," I said. "Was Jonah ever not honest with you about what he wanted? Ever?"

She sniffed and shrugged.

"He wouldn't ask you for those things," I said. "He wouldn't legally bind you for the sake of a stupid ceremony. He wouldn't ask you to have a kid and leave you to raise it on your own."

"I know he wouldn't, but…"

"No regrets, right? Isn't that what you told him?"

Kacey nodded. "It is. And it's true. Except the regret I didn't do enough. The regret I couldn't…."

Don't say it, I thought.

Her eyes overflowed. "I couldn't save him."

Kacey's hair fell over her face as she bent over, weeping.

I couldn't save him. What I had felt every day of my life since Jonah got sick. Only I couldn't cry it out like she could. If I touched her, if I touched her grief with mine, I'd rage and howl and lose my fucking mind.

Jonah… Come back, you asshole.

I sucked in a breath, used it to push the pain down. When I trusted my voice, I said, "You did everything right. Everything."

Kacey lifted her head. When she brushed the hair from her eyes, the look within their depths was desperate.

"You made him happy," I said. "Right at the time he needed it most. You made him happy. Quit worrying about what you didn't do, because what you *did* do was everything. Okay?"

She dragged the sleeve of her shirt across her face. "Easier said than done."

I could tell my words had helped to make her feel better. And making her feel better was as close to happy as I was ever going to get.

That night, we watched *Sixteen Candles* with a pizza and soda. Kacey sat beside me on the couch, half a cushion separating us, close enough to feel the warmth of her body.

"You're still flying back to Vegas on Sunday?" she asked as the credits rolled.

"That's the plan."

"Change of plan: I'm flying back with you."

I looked over at her. "Are you sure you're up for that?"

She sniffed a laugh. "No. But I need to see your parents. And Oscar and Dena. Put those wrongs right. Isn't that one of the steps in recovery? Make amends?"

"I guess," I said, staring at this woman who was so riddled with regret and shame, and so oblivious to her own strength. *That's part of the insidiousness of addiction,* I thought. *You remember the depth and blackness of the hole you were in and not the strength it took to pull yourself out.*

"I have a lot of apologizing to do," Kacey said. "I have to face Vegas at some point. Look the memories in the eye… Otherwise I'll hide out here forever, avoiding my feelings. Which is what drove me to drink in the first place." Kacey smacked the arm of the chair, her eyes shining. "See? Thousands of dollars' worth of therapy breakthroughs for the price of one Tarot card reading."

ALL IN

Before I could answer, she was out of the chair and climbing into my arms.

"Thank you, Teddy," she whispered against my neck.

My heart crashed against my chest. "For the five bucks? Easy money."

"No, you big dummy," she said, her laughter warm and soft on my skin. "Thank you for saving my life."

"It wasn't me, Kace," I said, and let my hand rest on her hair. "It was you. You did all the work—"

"Theodore," she said. "Just say, 'you're welcome' or when we get to Vegas I'll have someone tattoo the Hanged Man on your forehead."

"Well, when you put it that way… You're welcome."

CHAPTER 9

Kacey

The flight attendant smiled benignly at me. "Would you like something to drink?"

"That's a million dollar question," I muttered.

"Pardon?"

I smiled thinly. "Diet Coke, please."

The attendant popped a can for me and poured a bottle of water for Theo, then pushed her cart further down the aisle.

"You good?" Theo asked.

"I want to puke, my skin feels like it's a size too small for my body, and then there's that." I pointed to my jouncing leg. "I should've given you the window seat. I'm going to see Vegas get closer and closer as we land. We're crashing right into everything I'm scared of."

"Maybe it's too soon," Theo said. "It's only been a few days since you quit."

I shook my head. "I have to do this. If I stop to think too much, I'll chicken out. Plus, I'm already on the plane. Too late to have them swing around and drop me off in Oklahoma."

"Nobody's mad at you," Theo said after a moment. "My mother, especially. She'll just be happy you're okay."

"It's more than that," I said. I glanced out the little window where Texas was a vast, flat space of pale green and brown below us. "It's Vegas. And Jonah." My throat constricted and I gripped the armrest of my seat. "How do you do it?" I asked. "So many memories…"

He shrugged. "Work and school keep me busy."

I blinked. "What do you mean, school?"

He made a face. "Bound to come up sooner or later. I went back to UNLV to get an MBA."

"*Teddy.*" I socked his arm. "Shit, that's awesome. Why didn't you tell me?"

He smiled dryly. "You weren't really in the mood to make conversation."

I snorted. "Seriously, when did you start? How much do you have left?"

"January and I have a year to go."

I curled in my seat to face him. "Why did you go back?"

"So when I buy my own place, I won't be totally in the dark about how to run it."

I felt my cheeks stretch in the widest smile I'd worn in ages. "I'm so proud of you. Does that sound condescending?"

Theo said, "No," while nodding his head 'yes.'

I laughed and socked his arm. "Smartass."

I sat back in my seat, a strange, hopeful thought sparking in my mind. *If he opened a shop in New Orleans, I'd have a friend.*

My best friend.

What else would you call the person who dropped everything to fly across the country to save my life?

"Do you think you might want to open a shop somewhere outside of Vegas?" I asked slowly.

"Maybe. Mom's health isn't great." He waved his hand at my alarmed expression. "She's okay, she's just… She had the rug pulled out from under her, you know? She's shaky and scared all the time. I'd feel like shit leaving town."

Theo was stuck. Suspended. Just like the Tarot card said. My short-lived fantasy he might open a shop in New Orleans died a swift death. Family comes first, of course, but I hated the idea of him not pursuing his dream.

"I'm sure there's a way you can market a shop in Vegas so it stands out," I told him. "You're really talented, Teddy. I've seen your work. *Inked* has featured your work. If you open a shop, customers will come for *you*."

"Maybe. It's a risk. It was already risky. New businesses fail all the time. It would be different if it wasn't Jonah's money…" He shook his head, biting off his own words. "I'll get this degree first and go from there."

He clearly wanted me to drop the subject so I did. I turned my head to the window and watched the land slide beneath us. Soon enough—too soon—the plane began its descent and I watched Las Vegas—and all of the memories I shared with Jonah—growing closer and closer.

Tears blurred my vision but I blinked them back to watch the Strip with its lights—brilliant and colorful even at midday—glow against the yellow sands. Like colored glass glinting in the sun.

Las Vegas held all that scared me the most, and it was beautiful.

CHAPTER 10

Theo

We got my truck out of McCarran's long-term parking and drove to the hotel so Kacey could drop off her bags. She'd reserved a room at a little budget place off the Strip, not too far from my parents' house.

"They know I'm coming, right?" she asked, chewing her lip as we drove to the Belvedere neighborhood.

"I told them we'd head over after you got settled."

"But they don't know I was drunk for nearly six months."

"I didn't tell them anything," I said. "That's up to you."

Her hands twisted nervously in her lap, as she watched Vegas go by outside the window.

"It's going to be okay, Kace. I promise."

Kacey nodded. "Funny. Here, in the truck, with the windows rolled up? I feel secure. Barricaded. But when we step outside, when I breathe in Vegas… It'll be like breathing in Jonah. The memories. They're in the air, you know? Like I'll feel them in my chest when I inhale." She put her hand over her heart and rubbed as if it pained her.

I had no fucking clue what to say to that. Just as it had been with her withdrawals, there was nothing I could say to make the pain any easier to take. I just had to be there for her, if that helped at all.

As I turned onto my parents' street, Kacey sucked in a breath. By the time I parked, tears flooded her eyes.

"We're not even out of the car, yet." She stared out the car window. "I'm home," she whispered. "It's Jonah's home, but it felt like mine, too. Your parents made me feel welcome and loved. In a way my parents never did. And I left. I just…left."

I turned in my seat toward her. "Hey. Look at me."

She turned her head.

"You're here now."

She nodded, smiling weakly and then wiped her eyes. "Let's do this."

We climbed out of the car, and walked side by side to the house. The front door opened before I could knock. My mother walked straight by me and engulfed Kacey in a hug. They hugged and cried on the front stoop, then cried and hugged on the living room couch. Over and over, Kacey told her how sorry she was. Over and over, my mother hushed her, brushed back her hair and smudged away tears.

"I understand," she said. "You did the hardest thing. You stayed with Jonah to the end. For that, you'll always have a place in this family."

I rummaged in the fridge, trying not to listen until finally my mother clapped her hands and declared the crying was over. It was time to eat.

"Everyone out on the patio." She called to the back of the house, "Henry? Theo's back. With Kacey. Let's get the nice steaks, yes? Kacey, you like steak?"

Kacey nodded her head and I got the impression she'd have eaten them raw if it made my mother happy.

"Wonderful. Theo, dear, will you start the grill? Oscar and Dena will be here any minute."

My father emerged from the den and gave Kacey a hug and a peck on the cheek, and then we got down to the business of Sunday dinner.

I worked the grill, flipping six porterhouses over the fire while Kacey and my parents made small talk. I didn't listen but through the smoke of the grill, my eyes focused on the empty chair next to Kacey and to my dad's right from where he sat at the end of the table. Kacey's hand rested on the armrest, her fingers running along the wooden slat. My dad put his hand on the back of it as he leaned in to tell Kacey something.

Jonah was sitting in the chair. I could see him, plain as day, in the drape of our father's arm, holding Kacey's hand. He was right there, taking up that seat. It was forever his.

I brought the platter of steaks to the table and hesitated. Where was my place? My parents were on either end, two empty chairs on one side for Oscar and Dena, Kacey and Jonah's chair on the other.

I busied myself using silver tongs to plate the steaks.

"I'm so happy you're here," my mother said, cupping Kacey's cheek.

"It's all thanks to him." Kacey looked at me. "I was in a bad way.

Trying to stay numb." She smiled at me, shaking her head. "Teddy dropped everything and came to the rescue."

"He did, indeed." Dad turned to me. "Did you speak with your professors about the exams you missed?"

"It's fine," I said quickly, although the emails I'd received from my professors weren't fine in the slightest. Kacey gaped at me, alarm and regret twisting her features. I hated my dad a little just then.

"And your job is still waiting for you?"

"Henry," my mother said. "I'm sure he sorted everything out beforehand."

"Everything's fine," I said, the heat rising up in my face. I dumped my dad's steak on his plate harder than I meant to.

"I'm merely stating my concern for your responsibilities here," Dad said. "I'd hate to see you jeopardize your standing with the university. Tuition is expensive, and Jonah's contribution can only—"

"*Nothing* is in jeopardy, Dad," I said. "So just drop it."

"Drop it like it's hot?" asked a cheerful voice from the patio gate. "I see it's business as usual Chez Fletcher."

"Oscar," Kacey said, rising to her feet. "Dena."

She threw herself between them and they squashed her tight. The three friends embraced, the women holding on to each other the longest.

"Girl, you skipped town like the mob was after you," Oscar said. Over the six months Kacey was gone, he hardly mentioned her, or asked about her, and then usually only if Dena did first. He smiled his broad smile at her and I didn't doubt that he was happy she was back, but once the reunion it was over, it was business as usual.

My mother clapped her hands together. "Everyone sit. Eat before it gets cold."

I took the only seat available, the one that had been Jonah's and sat down, feeling like an imposter, despite Kacey's warm smile for me.

She filled everyone in on where she was living and working, and my mother crowed about how she'd always wanted to go to New Orleans. Kacey asked about Oscar and Dena's respective jobs—Oscar doing computer programming for the MGM Grand; Dena working as an adjunct literature professor at UNLV. The women fawned over Dena's engagement ring. Oscar and I made small talk about the Runnin' Rebels basketball chances this year. But underneath it all, was a sad truth: We were a bunch of people sitting around propping up the conversation with false smiles and high-pitched voices, trying to ignore the gaping black hole in our lives.

"I have a ticket to next week's game," Oscar said. "That is, if you don't already have a date lined up."

I felt Kacey's sideways glance at the same time Mom asked, "Are you seeing someone special, dear?"

"No," I said. "I'm too busy with work and school."

"Yeah, right." Oscar laughed while Dena regarded me with those dark brown eyes of hers—eyes that had a way of looking *through* you. I glanced away before she saw too much.

"So, listen," Kacey said. She tapped her fork against her water glass and threw a look around the table. "I need to say something. I owe you all an explanation."

"You don't owe us anything, dear," my mom said.

Kacey shook her head. "No, I do. For you and for myself." She huffed a breath and the entire table went still. I wanted to take her hand, let her know she had my support, but didn't dare. Not while sitting in Jonah's chair. I nudged her foot under the table instead.

She shot me a grateful smile.

"I told you I've been in New Orleans for the last six months. I headed east and kept driving until I landed there. Or maybe I just ran out of steam. I left Vegas because losing Jonah was harder than I could've imagined. I thought I was ready. Or at least a little bit prepared. I wasn't. Not even close."

I glanced around the table, all of them unmoving, unblinking but all of them—all of us—connected by our own memories of those fucking horrible days after Jonah left us.

"I tried," Kacey said. "I wrote a bunch of music really fast, as if I could outrun the grief and get it all out on paper. But it didn't work. The words weren't enough and I was too scared to face the enormity of the grief. I thought it would destroy me. So I fled to a different city, hoping to outrun the memories. And when that didn't work, I started drinking."

The table shifted now, leaning forward or back, tucking hair and scratching at chins. I pressed my foot to hers harder. Kacey sucked in a breath and I knew what she was going to say next. The hardest thing.

"I've been drunk for the last six months. Literally. Every day, all day." She looked at me, her eyes brimming. "Theo saved my life. I was slowly killing myself, and if Teddy hadn't found me…"

"Kace," I murmured. It wasn't a big deal and yet it was. I wanted to brush it aside and I wanted to be proud I helped her. I wanted to earn my seat, and yet I already belonged here.

God, when will everything stop feeling so fucked up?

Kacey smiled down at me. "He'll never tell you what he went through to help me sober up, but I'll tell you: it was hell. He never left, no matter how hard it got. I'll never be able to repay him for saving my life."

She heaved another sigh and wiped her eyes. "So I'm here now, thanks to him, but also because I missed all of you. And I wanted to say I'm sorry. I'm sorry for leaving. I'm sorry I made you worry or made you angry or hurt you. I'm sorry and… I'm sorry."

Mom took Kacey's hands. Dena's chair scraped on the stones as she stood up and came around the table to join the embrace.

Oscar, his expression subdued, was slowly nodding at me.

Dad shifted in his seat. "I had no idea her situation was so dire."

I braced myself for the "But…" The addendum that diminished what I'd done, or the rest of the lecture. But my dad stared past me, turning tonight over in his mind.

Do you see now, Dad? I thought. *I had to go. I made a promise. I went to her now, and I'll go to her again if I have to. I'll fail a hundred classes and be fired from a hundred jobs before I let anything happen to her again.*

CHAPTER 11

Kacey

"You'll come back tomorrow?" Beverly asked, hugging me goodnight. "How long are you in town?"

"Just a few days," I said.

Her face fell. "Oh. I thought you might be here longer. Or that you'd be moving back…?"

"Mom," Theo said. "She's tired…"

"I have to go back," I said, forcing a smile. "I'm booked for gigs and I'm trying to keep my obligations. "I'll visit tomorrow. For dinner? Can I bring something?"

Beverly hugged me again. "Just yourself, dear."

Dena pulled me in next. Her hug was like her gaze; warm and soft, and completely welcoming. Though she was only a few years older than me, she exuded wisdom I didn't think I'd ever know. Looking at her, I realized what it meant to be an old soul. "You did a brave thing," she said softly. "It might not feel like it, but it is."

"I don't feel brave," I said. "One minute I feel proud for getting out of the hole. The next minute I hate myself for digging in so deep in the first place."

"We all have our ways of coping," Dena said, holding me at arms' length. "You found something that felt like relief, something to numb you, and you clung to it, even as it dragged you down. But you climbed out, knowing how hard it would be on the other side. You should feel more proud than ashamed."

I hugged her tightly. "I missed you."

"I missed you too," she said. "And I miss Jonah. It's been harder than I ever imagined. But seeing you again reminds me how happy he was." She smiled and held my shoulders. "I know he carries that joy with him wherever he is. Take comfort in that if you can, love."

"I will."

ALL IN

But it was a lie. I didn't feel any comfort. I didn't even know what comfort meant anymore. Especially tonight, here at the Fletchers' house, where Jonah looked at me from photographs and dangled overhead in the glass lamps he'd made. Where he leaned over my shoulder and touched the small of my back. How I kept turning to look at him and ask what he thought, but it was Theo who looked back at me. I missed Jonah so badly, I could feel the cracks in my heart left by his absence. It felt impossible that they'd ever be healed.

Theo drove me to the hotel. He parked in front but I didn't move to get out.

"How bad is it?" I asked.

He frowned. "How bad is what?"

"The situation with your classes."

"Fuck, Kacey, don't…"

"Tell me."

He sighed. "I might have to retake one or two. Not a big deal."

I closed my eyes and slumped in my seat. "I owe you so much."

"You don't owe me a damn thing," Theo said. "Stop saying you do." His voice softened. "You look beat. Come on. I'll walk you up."

"Wait…" I glanced at the hotel. "I'm not really ready to be alone right now. It's so fucking hard. If I hole up in my room alone, I'll just cry all night."

Theo was quiet a minute. Then he said in a low voice, "I know a place we can go."

They call New York the city that never sleeps, but Vegas deserved the title more. The Strip was bustling on a Sunday night. Cars jammed the street in rows of red and white, and pedestrians streamed along the sidewalks. We passed the Bellagio Hotel and Casino, where Jonah and I had gone once. Our first date, I realized, when the lit-up fountains danced to a romantic ballad. Tonight it was Michael Jackson's "Billy Jean" accompanying them, but it didn't matter: I could still see us. Everything about that night was right there, perfectly preserved at the forefront of my mind. I could taste the cupcake he'd bought for me from an ATM.

I swallowed hard and looked away. Theo guided the truck down a side street next to the Wynn Hotel, and I knew where he was taking me.

"It's late," I said softly. "The Galleria will be closed."

"I got it covered," he said.

He parked the truck in a service lot, where employees parked, and came around to open my door.

"Do you moonlight here?" I asked, as he took my hand and walked me to a back entrance.

"They know me," he said.

That was true, but the security guard didn't know me. "Not sure about this, Theo," he said, stroking his mustache.

"She's Jonah's girlfriend," Theo replied.

The guard's eyes swept me up and down, taking in my bloodshot eyes and stooped shoulders. A smile unfolded beneath the mustache as he punched a code and let us in.

"Have a good night, Theo. You too, Miss."

"Thanks, Wilson," Theo said, and led me through the back corridors of the Wynn.

"They just let you in here?" I asked. I was already lost in the rights and lefts, but Theo seemed to know exactly where he was going. He was still holding my hand.

"I come here a lot," he said.

The Galleria was closed, but after a few words with the other security guard on duty, the door was unlocked for us and we went in. My hand slipped into Theo's as we walked the long leg of the L-shaped gallery, lined with stone sculptures. When we came to the bend, I stopped.

Theo's hand squeezed mine. "It'll be okay. I promise."

We rounded the corner.

I expected to cry and wail, to be flooded with pain and grief and collapse in a heap on the floor. I didn't expect my chest to tighten with exhilaration. I wasn't prepared for the smile that broke through my face like a crack in hard stone. Tears flooded my eyes but not for pain. For the breathtaking beauty of Jonah's masterpiece.

The water looked like it was in motion. The sea life at the bottom pulsed with life. I could feel the heat of the blazing sun slice through the delicate glass waterfall. A blur of yellows and blues, oranges and reds.

ALL IN

I sank down on a bench opposite the glass. I breathed through the tears and let it fill my eyes, let my eyes inhale the beauty of it.

"You were right," I whispered. "This is exactly the right place to be. Is that why you come here? Does it bring you peace?"

"Some." Theo sat next to me. An exhausted collapse of his limbs, as if he'd carried around a tremendous weight all day long, and only here could he set it down. As he stared up at the glass, he looked haggard and exhausted.

"I drank myself into a stupor to numb the grief," I said. "And I still want to. The fact we're fifty yards away from a casino filled with free booze is agonizing."

"You want to leave?"

"No, I have to deal with it. Being here helps. But what about you, Teddy? How have you been coping?"

He shrugged. "I just keep moving."

"Do you want to talk about it?"

"Not really." He was closed up tight, arms crossed, expression locked in determination.

You left when he asked you to stay. You weren't the only one suffering, about to shatter into pieces.

I leaned my head against his shoulder. "I'm sorry," I whispered.

"What for?"

"You know what for. You hurt as much as I do."

He shifted like he was going to say something dismissive. Instead, he sighed and said in a low voice. "Like I said, you're here now."

I nodded against him, my tired eyes wanting to close but if they did, the ache in my heart would pull me under. I drank in the beautiful glass instead.

We sat with Jonah for a long time.

CHAPTER 12

Theo

I went into work the next day at noon and Vivian told me Gus was already there, waiting for me.

"How bad is it?" I asked.

She shook the Magic 8-Ball on her desk, one of her many kitschy knick-knacks. She turned the blue triangle toward me: *Ask again later.*

"Thanks, Viv," I muttered. "That's super helpful."

She chucked me on the arm. "Go get'em, tiger."

I stepped into the back office that was hardly bigger than a broom closet, and just as cluttered. A bank of five lockers lined one wall, and the desk practically barred access to the bathroom.

"I'm trying to retire, Theo," Gus Monroe said, as I shut the door behind me. He leaned back in his chair, kicked his cowboy boots on the desk and smoothed his long, handlebar mustache with two fingers. A ponytail of thin brown hair hung over the shoulder of his plaid button-down. He pinched a quarter-inch of air between his thumb and index finger. "I'm *this* close to Belize's beaches for the rest of my life. I'm not trying to get back to inking."

"It was an emergency," I said. "I had to help a friend. She was in a bad way."

"*She*, huh?" Gus rolled his eyes. "For a chick you drop everything and take off for a week?" He shook his head. "Don't let women lead you around by the balls, Fletcher. They do it once, they won't ever stop."

"Good advice," I said, adding silently, *From the guy who's on his third marriage.*

"Here's another piece of advice: You take off like that again and I'm going to have to let you go. Can't be helped."

"It won't. I promise." A lie. I was thankful he wasn't firing my ass but if Kacey ever needed me again, I was gone.

Can't be helped, I thought and almost smiled.

Vivian poked her head in the door. "Sorry to interrupt, but she's here, Theo. Your brother's…girlfriend?"

Kacey mentioned she might stop by, but the last fucking thing I wanted was Gus to figure out she was the reason I'd taken off for a week. I turned to go. "Thanks, Viv."

"You just got back," Gus said. "Now you're socializing on company time?"

"She's a paying customer. She's here to pick a design."

He rolled his eyes. "Go." Then leveled a finger at me. "But I'll say it again, Fletcher. I love your work. You're a talented artist. And having *Inked* sniffing around here for news about you isn't exactly a bad thing. But no more taking off, you got me?"

"Loud and clear."

I slipped out the door and shut it behind me. Kacey stood in the little waiting area, making small talk with Vivian. Her hands gripped opposite elbows, hugging herself tightly. She looked frail and nervous.

"Hey." I came over to her. "You good?"

"Sure," she said, smiling weakly. "Just…more memories."

My stomach twisted around one of them—an ugly memory. The day Jonah and Kacey came here together was the day we had to admit Jonah was getting worse. The day that marked the beginning of his downhill slide.

"Come on, I'll introduce you around." I led her down to my station. The shop was slow that day, and both Zelda and Edgar were between clients.

"Guys, this is Kacey Dawson," I said. "Kacey, that's Edgar Morrello and Zelda Rossi."

"Nice to meet you both," Kacey said.

Zelda smiled and gave a small wave. "Hi."

"Good to meet you, little lady," Edgar said, in a warm, genuine, with no trace of a joke imbedded in it.

Kacey perched on the side of my chair, swinging her legs back and forth. She wore skinny jeans, black ankle boots, and an oversized Rocky Horror Picture Show T-shirt. Her hair was down, her makeup spare. She looked effortlessly sexy.

"Did they know Jonah?" she asked softly, with a backward nudge of her head. "I don't remember them at the funeral. Then again, that day is all a blur."

"They were there," I said. "And I don't remember much about the funeral either. I've dedicated the last six months to blocking it out."

She smiled and a short silence fell between us.

"Do you know what you want yet?" I asked. "I owe you a tattoo."

"I still haven't decided."

I jammed my hands into my jean pockets. "Maybe the glass that Jonah gave you? The universe orb?"

Dumb suggestion. You'd never capture it perfectly.

Beneath that thought, I hoped she'd say no. I didn't want to use my art to render Jonah's on her skin.

Kacey frowned and thought for a moment. "No. I don't know what I'm supposed to get but that's not it."

"What you're *supposed* to get?"

"Yeah, I have this weird feeling that it's something specific. Something only you can create for me. But I don't know what it is yet. It'll come to me." She looked up and laughed a little. "Maybe I need to pay Olivia the Fortune Teller five more dollars and let her tell me."

I smiled, trying not to look too relieved. *The heart wants what it wants.* I think I read that somewhere. My heart, apparently, was a selfish asshole.

"Speaking of advice from the Other Side, have you thought about maybe buying this place?" Kacey asked. "Vivian was telling me your boss is on the verge of retirement. Maybe he wants to sell."

I cleared my throat with a glance toward Zelda and Edgar. Thankfully both were preoccupied with new clients.

"Hadn't thought about it. This place is pretty small and not really what I had in mind, in terms of style." I leaned closer to her. "And it's not exactly common knowledge around here that I'm looking to get my own shop."

"Why not?"

I opened my mouth and then shut it again. "I don't know. It's just…not something I talk about."

She arched her eyebrows.

I held up my hands. "What? I don't need a bunch of people knowing my business."

"Aren't they your friends?"

"I guess."

"You don't like to talk much about yourself," Kacey said, a smile lifting her sad expression to something warm. "In fact, I recall you hardly said two words to me when I first started seeing Jonah." Now the smile stretched to a grin. "Strong, silent type."

"I talk when I have something to say."

She rested her chin on her shoulder. "I like that. I'm the exact opposite. I'll miss talking to you when I go back to New Orleans."

"When?"

"Tomorrow."

My heart sank into my guts. "So soon?"

She nodded. "Already bought the flight. I'm glad I came back, but I have responsibilities back there." She smiled ruefully. "I'm trying really hard not to be a giant fuck-up anymore."

I toyed with a chipped piece of wood on the armoire. "Think you'll ever move back here?"

She sighed as her legs swung back and forth like two pendulums. "I honestly don't know, Teddy. I want to. I miss you and Beverly and everyone. But being here is really fucking hard." Her shoulders rose and fell, a pained, sad shrug. "I'll miss the hell out of you, but I think it'll be easier to heal in a place where I don't see him everywhere I turn."

I nodded. "I get it."

"You guys are so brave. You live with the memories—a lifetime of memories—surrounding you. I'm not strong enough for that. Not right now."

I tried not to let the crushing disappointment show on my face. "I get it, Kace. We all do."

She smiled a little brighter then.

"You need a lift back to the hotel?" I asked.

"I have an Uber picking me up."

"Mom wants dinner again tonight. With all of us."

She nodded. "I'll tell them I'm not staying."

"You sure you don't want your tattoo while you're here?"

She grinned. "I'm not going to get one in New Orleans, if that's what you're so worried about." She reached around and tapped her right shoulder blade. "This spot is reserved for a Theo Fletcher original."

A fierce desire rose to see that plot of her body she was saving for me, and I had to kill it quickly.

Kacey slid off the chair. "I should wait out front."

We started walking toward the entry, every bone in my body

screaming, *Stay. Please stay.*

"I'll make you a deal," she said.

"What's that?"

"When you buy your own place, I'm the first customer."

"That might be awhile."

She stopped by the reception desk and stretched up to kiss my cheek. "I can wait."

Her perfume filled my nose, and the whispered words sank into my skin and dropped straight into my groin. I stood there watching as she left the shop. Then my eyes noticed Gus, his arms crossed over his narrow chest, his expression 100% I-told-you-so.

"Uh huh," he said. "By the balls, Fletcher. She has you by the balls."

I wish, I thought.

"She'll come back." I picked up Viv's Magic 8-Ball and gave it a shake.

Outlook good.

I shook my head as I set it down. I was becoming a chump. First Tarot cards, now stupid toys. But I smiled all the way back to my station and the smile hung around as I set up for my first client.

When little slivers of hope put in an appearance, you have to grab them and hold on. Give them a smile. Otherwise, what's the fucking point?

CHAPTER 13

Kacey

At dinner that night, I told the Fletchers, Dena, and Oscar that I was definitely going back to New Orleans. Beverly was disappointed but told me she understood, so long as I came back to visit.

"And I'm not going to give up on the idea of you moving back here," she told me when it was time for me to head back to the hotel. She hugged me tight. "For what you did for Jonah…"

I hugged her back. "I didn't do anything for Jonah that he didn't do for me."

Beverly pulled away and cupped my face in her hands, her face threatening to crumple into tears. "Oh, my sweet girl…" she managed, and let me go.

Dena pulled me close. "Our wedding is in one month. I want you to be one of my bridesmaids."

I recoiled a little but tried not to show it. The wedding of Jonah's best friends, without Jonah present, would be so fucking hard…But I smiled and nodded, my happiness for them surfacing from beneath the grief.

"I'd be honored, Dena."

She smiled at me and then said, as if she could read my thoughts, "It will be a bittersweet day, but in the end, love must triumph, yes? For *all* of us, Kacey," she added in a whisper, as if it were a secret.

Theo was at my hotel before sunrise. He took my trundling luggage out of my hands and stowed it in the back of the truck, then opened the passenger door when I paused to rummage in my purse, making sure I had everything.

"You're a true gentleman," I said, climbing in. Two coffees were sitting in the cup holders, filling the cab with their heavenly scent. "I take that back. You're a saint."

Theo grunted a reply. He said almost nothing the entire drive to the airport. His expression was hard and his eyes full of thoughts he wouldn't share with me. At the security checkpoint at McCarran, I faced him, tucked a lock of hair behind my ear.

"Teddy, I can't thank you enough."

"Don't," he said, his eyes looking everywhere but at me. "Don't thank me, Kace. Just…"

"What?" I chucked his arm lightly. "Talk to me, Goose."

He shook his head. "Nothing."

"Okay." I stepped closer and tentatively gave him a hug. It felt like hugging a boulder. "Goodbye."

I released him and turned to go, but his hand slipped into mine and he pulled me back. His light brown eyes looked backlit from within, as if all the thoughts he never said were on fire. His jaw worked for a moment before he said, "Remember the other night. Outside your hotel, when I said you didn't owe me anything?"

"Yes."

"I take it back. You owe me one thing."

His hand was still holding mine. "Okay."

"You have to promise me that if shit gets tough, and it feels like you're going under, you fucking call me."

"So you can fly back to New Orleans and fail more classes? Or maybe lose your job?"

"*Yes.*" His hand squeezed tighter. "I don't blame you for taking off the first time. Hell, some days I want to jump in this truck and start driving, just to get lost for awhile. Don't beat yourself up. You did what you had to do to cope." The hard edges of his voice softened, as did his gaze on me. "But don't do it again."

I nodded mutely. "I won't."

"Promise me, Kacey. Don't ever disappear on me, okay?"

"I promise."

He kept his gaze locked on me a moment more, then nodded, as if satisfied. "Good. Then we don't need to talk about it anymore."

He let go of my hand and hugged me. I walked down the gangway to my plane, turning his words, and the conviction behind them, over and over in my mind.

He's intense because he has so much at stake, I reasoned. *He can't lose more time from work or school to bail my ass out of trouble again.*

But it felt deeper than that. I tucked the hand he'd held under my arm to keep it warm, thinking about all the promises tucked into a goodbye.

Stay here, Theo said, the night we scattered Jonah's ashes to the desert.

I will, I said.

I turned to the window as the plane took off and watched Las Vegas, and all its goodbyes and promises, grow smaller and smaller, until it was gone.

Promise me, Kacey...

CHAPTER 14

Kacey

To my sober eyes, my little shotgun house seemed shabby and dilapidated. With the beer (and vodka and whiskey) goggles off, I could see it was a cute little place with a lot of potential, if only I bothered to give it some attention.

I walked around, thinking about paint and curtains and rugs, when the doorbell rang. In the peephole was an African-American woman with close-cropped hair. She looked to be in her early-thirties. wearing a denim jacket. Her smile was bright white but for tiny gap in her otherwise perfect front teeth. A foil-covered pan balanced in her oven-mitted hands.

I opened the door. "Yes?"

"Hi," the woman said. "I'm Yvonne Robinson. I live next door." She inclined her head, then held up the pan, which smelled like tuna casserole. "Welcome to the neighborhood."

I frowned. "I've been living here six months."

Yvonne gave me a dry look. "Honey, you may have *resided* here, but you weren't really *here,* now, were you?"

I grinned despite a blush creeping up my neck. "No, I guess I wasn't. Would you like to come in?"

"If you please. This pan is heavy."

Yvonne strode past me, straight to the kitchen where she set the pan on the counter. Already the casserole was filling my little house with a delicious scent.

"It just came out of the oven," Yvonne said, taking off the oven mitts and tucking them under her arm. "So you'd best wait a bit before digging in."

"I'll try," I said, indicating for her to sit on the couch. "It smells amazing. Tuna casserole is my favorite. My mom made it all the time when I was a kid."

"No offense to your mama, but I got them all beat," Yvonne said with a laugh.

"So… How did you know…?"

"That you were in a bad way?" she finished, leaning forward on the couch. "You don't remember me, do you?"

I searched my memory, then shook my head. "I'm sorry. I've been…out of it."

"Honey, I know," she said. Her words came out rapid-fire, every other sentence curling up at the end, making questions out of statements. "I used to see you coming home late at night, kind of stumbling? I wanted to help but I work all hours. I'm a nurse down at Ochsner Medical? A few days past, I heard you having a hard time. When your fellow was here? Theo? I thought he was the cause of it. I heard you yelling bloody murder and came over with a baseball bat, ready to knock his teeth in."

She shook her head, laughing at the memory. "You should've seen the look on his face, poor baby." Her chuckling faded. "But turns out he was helping you, not hurting, wasn't he?"

I nodded, trying desperately to remember. The shame climbed up my cheeks because I couldn't.

"Anyway, he told me the situation, and I gave you a look over." She glanced around. "Where's your man now?"

"Oh, no, he's not…my man." I tucked a lock of hair behind my ear. "Teddy's just a friend. No, more than that. My best friend. He's actually my boyfriend's brother. I mean, he was. Jonah…he's my boyfriend… Was my boyfriend. He…passed away."

It was the first time I'd had to say the words out loud. I had zero practice talking about Jonah's death. I had no canned response, no rehearsed story. I couldn't even get the tense right. When I could say my boyfriend had passed away without bringing the world to a screeching halt? It hurt, like a hammer striking my chest with every syllable.

"Anyway…well, I used to live in Las Vegas but I moved here after Jonah… I wasn't doing so well and Theo helped me. What you heard and saw was me coming off the booze. I'm sorry. It must've been awful."

"Not as awful as it felt for you, baby." Yvonne reached across the space between us to take my hand, her dark eyes warm. "It wasn't pretty, but you came out the other side, didn't you?"

"Barely," I said.

"Barely is still a 'yes.' Remember that." Yvonne's grip on my hand became a pat and her eye caught the watch on her wrist. "I wish I could stay longer but my shift starts in forty. Don't be a stranger now." She chuckled. "You know I won't."

I hurried to catch up and open the door for her. "I won't either. Thank you. For the casserole. And for helping me when I was…"

"Down? You're welcome. And honey? If you need anything? If you want to talk or if the craving gets bad? Give me a holler or knock on my door." She peered at me intently. "Are you in a program?"

I wanted to tell her I was determined to do this on my own, but to a healthcare professional like Yvonne, it would sound like an excuse. You can't bullshit a nurse.

"I haven't decided yet," I said

She pursed her lips. "Think about it. And don't think you're alone. This is New Orleans, baby. We stick together." She started down the steps of my porch, shaking her head. "Boy, do we."

"Thanks, Yvonne."

She waved over her head and marched the five steps to her own shotgun house. It wasn't as garishly colorful as mine, but it was ten times better maintained.

I closed the door and stood inside the quiet of my home.

Alone and sober.

Not entirely alone, I thought, and pulled the foil off the casserole. I cut a block of noodles, covered with crispy croutons, and ate it straight from the dish. It tasted heavenly. I ate that piece and another, standing up in my kitchen. I noticed my window faced Yvonne's house. Only three feet separated our kitchen windows.

I threw open mine. "Yvonne!"

From inside her house. "Yeah, baby?" She came to her window and opened it, leaned her forearms on the sill. "Good, right?"

"It's perfect."

She laughed and made a shooing motion, then retreated back into her place. I laughed and shut my window.

My new cellphone chimed a text. It was Theo.

Wanted to make sure you got in okay.

I smiled. *Nope. Not alone at all.*

ALL IN

On Thursday, I showed up for work at Le Chacal, right on time.

Singing sober wasn't as hard as I thought it would be. The tears still came at the end of "The Lighthouse." But instead of being walled off from my audience by alcohol, I could feel the intense emotion working its way through the crowd. No one drank, whispered or moved during the song. When it ended, I heard a collective intake of breath before the applause.

"Thank you," I murmured into the mic, feeling strangely shy. I left the stage and took my guitar to my usual seat at the bar.

Big E planted his hands on either side of the old wood, grinning. "What'll it be, sweets?"

"Seltzer with lime, please." I slapped a ten-dollar bill on the bar. "And keep'em coming."

He bellowed laughter and set the drink in front of me. "You done good, kid. How do you feel?"

"It's weird," I said. "I've played shows a hundred times bigger than this, but this was the first time I felt nervous. It's so…intimate in here. I can't hide anything. I either play my guts out or stay home."

"I'm glad you didn't stay home," Big E said. "I'm proud of you."

"Thanks, E," I said. "And thanks for—"

He held up his hands. "Nope. No thanks required. Just doing my job."

"What *is* it with guys and gratitude? Teddy's the same way. Wouldn't hear a thank you if I paid him."

Big E shrugged. "Real men take care of the women in their lives as a matter of course. Not because they want something in return."

His words warmed me better than a shot of whiskey. "Not even a thank you?"

"Not even that."

I laughed and rolled my eyes. "Theo definitely takes care of the women in his life," I said. "His mother, me… If he ever settled down with a woman, I'll bet she'd be spoiled for the rest of her life."

Big E frowned. "What about you?"

"What about me?"

"I thought…" He looked about to say something else, then

shrugged. "Never mind."

I was about to press him when I felt a tap on my shoulder. I turned to see a young couple, maybe in their late twenties. The guy had short dark hair and black-framed hipster glasses—a Buddy Holly throwback. The girl had long, free-flowing red hair and a bohemian-looking dress splashed with flowers.

"Miss Dawson?" the guy said. He had to pitch his voice high above the jazz trio now onstage. "My name is Grant Olsen. This is my sister, Phoebe."

"Nice to meet you," I said, smiling politely. Grant said nothing else. I looked from one to the other, my smile starting to slip.

Phoebe elbowed her brother in the side. "*Talk*," she hissed.

"Uh, right." Grant adjusted his glasses. "We own a small recording studio."

"Like, totally small," Phoebe added, "but still legit."

"Yes, uh…legit." Grant fumbled in his pocket for a business card and handed it to me. "I'm a sound engineer, Phoebe produces. Can we talk with you a minute? Buy you a drink?"

I agreed to the first, declined the second. We sat at a small table, where the Olsens described their studio and their commitment to producing local indie artists.

"We really love your work," Grant said, pushing his glasses higher up on his nose. "Your voice. The lyrics. Very unique. Poignant."

"You're like if Brandi Carlile and Adele had a love child," Phoebe said.

"Oh, no," I said, shaking my head. "That's nice of you to say but…"

"But nothing," Phoebe said, fishing a cherry out of her drink. "Great vocals *and* emotional lyrics. Dream combo." She bit the cherry and pointed the stem at me. "And you used to play for Rapid Confession."

"A lifetime ago," I said. "I'm not interested in playing off that. I'm doing my own thing now. The band is doing theirs."

She exchanged looks with her brother, and then Grant said, "We love that. Honestly, we want to help you do your own thing now. We noticed you don't sell CDs prior to your shows and we can't find any digital tracks anywhere either."

"Because I don't have any," I said.

"We'd like to change that."

We talked for an hour, Grant and Phoebe laying out a plan for me to record and produce an album—all the songs I'd been playing at these clubs. It could be sold both digitally and as a physical CD.

"Can we give you a tour of our recording studio tomorrow?" Grant asked at the end of his pitch. He held up his hands. "Or later in the week? No pressure. No obligations. Just come over and check it out."

I twirled my empty seltzer glass around and around. I'd never heard these songs from an audience perspective. Recording and then listening to them filled me with a strange fear. It would be easy to say no. Easy to say thanks, but no thanks, I was happy as is.

But I wasn't happy.

And doing what scared me was the only way I was going to recover. I didn't need a Tarot card to tell me.

"Tomorrow is good," I said to Grant and Phoebe. "Why wait?"

※

The Olsens hadn't been lying. Their studio was tiny, but it was also completely professional. It looked like a miniature of the studio where Rapid Confession recorded before the tour. A dim, windowless rectangle, separated by glass into two spaces. The recording area was hardly big enough for a band, but would accommodate one chick on a stool with her guitar perfectly well. On the other side of the glass, the soundboard took up half the space—a vast array of knobs, buttons, sliders and other functions I had no clue about.

Posters of indie shows and bands papered the walls of the soundbooth, while dark gray foamy-looking stuff, like the inside of egg cartons, covered the walls in the recording space. The whole place reeked of old incense. I loved the vibe of it immediately.

Grant rubbed the back of his neck and gave Phoebe a dark look. "I know it's not much, and I keep telling Phoebe to chill with the incense…"

"Start wearing deodorant and I'll consider it," Phoebe snapped.

"I wear deodorant. Christ, you say something like that in front a potential client?"

They bickered under their breath at each other until I unstrapped my guitar case and set it down like I was unpacking a bag. Then they stopped and stared.

"So," I said, taking a deep breath. "When can we start?"

Back home, I curled around the universe orb and told Jonah about the new developments.

"It might be the right thing for me," I said. I usually had a cocktail in hand for these conversations. I clutched the glass tighter instead. "Or it might not. See, those songs…I've never heard them outside of myself. What if it's too hard?"

It was already too hard.

I wiped my tears. "Teddy took me to see your glass when I was in Vegas. And it was so beautiful, Jonah. Your legacy. But remember what you told me in your letter? That our love was your legacy too?" The tears were streaming now, but somehow a smile stretched my lips. "These songs, they're *our* legacy. They're us. Love. You and me. And I think I should share them. How does that sound?"

It sounded good to me. It sounded *right.* Maybe recording this album, making those songs permanent, instead of watery breaths in a darkened club that dissipated into the smoky air, was what I was supposed to do. It could be a way to let him go.

I sighed and laid my head next to the glass. My sore eyes grew heavy watching the glowing stars swirl around the planet. I slipped into the twilight space between sleep and awake and felt Jonah with me.

And he was smiling.

CHAPTER 15

Kacey

Three weeks later the album was nearly finished. I still hadn't heard the whole thing mixed—I'd laid down the guitar track first, then the vocals. Only bits and pieces got played back for me.

I didn't know what kind of impact it would make on the music world either, despite the fact that Grant and Phoebe were in a state of perpetual giddiness. They assured me over and over again it was going to be a huge hit.

"Even at ninety-nine cents a song, you can make a killing if just one goes big," Grant told me, his eyes bright behind his glasses.

You can buy a lot of booze too, I thought. An echo of my Rapid Confession days when success wasn't necessarily a good thing.

We wrapped it up on a Thursday night. Back home, I changed from my recording attire of sloppy jeans and T-shirt, to the nicer jeans and blouse for my gig at Le Chacal that night. My cell phone buzzed a text from Theo: **You up?**

I typed back, thumbs flying. **You realize that's the internationally-recognized code for booty call, right?**

Nothing for a minute, then: **Dirty mind. I was innocently asking if you're awake.**

There's nothing innocent about you, Teddy. It's only eight pm here and you know it. What's up?

You working tongue?

I laughed. **No, my tongue has the night off.**

Tonight. I meant tonight. Fucking autocorrect. Calling...

Theo hated texting because he made so many typos. Which was fine with me, I preferred hearing his voice anyway. I liked its deep roughness in my ear.

My phone rang. "Yes, I'm working tonight," I said. "I need the money to pay my gigantic phone bill."

"You're telling me," Theo replied. "I had to take out a small loan after you kept me up until four in the morning last week."

"All you had to do was concede *The Princess Bride* is the most quotable movie in existence and I would have let you off."

I grinned, remembering how Theo tried to argue *Monty Python's the Holy Grail* had earned that title. I'd badgered him with "Inconceivable!" until he gave up.

"Don't start," he said, "or I'll fart in your general direction."

I'd no idea stern-faced Theodore was a huge Monty Python fan. But during our marathon conversations, I learned he could quote the entire *Holy Grail* and *Life of Brian* movies almost verbatim, accents and all.

These monster phone sessions started out as him checking in on me. Brief chats, once or twice a week, making sure I was okay. The craving for booze was a constant. On bad days it flared into an insatiable thirst, laced with grief for Jonah. On good days, it was background noise, sometimes hardly noticeable.

The good days, I noticed, were growing more and more frequent. I had friends now: Yvonne next door. Big E. Even Grant and Phoebe were more like friends than business partners.

And I had Teddy, who now called me almost every day.

"So," he said. "Oscar and Dena's wedding."

"Yes. Next Saturday. I'm so excited. Especially since my bridesmaid dress isn't a total nightmare." I glanced at the coral-colored, strapless dress hanging high on the door of my bedroom. "Not really my style but it's pretty. Just the right color for a spring wedding."

Theo grunted an acknowledgement of the girly dress talk, and then said, "When are you flying in?"

"Friday," I said. "I'll be there in time for the rehearsal dinner."

"Cool."

"You don't sound super thrilled about it."

"I never should've agreed to be the best man. It's going to suck."

"Why? Not a fan of making toasts in front of hundreds of strangers?"

"Something like that," he muttered. "Anyway, are you bringing anyone?"

I blinked. "You mean like a date?"

"Yeah."

"God, no. I'm *soooo* not ready for that." I plucked at my duvet, making little wrinkles in the material. "Are you?"

"No," he said.

A small smile spread over my face and I smoothed the duvet down. "Why not?"

"There's no one I want to fly all the way to New York," he said. "That's an expensive date."

"Good point," I said.

Oscar and Dena were getting married at an exclusive club Oscar's parents belonged to in upstate New York. The east coast location was easier on Dena's grandparents—both in their eighties—who had to fly from Tehran, via London, to the US.

"So, we can be each other's date," I said. "At the least, you can save me a dance or two, so I'm not sitting alone at the table all night like a pathetic loser."

"You're not a pathetic loser," he said darkly. "And I don't dance."

"Yeah, right," I laughed. "You'll have to beat the single ladies off you with a stick. Maybe the married ones too."

"That's not happening."

"You sure about that?" I said, grinning. "Admitting you have a problem is the first step toward recovery. You're going to look amazing in a tux, Teddy."

"Yeah, yeah."

I glanced at the clock. "I gotta go soon. I have my Le Chacal gig tonight."

"You don't sound super thrilled about it," he said.

I smiled at his echo of my words. "I know. I've been more focused on recording. We finish tomorrow. The Olsens I keep telling you about? Turns out they really know their shit. They said the album might be ready by the time I get back from New York."

"Already?"

"Not a lot of mixing and mastering to do when it's just one voice and a guitar. Although they did talk me into letting a local violinist play background on a few tracks. I'm actually kind of excited about it."

"That's a good thing, then."

I plucked the duvet again. "I think so. I'm nervous to hear it. Okay, no, I'm scared shitless to hear it. From an outsider perspective."

"Take your time. Don't listen until you're ready."

"When did you become so wise?"
"Born that way."
I caught sight of the clock again. "Oh, shit. I really gotta run."
"Tell Big E I said hi," Theo said.
"I will. Text you later?"
"I'll be here."
"Bye, Teddy."
"Bye, Kace."

CHAPTER 16

Kacey

My flight landed in Albany the afternoon before the wedding, and I just made it to the rehearsal dinner at a ritzy steakhouse. Dena had six bridesmaids, and I was thrilled to see Tania King, Jonah's former assistant, was one of them. We hugged and cried a little—just seeing her brought back a flood of memories. She confided she was thrilled I was there for a more practical reason.

"Aside from the Fletchers, I literally know no one here," she said.

"Hey, I'm in the same boat."

She looped her arm through my elbow. "Oh, thank god. You're mine."

We stuck to each other at dinner too, and Tania told me all about working for the Chihuly Studio in Seattle.

"It's incredible," she said over clam chowder. "I wake up every morning thinking, *Holy shit, this is my life now.* Thanks, in no small part, to Jonah." She leaned in close to me, her voice dropping. "Honestly—and I hate to even say this—but tomorrow is going to be hard without him here. The gaping hole in my life…it's easier to ignore it in Seattle. But here, around all his old friends…" Her dark eyes trailed down the table, taking inventory of each guest. "I can't even imagine how hard this must be for Oscar and Dena."

My gaze trailed to the happy couple at the end of the long table. On Oscar's left sat Theo, looking handsome in slacks and a dress shirt. No tie, his sleeves rolled up to his forearms, dark ink swirling down to his wrists.

"And how are you?" Tania asked gently. "I heard you moved out of Vegas?"

She'd probably been too busy with her job to know too much about my situation, and part of me wanted to smile and make light of it. But my personal recovery plan was to be as honest as I could. With everyone.

"Yeah, I moved. I couldn't hack it. I live in New Orleans now." I stirred my soup. "That's the sanitized version of what happened. The Black Plague version is, I ran out of town without telling anyone where I was going and spent the last six months in New Orleans, drunk off my ass."

Tania's eyebrows shot up, but then she nodded. "Okay."

"Theo found me, dropped everything to help me sober up—and it wasn't any goddamn picnic for him, I can tell you. Now I'm here, all dressed up for a wedding, instead of dead in a ditch somewhere."

"I'm so happy you're here." Tania's eyes glanced at Theo. "He's a rock, that guy."

"How so?"

She spooned a bite of soup then dabbed her napkin to her mouth. "You know I was Jonah's assistant in the hot shop. Carnegie Mellon paid me to do that job. But for an installation the size Jonah envisioned, I didn't think two people could complete it on time. I couldn't be there every minute—I had my own classes at UNLV. So Theo stepped in. He'd never worked with glass before. Jonah and I showed him the basics, and it just clicked for him. The job needed to be done and he was going to do it. He just went for it. All in. And when the installation was finished, I got all the credit for the assist. I tried to get Theo to put his name on the paperwork for the Wynn show. Jonah tried. Hell, Jonah was about to do it without Theo's permission. But Theo side-stepped us, went to Eme Takamura directly, and told her his name wasn't to appear anywhere with relation to the installation."

"Why wouldn't he take any credit?"

Tania shrugged. "That's just how he is. So it doesn't surprise me in the least he dropped everything to fly to you when you needed him. It's what he does. If there's a job to do, he does it."

I nodded, thinking about Theo being best man for Oscar. *Jonah would have done it.*

Tania had grown quiet. I saw her jaw work and her eyes fixed on the water glass in front of her.

I covered her hand with mine. "Hey."

She smiled, not looking at me. "God, I miss him like hell."

"I know." The words held the deepest, hardest truth for everyone in this room.

I miss you, Jonah. We all miss you.

It was easy to feel like I suffered the most. To believe the bulk of the pain was mine to choke down—an enormous mouthful, while everyone else only had to chew little bites. But everyone who'd known Jonah had a plate of pain to swallow.

Every instinct screamed to change the subject before I started crying again, but instead I squeezed Tania's fingers.

"Jonah couldn't have finished the installation if it hadn't been for you," I said. "I know for a fact he considered you one of his best friends. He loved you like hell. That's why you miss him like hell."

"Thanks, Kace." Tania smiled and swiped away a tear. "I know he did, but it's nice when someone else says it."

The next morning, we drove in a cavalcade of sedans to the Centennial Club, twenty minutes outside Albany. The club was a stately, 18th century manor, with many gables piercing its red roof. It sat on a huge field of grass, like an island floating on a flat, green sea.

Dena and her bridesmaids, along with her mother and grandmother, were ensconced in one wing of the big manor, while Oscar and his menfolk were on the other. The ceremony would be in the sprawling backyard that looked more like a football field, and the reception in the grand ballroom.

In the east wing, the bridesmaids slipped on our coral-colored dresses, while Dena had her hair and makeup tended to. The strapless dresses had crisscrossing folds over the bodice, cascaded to the floor in soft lengths of silk.

Dena's mother—an elegant-looking woman in a more modest dress the same shade of orange-pink as ours—fussed over her daughter, while Dena's 80-year-old grandmother sat in a chair and watched. Both the mother and grandmother gave me a few side-glances, as did two of the bridesmaids I'd never met before.

I looked at myself in the full-length mirror. The tattoos swirling down my right arm and the guitar on the inside of my left wrist painted a stark contrast to the billowy pastel of the dress.

Dena approached me, her knowing, peaceful smile on her face.

She looked radiant and far calmer than any bride-to-be I'd ever seen.

"Kacey," she said softly. "You look beautiful."

"That's my line. Dena…you're stunning." I rubbed my arms, as if I could rub out the tattoos just for today. "Not too sure the ink goes with the dress."

Dena reached for the tray of hairdresser's ribbons, pins and brushes, and took up a black silk rose. "Do you think I'd forgotten you had these tattoos when I picked out the dress?"

"No, but I can feel your grandmother staring," I said. "I want this day to be perfect for you."

Her grin widened as she affixed the silk flower behind my left ear. "Today will be perfect because the people I love are here, just as they are."

I inspected myself in the mirror. None of the other bridesmaids had a black flower, but none of them had ink all up their arms, either. But I had to admit, the black rose was a perfect accessory, complementing my tattoos and bringing the whole look together.

Tania approached. "You're the most badass bridesmaid I've ever seen," she said, looking resplendent in her own dress. She linked her arm in mine. "Come on. It's time to rock n'roll."

We descended the stairs and a harried-looking wedding planner jostled us into place. Dena was like a cloud of calm, floating among us in her white silk dress, while the rest of us fluttered around her like nervous birds.

A cellist played Pachelbel's Canon in D, and we took our turns marching out of the house and between the rows of white chairs set up on the lawn. Oscar and his groomsmen were already under a white awning, wreathed in green vines and pink flowers.

I took my turn down the aisle, paranoid my heels were going to dig too deep into the lush grass and send me sprawling in front of everyone.

How would that be for badass?

Oscar looked handsome in his tux but a bit petrified. My eyes found Theo standing beside him. In a tux.

Oh, wow…

He looked devastatingly handsome. His dark hair slicked back, his hands clasped in front of him where cufflinks glinted in the sun. His expression was flat with boredom, until he caught sight of me. His mouth fell open a little and his eyes widened.

I smiled at him, tried a little wave behind my small bouquet of white roses. Theo didn't respond but stared at me in that way he had, like he couldn't believe I was real. I thought he was playing around but as I neared my place on the platform, his stare hardened and then he suddenly looked away.

Okay, then.

The ceremony was the perfect length—not too short to make all the fuss seem excessive, and not too long that anyone grew impatient. Oscar and Dena exchanged traditional vows, then kissed as the sun sank beneath them. The crowd cheered and the procession returned to the house for the reception.

For the recessional, I was paired up with a buddy of Oscar's. Theo naturally escorted the Maid of Honor, who clutched his arm extra snugly, I noticed. She giggled something in his ear that he ignored.

Once inside the manor house, Theo ignored me, too. The bridal party took photos with Oscar and Dena, then we were free to enjoy the cocktails and hors d'oeuvres being served in a grand sitting room. A cellist played in the corner under the muted conversations of a hundred guests.

Over a little plate of snacks, Beverly gushed over Theo, Tania, and I. Henry made me promise to save him a dance, even though his eyes strayed to my tattoos more than once while we chatted. Theo didn't say a word.

"What's wrong, dear?" Beverly asked. "Nervous for your toast?"

"Yeah," he muttered. "I guess."

I pulled him aside. "Hey. How you holding up? For real."

"For real? I fucking hate giving speeches."

"Picture everyone in their underwear. I hear that helps."

"I picture everyone thinking, *Jonah should be up there."*

The smile fell off my face like a paper mask. "Teddy," I said softly.

"It was already hard without him here. I'm making it ten times worse."

"That's not true," I said.

He glanced around darkly. "Isn't it? It's what I'm thinking. Jonah and Oscar were best friends. I'm like a bad stand-in."

"That's not true," I said, gripping his arm. "We all miss Jonah, but no one thinks that you're…"

"The consolation prize?" Theo said, meeting my eyes for the first time. "Forget it. I just want to get this over with." He downed his flute of champagne and set it down on a small table.

"You're going to do great," I said.

His expression softened as he took in my dress, my hair, and then his gaze swept over my face. He looked about to say something, but changed his mind, his features hardening again. "Oscar should've picked someone else," he said, and walked away.

I started to follow after, to tell him that Oscar picked him because he wanted *him*, but the wedding planner threw open the doors to the grand ballroom and the guests flowed in, carrying me on the current.

A collective gasp went up as we stepped inside. The wooden floors gleamed in the light of a dozen different sources—delicate chandeliers on the ceiling, sconces on the wall, and incredible centerpieces on each of the round tables. Flowers, silverware, and delicate porcelain place settings were simply arranged but incredibly elegant. I could see Dena's hand in all of this. A round table swathed in shimmery red gold tablecloth, was laden with bowls of poppy seeds and rice, little cups of rice, black tea leaves and other seeds I couldn't name. Silver platters held Baklava, rice cookies and almond cookies. A mirror in a silver setting and two candelabras made up the centerpiece. I overheard a man tell his partner that the mirror and candles represented light and fire.

"Light and fire," I murmured to myself when I saw that my place card had me seated between Tania and Theo.

But my smile faded when it was clear Theo wouldn't even look at me, and when he did, he squinted and looked away, as if I hurt his eyes. When it was time for his toast, he stood up with grim determination, a piece of paper from one hand and a glass of champagne in the other.

He's a rock, I thought. *He does the job.*

The room grew hushed as Theo studied the words written on the paper. "Fuck this," he muttered under his breath, and tossed the paper down, then faced the crowd.

"I've known Oscar for about twenty years," he said. "Since we were kids. I met him through Jonah. For those of you who don't know who Jonah is, he was my brother and Oscar's best friend. For those of you who *did* know Jonah, you know I'd much rather be listening to him get up here and talk instead of doing it myself. I can't help but feel he's laughing at me wherever he is, because he knows how much I hate this kind of shit. Sorry."

The crowd murmured laughter, and I thought I could feel a collective sigh of relief. As if the elephant in the room had been acknowledged.

"Oscar and Dena were made for each other," Theo continued. "There's not a whole lot more to say than that. She's the calm to his storm, the poetry to his dirty jokes, the opera to his football game. Each fills the gaps in the other. They lift each other up and stick together when shit gets rough." He coughed another 'sorry' and the audience laughed.

"But they have more in common than you think. They're both the best people I've ever known. They're both generous to each other, and to their friends. They have more love in their hearts than many people have in their little finger. We should all be as lucky to find someone who is the other half of ourselves. To be as a much of a matched set as Dena and Oscar." He raised his glass. "Congrats, you guys. I'd say I hope you have a long and happy life together, but I don't have to. I know you will."

The guests made a resounding toast and Theo quickly sat back down.

I touched his arm. "That was perfect."

He looked as if he were going to say something harsh to me, or maybe nothing at all. But he eased a sigh and nodded grudgingly. "Just glad it's done."

The DJ played, people ate and danced and laughed, and I tried not to think about how much I wanted Jonah to be there. How I tried not to look for him, or turn my head and expect to see him there, holding his hand out to me, asking me to dance.

Finally, I couldn't take any more sitting and nursing the ache in my heart.

"Hey." I tapped Theo's shoulder. "You promised me a dance."

"Sorry," he said. "Don't feel like it."

"Hey," I said again, my voice cracking. "I miss him too."

Theo looked at me then, his eyes softening the way they had earlier, but this time they stayed soft. "Yeah," he said.

The DJ played Bryan Adams' "Everything I Do." I got to my feet and held out my hand. "Dance with me."

Theo took my hand and let me pull him to his feet, but then he led me to the dance floor, cutting through the swaying couples to an empty spot.

His hand was heavy on my waist, and he held our clasped hands out stiffly so they floated in midair. That wasn't going to cut it for me. I needed to hold and be held.

I moved in close, put my head on Theo's chest, pulled our clasped hands in to rest on his heart. He stiffened, then relaxed against me, still strong and solid but molding his body to fit mine.

"That's better," I said, tucking my head under his chin where it fit perfectly.

"Yeah," he said softly. "It is."

CHAPTER 17

Theo

Thank God.

I didn't know I needed this. Not until Kacey rested her head against my chest. A communion with another person in pain, the only other person on the planet who'd been as close to Jonah as I'd been.

I let my cheek rest against Kacey's forehead. We turned in a slow circle, hardly moving, just holding each other. My body should've been rampaging with her pressed against me this way. But nothing sexual was in the warmth flooding me. Only comfort. This woman knew exactly how I felt. I didn't have to say a word. I didn't have to explain why I felt like shit, out of place, or why I'd spent the whole night listening for Jonah's voice, straining to hear him among the crowd, craning my neck to see him laughing with Oscar.

He should've been here. To give the toast, to dance with our mother, with Dena, and especially with Kacey. It would've broken my damn heart, but I would have given anything in the world to look over and see Kacey wrapped in Jonah's arms.

Instead, she was in mine, my body absorbing her peace like a sponge soaked up water. Part of me felt like a fraud. Like a con man. A consolation prize.

The other part of me felt like I was home.

"This feels nice," Kacey murmured. "Whenever I feel I'm coming apart, you always hold me together."

"Same for me," I said. "Right now…this feels good."

She nestled closer to me and I held her tighter, not wanting the song to end. If I closed my eyes, I could shut out the world for a little bit longer. But I looked up and found Oscar staring at me, his eyes hard, his brows furrowed in confusion. As Kacey and I turned, I saw our table, where my parents were sitting. They were watching us dance, my father with pursed lips, and my mother with a nervous smile for me when our eyes met.

I pulled away from Kacey—unmolded myself from her body. The song ended at just that moment, but my sudden break startled her. She stared up at me, and whatever sense of peace she'd had during our dance seeped out of those incredible blue eyes and the real world—the one without Jonah—flooded back in.

"Sorry," I muttered lamely. "Sorry, Kace... I..."

"It's okay," she said softly. "It was nice. For a few minutes, anyway, wasn't it?"

I led her back to the table and she excused herself to use the restroom. Tania jumped up to go with her.

"It's so sweet of you to comfort Kacey like that," my mom said. "She must be hurting so badly."

I nodded, jaw clenched. All the old pain and anger came roaring back, burning up the last of my peace with Kacey. "Yeah," I said, biting off each word. "She is."

"You're wonderful to take care of her," my mother said, looking relieved. "I know Jonah must be glad for that."

"He is," I muttered, easing a sigh, forcing myself to calm down. "I know he is."

Because that's what I promised him: to take care of Kacey.

The other half of Jonah's promise had never felt more impossible to keep.

Tania and Kacey came back from the bathroom just in time for the bouquet throwing. Kacey tried to refuse, but Tania tugged her arm. "It's just silly fun. Or in my case, it's looking for all the help I can get."

Kacey laughed a little and relented, but both came back empty handed. My mother actually looked relieved, as if catching a bunch of damn flowers meant anything.

"I did my best," Tania said, with mock sourness. "But Oscar had a secret Olympian high-jumper on his side of the family. I'm telling you, this was fixed."

Everyone laughed, but Kacey only smiled, her eyes distant.

She looks tired, I thought. My phone's face read midnight when Oscar and Dena changed into more casual clothes and left for the airport. The guests watched from the front porch of the Centennial House as they drove off in a sedan, *Just Married* soaped up on every window. Some people threw rice, others sugar—an Iranian tradition meant to wish them a sweet life.

I leaned over to Kacey. "You want a ride back to the hotel? It's late."

She smiled wanly. "God, yes, I am so done."

I drove my parents, Tania, and Kacey back to the hotel in Albany. We made plans to have breakfast the next morning, and said our goodnights with a palpable sense of relief the night was over. The first big event in our lives Jonah wasn't there for.

I walked Kacey to her room. Outside the door, she paused. "Now that we're here, I'm strangely awake. I'm going to watch a movie. Want to watch with me?"

That's a bad idea, said an inner voice, remembering Oscar's hard look and my mother's nervous smile.

"Sure," I said. Nothing was happening with Kacey and me. She was my friend and she comforted me like nothing and no one ever had before. I wasn't about to let anyone make me feel like shit about it.

In her room, I shook off my tux jacket and tossed it and the tie onto one of the double beds.

"Tania was so funny about the bouquet," Kacey said, pulling the pins out of her hair on her way to the bathroom. "You should've seen her. When the other girl caught it, I thought Tania was going to tackle her. I didn't even try for it."

"Why not?"

"For one thing, I'm not in the market. For another…it felt wrong. I had the feeling if I came back to the table with the bouquet, it would've hurt your mom's feelings."

Before I could reply, she came back out and pointed at the TV. "The hotel has HBO On Demand. Can you see if they have *Dirty Dancing*?"

"Again?" I asked. "I've seen it twice with you. God knows how many times you've seen it alone."

"Fifteen." Kacey grinned. "Sixteen's the charm."

"If you insist."

"Thanks. I gotta get out of this dress."

I kicked off my shoes and settled against the headboard while Kacey rummaged in her luggage for something to sleep in.

I hoped she didn't need help unzipping her dress.

I hoped she did.

Some friend you are.

She managed it on her own and came out of the bathroom wearing shorts and a T-shirt. Her hair fell around her shoulders in honey-colored waves from being pinned all day.

"It was a beautiful ceremony, wasn't it?" she said, settling herself on the pillows of her bed.

"Yeah," I said, though I couldn't recall much of it. I'd watched Kacey come down the aisle, looking radiant in her dress that made her eyes stand out like sapphires, and just about lost my damn mind. The rest of the ceremony was a blur.

I punched in buttons on the remote and called up the movie.

"Oscar and Dena are going to make the most beautiful kids," Kacey said after a few minutes.

"Probably," I said.

"How about you? Do you want to get married some day? Have kids?"

"Yeah, I do. You?"

Kacey smiled sadly. "I don't know. I never thought I'd be the marrying type. Or the kid-having type, either. I was too messed up for too long to be responsible like that. But maybe. Someday."

"*Someday* should be my motto."

"You're actually willing to give up your rep as a ladies' man and settle down?" she asked with a grin that pushed back the sadness for a heartbeat.

"I'm not like that," I said. "Not anymore. I got it out of my system."

"Yeah? The way Oscar talks, I imagine you out with a different girl every night."

"He's just messing around."

She nodded. "Well, I can see you getting married."

"You can?"

"Of course. You told me once, you like permanence."

"Yeah," I said, feeling a familiar fire simmer in Kacey's presence, the same I'd felt on the dance floor. A peacefulness and an urge to trust her with the truth. "I want something real."

She curled toward me on her bed. "I have this image of you holding a baby, tucked in the crook of your arm like a football while snagging the diaper of another toddler before he tips over and clocks himself on the edge of the table. And you do it with zero stress. Don't even blink an eye." She laughed a little. "I don't know where that came from."

"Oh yeah?" I was going to leave it at that, but it was easy to talk to Kacey. "Buddy of mine has a new baby. He posts pictures of him napping with her on his chest, holding his finger in her little fist. I could handle that."

"How many kids do you want?"

"At least two," I said. "I think they should have a brother or sister. I'm glad I did."

Understatement of the century.

Kacey's smile faded. "I'll bet. I always wanted a brother or sister too. But dad could barely stand me as it was. It's not surprising my parents only had one kid."

"Have you talked to them lately?"

She shook her head. "Not since…I don't even know when." She shrugged, a tight, helpless gesture. "Not a word in a long time."

"Such bullshit," I muttered under my breath. The pleasant warmth in my chest from this conversation heated to anger.

"What did you say?"

"I said, it's fucking madness they won't even call you back. It'd been, what? Six months since you heard from them?"

"Longer," she said. "I stopped calling them right around the time I met Jonah. We saw them on our trip to San Diego. Did he tell you about it?"

I shook my head. "He didn't tell me anything but his face was like a postcard when he got back."

She tilted her head.

"I remember he looked…content. In a way a man in his position didn't have any cause to look."

She stared at me blankly, and I watched my words sink in, spread over her face, and draw a beautiful smile to the surface. "Thank you, Teddy," she said softly.

I waved my hand. "Anyway," I said. "You saw your parents then?"

She nodded. "We *saw* them," she said. "Literally. From across the street. I didn't want to talk to them. They looked happy so I let them be. Maybe I should do that permanently."

"You want to?" I asked gently.

She shrugged again, her hands toying her long hair, examining the ends. "Might be easier than being rejected over and over again."

"I know what you mean," I said.

"You do, don't you?" Kacey sat up on her pillows. "This is a personal question, but has Henry always been hard on you?"

I nodded. "Since Jonah and I were kids. Nothing's ever good enough. I get sick of it. I'm so sick of giving a shit about what my old man thinks of me, and yet I can't stop." I snorted. "Sounds like such self-pitying bullsh—"

"Hello, look who you're talking to," Kacey said. "It's frustrating as hell, right? Like you don't want to care but you do. A lot."

I looked. At her beautiful, open face; her simple words resonating in my heart. "Yeah, I do."

"Why is he hard on you?" she asked. "Harder on you than on Jonah?"

"Definitely not. I never resented Jonah for it. Not even when we were kids. He stood up for me but he never pitied me. I could never hate him. Or be jealous of him…"

The pain I kept so tightly locked down threatened to boil out. I kept the lid on tight.

"Dad's never approved of my art and he never will. I should get used to it or get over it. If it weren't for my mom, I'd move the fuck out of Vegas and open a shop somewhere else."

"Oh, really? I can think of a city that could use your talents," Kacey teased, and then waved her hands, as if she could dispel the words like smoke. "No, Beverly needs you. And I think Henry is reachable. I feel he's got it in him to come around."

"What makes you say that?"

"When I compare him to my dad." She flumped back on her pillows. "Dad and I are a lost cause. I think my mother and I are becoming one, too. Every day I don't talk to her makes it easier for her to let me go."

"Let you go for *what?* Why did he cut you off? Why has he been a dick to you for so long and why does she go along with it?"

She shrugged. "I don't know. I feel like my mother's not telling me something about my dad. When I was a kid, still living at home, he could hardy look at me. Like it hurt his eyes. And sometimes I'd catch Mom staring at me like the way you do an old photograph. With nostalgia." She shook her head. "I know that makes no sense at all, but I get this *vibe* from her. As if she missed me…even though I was right there the whole time."

"Maybe she was feeling shitty for not standing up for you," I said.

"Maybe." She smiled a little, turned on her side to face me. "You and I are a lot alike, Teddy."

I stared at the TV where the movie was playing without an audience. Baby trying to learn the steps to that first dance with Johnny, nervous and faltering. "We both have a parent we can't please," I said.

"Yeah."

"And we both miss Jonah."

"God, yes, I do. It comes over me in waves. Unpredictable. It ambushes me when I'm with my friends in New Orleans, or when I was recording that album…Oh my god. I'd be singing one track, and I think, 'This is getting easier. Our time together was so short, but instead of feeling bad that it ended, I'm just happy it happened.' Like my heart was healing after all. And then I'd ruin the next track completely with a total sniveling ugly cry, and I'd think, 'I'm never going to get over this. I'm never going to keep that promise I made to him.'"

I jerked my head in her direction. "What promise?"

Her blue eyes shone like glass. "He was extracting promises at the end. Remember?"

"I remember," I said quietly.

Kacey's smile was heartbreaking as she dropped her gaze to the blanket. "Mine was to promise to love someone else."

My heart began to jackhammer and the blood rushed to my ears. Her promise and mine linked themselves in my mind. In my goddamn heart.

"I promised," she was saying softly. "I said yes. I didn't want to and I didn't mean it. It felt impossible. But he was so tired…" The tears were coming again and her voice turned weak and watery. "He was so tired. But then I promised and he was happy."

A thousand different emotions were boiling in me. My guts churned as if I'd eaten and then jumped on a roller coaster.

He asked her to love again.

He asked me to love her.

What the fuck, Jonah?

Kacey wiped her face on the pillowcase. "My hope is someday the promise will stop feeling so impossible to keep. But whether or not I do, at least it made him happy at the end. That's all that matters." She looked up at me. "Isn't it?"

"Yes," I said, like a croak. Then louder, "Yes, that's the most important thing."

She became engrossed in the movie, while I stared straight through the TV. Lost in my head, unable to fathom the depth of my brother's heart. A man who told the love of his life, at the moment of goodbye, to love someone else.

And to his brother, a promise to love her…

The movie ended. Kacey had fallen asleep. I slipped out of the bed I was lying on, put on my shoes, grabbed my jacket and tie. The door squeaked like a goddamn hyena, but Kacey only stirred and slept on. I closed it tight, making sure it locked behind me.

In the silent hallway to my own room, our promises—Kacey's and mine—linked themselves again in my mind, around and around, like dancers at a wedding.

CHAPTER 18

Kacey

I came home to a wet and rainy New Orleans. No sooner had I trundled my suitcase into my living room and shrugged off my jacket than I heard Yvonne shouting for me. I went to the kitchen and threw open the window.

"This came for you," she said. "Two days ago." She tossed a small, flat, square package wrapped in brown paper across the small divide between our houses. "The rain was coming down fierce, so I rescued it."

"Thanks, Yvonne." I knew what it was—a CD—and my heart skipped a beat.

"How was the wedding?" she asked over the light rain smattering against our roofs.

"It was nice," I said, "but I'm glad to be home."

"Glad you're back too, baby," she said. "Come over tomorrow for beignets and tea, and tell me all about it."

"Deal."

In my living room, I sat on the couch, turning the small package over in my hands. A small note was scrawled onto the front.

It's better than you can even imagine!!!

I wasn't so sure. To Grant and Phoebe, this was an indie album we all hoped might sell a few copies. To me, it was a love affair—mine and Jonah's—put to words and music, start to finish.

I took the CD case to my bedroom and set it on the bed next to the universe orb.

"It was a beautiful ceremony," I said as I changed out of my jeans and black silk blouse. "You should've seen Dena. She was radiant. And Oscar looked scared shitless but also madly in love. And Teddy…"

I pulled on sleep shorts and my faded *Wham!* T-shirt. "You would have been so proud of him. He felt bad about being best man. He said he could feel how everyone was thinking about you. But he gave the most perfect speech." I sank onto the bed beside the orb, running my fingers over the smooth glass. "But you know this, right? You were right there. You saw how he talked about you. We all did, all night. We miss you so much. You must know that."

I sniffed as the tears dropped onto my white duvet. I pulled my laptop off the floor and slipped the CD into it.

The first song, "Riot Girl" began to play, and I curled around the universe orb and listened.

I listened to a girl sing about the wreck she'd been and the sweet, noble man who'd given her the strength to stand on her own two feet.

I listened to a girl sing about a love that altered her forever, down to her soul.

I listened to her sing about moments slipping through her fingers like sand, and a grief so deep, it nearly drowned her in an ocean of tears.

I listened to a girl sing about her love's impossible courage. How, even at the end, her man's failing heart had strength to show her a future, even without him.

I held the universe orb, clutched it to my heart, and listened to a girl fall apart in a song called "The Lighthouse."

When I sang the song at the clubs, it was always the emotional anchor that dragged me down and brought out the tears. I cried that night—great heaving sobs that made my stomach ache. But as I listened to this version of "The Lighthouse"—clean and pure with no background noise—I heard something new. A violin behind the sad strum of a lone guitar and the girl's breaking voice. Its strings rose an octave higher than the guitar, rising in perfect harmony. It lifted up the refrain, when, in the live performances, the refrain fell down.

This time, I heard hope.

As the last notes hung in the air and then dissipated, I felt a shift in my heart. A soothing hand closed around the deep ache. I picked up the universe orb. Cradling it in my arms, I carried it across the room and set it on its stand on the dresser.

"Jonah," I whispered. "I'm going to try this. I have to try to let you go now. Because, I think…it's what you want. Isn't it? It's what you've been trying to tell me. I don't know if I can let go entirely. But tonight, I'm going to try."

I kissed the tips of my fingers, placed them over the orb and its lonely planet and swirling constellations.

"Live in the stars, baby. Okay?" My voice cracked but didn't break, and I smiled through my tears. "You're free. You made me free."

I know it was the trick of the bedroom light blurring my vision through my tears, but I swear I saw the luminescent swirls of a million stars in that glass orb flare brighter, all at once.

I closed my eyes.

I inhaled. *You are a universe…*

I exhaled. *No regret, only love…*

And on the currents of that soft breath, I whispered to Jonah, "Goodnight, love. I love you. I will always love you…"

EMMA SCOTT

The Lighthouse

The bottom of the bottle
Is where I don't have to feel
At the end of every night
I can pretend I'm not real

The shore is growing distant
The planks beneath me break
I sink into the deepest dark
And beg the stars to take

Me, into their infinite silence
Where it is quiet upon quiet
In your still glass orbs
Where no one can hear me cry

(chorus)
The lighthouse
At the edge of my world
Has gone dark,
I break myself on the rocky shores
Sink beneath the waves
Drowned in the downpour
Of my own tears
An unending rain
Falling and filling an ocean
Of unbreathable pain

Your light went out forever
I could close my eyes
The black is black is black
Like ashes against a night sky

A darkened lighthouse
At the edge of the world
Is all that's left
Of this drowning girl

PART 2

You will heal and you will rebuild yourself around the loss you have suffered. You will be whole again but you will never be the same.—Elisabeth Kübler-Ross

CHAPTER 19

Kacey

Two Months Later

Teddy, I texted. **Guess what?**

I give up.

I could practically see his smug little smirk. I rolled my eyes at my phone, and typed back: **You didn't even try.**

There's an 80's movie marathon on cable this week?

Almost as awesome. I bit my lip, not wanting to come across as bragging, but he was the first person I wanted to share the news with. **My album, *Shattered Glass*? It's number one on CDBaby and Beatport. Number six on iTunes.**

I squinched my face up and hit send. Then grinned ear to ear at Theo's reply.

Holy shit! Calling…

My phone lit up and I answered, "Holy shit."

"That's fucking awesome, Kace."

"Thank you," I said, plucking at a stray thread on my couch

pillow. My smile wouldn't dim. "It took a little bit of time to get the ball rolling, but now the downloads are really steady. It's pretty crazy. Grant and Phoebe said 'The Lighthouse' and 'One Million Moments' were bestselling singles."

"Hell yeah, they are," Theo said. "Any record execs calling you yet?"

"No."

"They will."

"Grant thinks a video on YouTube will get their attention. He's full of ideas. Before we released the album, he talked about just me and a guitar and some candles in an empty room. But now that some money's coming in, he's thinking water tanks and special effects. Can you believe that?"

"I'm really damn happy for you, Kace."

"Thanks, Teddy."

"So are these Olsen people legit? They're not ripping you off, are they?"

"So far, they're great. We have a contract. I pay them 15% of everything I make plus a flat fee for the use of their studio and for production of actual CDs."

"Sounds fair."

"Sounds on the low-end to me. If I ever make a shit-ton of money, I'm going to take care of them. I wouldn't even be taking this next step if it weren't for them."

"What is the next step?"

I flumped back in the chair with a sigh. "Grant wants to do a release party."

"Where? When?"

"Next Friday. Le Chacal. I had Grant do it there so I can hang with Big E. I need all the friends there I can get. *Hint, hint.*"

I was teasing and I wasn't.

"Shit, I wish I could," Theo said. "But Gus is already up my ass about missing work. And I have class. I'm sorry…"

"Don't be sorry," I said, keeping the disappointment out of my voice. "It's expensive, and it's short notice. I don't actually expect you to drop everything and fly out for a silly party."

But I wanted him to, I realized. I missed him a lot, and our phone conversations were starting to feel like little crumbs of food when I wanted a big feast.

When did that happen?
I cleared my throat. "So anyway, I'll call you after? It'll be late."
"I don't care," he said. "I'll be here."
"You're always so good to me."
"I try to be, Kace," he said softly.
A short silence fell, waiting, like we were both holding our breath. I broke for air first.
"Okay, I should go," I said quickly. "Give your mom a kiss for me."
"Yeah, for sure, I will," he said just as fast. "Goodnight, Kace."
"Goodnight, Teddy."

The night of the party arrived and I was nervous as hell. I put on black leather jeans, and a silky gray blouse, off-the-shoulder with billowy sleeves. I piled my hair on my head, pulling loose tendrils to frame my face. With a pang, I tucked the black rose Dena gave me at her wedding behind my ear. I wished she and Oscar were coming to celebrate with me. And Theo.

And Jonah.

A text came in on my phone before I headed out: **Enjoy your party. You deserve this.**

A warmth bloomed in my chest as I replied: **Thanks, Teddy. <3**

Le Chacal was packed to capacity. I'd never seen the club so full before. Jonathan, the skinny and balding owner, practically had dollar signs in his eyes at the amount of booze flowing. The doors and windows were open, and people and music spilled out onto the street. Passersby who had no idea what was happening stopped to listen, and many stayed.

I headed for the table Grant and Phoebe set up near the bar to sell CDs. I'd given myself a hand cramp signing 500 covers, thinking it was too much, no way we'd sell a fraction of them.

"Five hundred CDs, sold out," Phoebe said, showing me the empty box. "In record time."

"At ten dollars a pop." Grant held up his hands, grinning wide. "I know it's vulgar to discuss money, but let's just say it's not bad for a night's work."

Phoebe pressed a seltzer water with lime into my hand, which nearly sloshed all over the floor a minute later when Big E picked me up and swung me around. Yvonne had arrived too, with a couple of her friends, and we laughed and shout-talked over Louis Prima on the sound system. Ten minutes later, my phone vibrated from my back pocket with a text from Theo.

Having fun yet?

My brow furrowed. **It's early, but yes.**

I started to send another but he beat me to it.

You wore that flower in your hair at the wedding.

My head jerked up, my eyes scanning the crowd as my heart began to pound.

No way.

My eyes scanned the bar. Then tracked back. Theo was standing with Big E, both of them grinning like dopes.

My mouth dropped. "No. Way."

Theo was ridiculously handsome in a red wine-colored dress shirt, rolled up at the sleeves, and dark jeans. He gave me a cocky grin and waved hello with his phone.

My heart, already so full of happiness, expanded in my chest as Theo's eyes held mine and his smile pulled wide. I pushed through the crowd as fast as I could and flung my arms around his neck. "Are you *kidding* me?"

I held him tight, breathing him in, his skin, his cologne. Feeling his strong arms around me and the laughter coming through his chest.

"I can't believe you're here!" I cried.

"I'm here."

"You told me you had too much school, you big liar."

"I do," he said. "But funny thing about UNLV—they give us the weekends off. Weird, right?"

I laughed, smacked his arm, then hugged him again.

"And you," I said, turning to Big E. "You're his accomplice."

The big bartender held up his hands. "I'm just as happy to see this guy as you are." His warm gaze went between us. "Well, maybe not *quite* as happy…"

I took Theo's hand. "Come on. I want you to meet Grant and Phoebe, and I'm sure Yvonne would love to see you."

Theo made a face. "Hope she left her baseball bat at home."

I introduced my Las Vegas friend to my New Orleans friends, and spent the rest of the night laughing and talking, surrounded by the people I loved. The crowd swelled and soon Rufus signaled from the booth that it was time to play.

I blew air out my cheeks. "Is it just me, or is this crowd really big?"

Phoebe took my drink from my hand, as Grant looped my guitar over my shoulder. Theo leaned in to be heard over the noise, his breath warm on my cheek, like a kiss.

"Knock'em dead."

I glanced up at him. "Thanks, Teddy." The crowd was too loud but I know he heard me anyway.

I sang a few songs from the album, including "The Lighthouse." The huge crowd gave me their silence and I gave them everything I had. But I wasn't the Drowned Girl anymore. While I felt the ache of Jonah's absence in every word, in my mind I heard a violin, lifting up the refrain with hope. I infused the words with rich emotion, but I didn't cry.

After I finished my set to resounding applause, a zydeco band took the stage. They insisted I join in for a set. I wasn't fluent in their style of music, but I heard the changes and felt the flow, and soon was jamming with them. The crowd went crazy.

My eyes kept seeking Theo in the crowd. Every time I did, I found his eyes on me, that intense look that only Theo Fletcher possessed. The look that made me feel, for a few brief moments, as if no one existed in his world but for me.

CHAPTER 20

Theo

The next day, Kacey took me around New Orleans to all her favorite joints. Now that she was sober, she said, she could enjoy the city. She looked beautiful in a simple T-shirt and denim skirt, her skin glowing with health. The incredible blue of her eyes was brighter than I'd ever seen it.

"I love it here," she said over beignets at a small café. "The city is so different from anywhere else I've ever been." She took a generous bite from her pastry. "Full of dancing ghosts."

I nodded absently, only half hearing. "You have some powdered sugar…" I gestured at her lower lip that was dusted in white.

She took a napkin and wiped it away. "Gone?"

"Gone."

She'd wiped the powdered sugar from her mouth but my imagination conjured me leaning over the table and sliding my tongue along the seam of her lips, tasting the sweetness…

I was suddenly extremely grateful for the table concealing my lap, and took a long drink of ice water. Since Kacey's revelation of her promise to Jonah, the little flicker of hope in my heart had flamed up into something constant. Something permanent. It no longer felt like she and I were impossible.

But what do I do? Tell her what I feel? I can't tell her. It's too soon. I'll fuck it all up.

With any other girl I'd already have had my hands in her hair and my tongue in her mouth because I wouldn't give a shit what happened later. With Kacey, I cared about all of it; this moment and everything after.

"I'm so happy you're here," she said suddenly. "I know I'm a broken record but I miss you." She frowned, her brows furrowed as if she were trying to work out some complex problem. "I miss you a lot, actually. More than a lot. Is that weird?"

"No." I coughed. "I miss you too." I stirred my coffee to conceal how her words hit me right in the chest. "But it sort of seems like you're done with Vegas."

"I guess so," she said, still distracted by her own thoughts. "I'm doing okay here. I'm not drinking, I'm holding down my jobs, making friends. Building a life."

I nodded. She was closing a door and opening a new one, like that damn Tarot card had said. Meanwhile, I was the Hanged Man. Getting a degree wouldn't help me if it meant buying a business in Vegas that would likely fail.

If I moved to New Orleans, I could build a life here too.

"Are you finished?" Kacey asked suddenly, indicating my food. "I need to walk."

"Let's go."

We left the café and walked along the French Quarter. I thought we were strolling aimlessly, enjoying the spring Saturday, but Kacey had a plan. I realized we were walking along the edge of one of those famous New Orleans cemeteries, with row after row of little house-like crypts, sagging with time. It had to be eighty degrees out but my skin broke out in gooseflesh.

"Let's go in," Kacey said.

"You sure?"

She shot me a grin. "Why? Are you scared?"

"No," I snorted. "It's just…" *Graveyards give me the fucking creeps.* "…a weird place to hang out."

"It's historical," Kacey said. "Suits my mood, too. Come on."

I followed her through the open gates. The late-morning sun glinted dully on a stone plaque, *St. Louis Cemetery #2* chiseled into it.

We walked among the rows of crypts. Flowers, beads, and candles were strewn at their doors. Some were fenced in with spike-tipped iron, some with pristine white marble. Most were browned with age, probably erected before Las Vegas was even founded.

"Marie Leveau's crypt is in the St. Louis #1," Kacey said. "She's the voodoo queen. We should go there sometime."

I made a sound that could have been yes or no. I didn't even want to be in *this* cemetery, but it'd be a cold day in hell before I admitted that to Kacey.

We found a bench and took a seat as the sun rose higher behind the rows of crypts.

"This place has restless spirits," Kacey said. "Can you feel them?"

Well shit, I can now, I thought, glancing around and rubbing my arms. Thankfully, Kacey was lost in her own thoughts and didn't notice.

"I'm restless too," she said. "I feel like I'm always on the verge of something big. Then something big happens, like the album selling well, or the show last night. I think, *Okay, that was it. That was the Big Something.* But the next day, or next hour even, the feeling is back. I'm always waiting for something else but I have no idea what. It's unsettling."

"I sort of feel the same way," I said. "But for me, I think the Big Something is what happens when I graduate."

"Then you start your own business," she said.

"Yeah, I guess. But fuck, it's risky. I can't tell if it's the wrong thing to do, or if it's just my nerves trying to talk me out of it. Or my *dad* trying to talk me out of it."

"Don't let him talk you out of it," she said. "It's your dream. Don't let it go."

She sounded like Jonah. Her conviction and her belief in me exactly like his: unconditional.

Kacey regarded me a moment, then glanced down at her hands, that same confusion as earlier twisting her features. "You're my best friend," she said. "And when I saw you at the bar with Big E last night, I felt so…happy. More than happy. Overjoyed."

"Oh yeah?" I said, trying to keep my voice level. "I get that a lot."

She elbowed me in the side. "I'm being serious. I haven't felt like that in a long time." She looked up at me. "Is that what we are? Best friends?"

"Well, I think…yeah, Kace. You're my best friend."

She bit her lip. "Are you seeing anyone? Someone special?"

"No," I said slowly. "Not anyone special."

"Oh," she said, tucking a lock of hair behind her ear. "Oscar makes it sound like maybe you are. Or… I don't know."

"He's wrong," I said, harder than I intended. "He likes to take a joke and run it into the ground."

She nodded. "It's none of my business, anyway. I was just…wondering."

"I haven't seen anyone seriously since Holly."

What the hell...?

But the words escaped and there was no taking them back.

Kacey stared. "That was almost a year ago. You broke up with Holly that night at Grand Basin." She glanced up at me. "Why? I mean, why then and there, in the middle of the woods?"

Because I heard you sing. And I knew I'd never be the same.

I shrugged, keeping my eyes fixed away. "It wasn't going to happen between us. It felt wrong to string her along."

"But why that night? Why not wait until after the trip?"

I tried to think of a plausible reason. The truth—or part of it— seemed the only way to go. "I knew she'd want to have sex that night. But it was already over for me."

Kacey raised her brows with a knowing smile. "So you could've gotten laid one last time, but took the high road instead."

"I'm not a total lowlife."

"You're not any kind of lowlife," she said. "Funny, at the time, Dena and I thought what you did was kind of harsh. Turns out, you were doing the right thing."

"What about you?" I asked slowly, the words sticking to my teeth. "Seeing anyone?"

"No, no," she said, hugged her elbows. "I'm not ready. I think about what it would be like, being on a date with another man. Holding his hand or kissing him goodnight, and I just…I can't do it. My mind won't even go there."

"Because of Jonah," I said quietly.

She nodded, dropped her gaze to her hands again. "I'm trying to let him go, you know? But I don't think that's something I can *do*. Like flipping a switch. I think it's just something that will happen gradually, and I'll know it's happening because I'll start doing things again. Going on dates, thinking about other guys…"

A thought pulled her lips down and she looked up at me. Our eyes met and my guard started to slip, the walls coming down. She sat so close, watching me, a vague notion starting to take root, realization creeping into her gaze.

Say something, Kace. Do something, because I can't. It has to come from you. It has to be real…

She leaned toward me. "Teddy…"

I felt pulled down toward her. "Yeah?"

"Do you…still visit Jonah's installation a lot?"

I blinked and Kacey's sheepish laugh broke the tension hanging in the air like spun glass. "Sorry, totally random. I just…You've always been there for me. I wondered if you wanted to talk about it. Or him."

Disappointment crashed me back to earth. "No, I'm good."

"That's what you said last time," she said. "Are you really?"

"I'm fine, Kace. Promise."

Kacey turned on the bench to face me. "Teddy. I'm here for you. Even hundreds of miles away, I'm here. If you ever need me like I needed you…"

I wanted to touch her face. I wanted to tell her I needed her in a way she couldn't imagine. I wanted to tell her the truth.

"Kacey…"

But I couldn't say it. The words, born in my heart, rose up and became stuck in my throat, trapped by excuses. *It's too soon. She's not ready. She said it herself…*

"Thanks. I'm here for you too."

God, you're pathetic.

Kacey nodded. "Because we're friends. And friends miss each other when they're apart, and they're happy to see each other when they're together. It makes sense. Right?"

"Sure," I said slowly.

She sighed. "I guess that's it then."

We started back for her house. But the perplexed look on her face wouldn't leave.

Friends love each other too, I wanted to tell her, but it was too late. The moment had slipped out of my fingers and I'd let it.

CHAPTER 21

Kacey

Grant Olsen's grin was so wide I thought it would tip his glasses off. "And that, as they say in the business, is a wrap."

"Thank God," I said, as a production assistant wrapped a towel around me. "I look like a drowned rat."

Phoebe handed me a hot coffee. "I would tell you that's not true, but I like to keep my relationships honest."

I stuck my tongue out at her.

The set for the music video to "The Lighthouse" was a black, windowless boxy room with cables and lines snaking all across the floor. Two flood lights with blue and green filters beaming down on the water tank I'd spent the last three days in.

The director Grant hired had envisioned a girl trapped in the tank while a man—his face always obscured by shadow—was just out of reach on the other side of the glass. Using some fairly expensive CGI, they were going to pull the video of me in the water and superimpose it on shots of people in everyday life: at a cocktail party, at an apartment, in the bedroom of my cheating boyfriend and his lover. I would be the Drowned Girl, always submerged, while life went on around me.

I appreciated the theme of a cheating boyfriend and not a dead one. I wouldn't have agreed to do it otherwise. I would never have let some actor portray Jonah in a dramatic rendition of us. It would've felt cheap and disrespectful, exploiting what we'd had for a silly video.

Even with the changed narrative, I thought the shoot would be emotionally draining. But the video was shot out of order, chopping and shuffling up the story until it was unrecognizable. Take after take, until the takes blurred together. The constant technical adjustments. The stops and starts. The dauntless struggle not to let air bubbles leak out of my nose and ruin a scene. After three days, I was tired of "The

Lighthouse."

I dried off while the Olsen's updated me on record sales. "You're a hit, girl," Phoebe said, shuffling some papers. "This video is going to put you over the top."

"Thanks to you guys. None of this would have been possible without you."

"Just don't forget us when you're accepting your Grammy," Grant said, still grinning.

"I won't."

"You can't," Phoebe said, her eyes flashing. "We put it in your contract." She flicked her fingers at her brother then. "Go away. We have girl talk."

"We do?" I asked.

She waited until Grant was out of sight. "Matt Porter asked me if you were single."

Matt was the graphic designer doing the cover for *Shattered Glass*. Cute, dry sense of humor, nice smile.

"Oh yeah?"

"Yeah." Phoebe nudged my arm. "So?"

"I don't know," I said. "I'll think about it."

Even saying that sent guilt curling around my heart, and that unsettled feeling I'd told Theo about hit me with a vengeance. If I wanted to shut that door the Tarot card told me about and start a new chapter, I had to *do* something. Or maybe a bunch of Big Somethings.

I drove my little car home, where I stood in the entry. Home, yet feeling untethered. I had success now. Money in my bank account, good friends and a career that seemed to be taking off.

Shut the door. Do something big.

Before I could talk myself out of it, I called my parents' house in San Diego. The ringing went to the answering machine. After my mother's halting voice said to leave a message, I sucked in a deep breath.

"Hi, Mom. Hi, Dad. It's Kacey. I haven't called in almost eight months. I don't know if you tried to call me. I got rid of my old cell phone, but I have a new number now. I'm living in New Orleans. My music career is taking off—as a solo artist this time—and I'm taking care of myself."

I took another breath, feeling the urge to hurry. If the machine cut me off, I wouldn't have the guts to call again.

"I'm doing really well, and I just wanted to let you know. I'm okay. And also…" I exhaled and sat up straighter. "This is the last time I'm going to call you. I can't keep trying and getting no response. If you want to talk to me, I'm here. Okay, Mom? If you want to talk, you call me. If not…Well, then I hope you both have a long and happy life."

I left them my new cell phone number and hung up. My heart was pounding and tears stung my eyes, but I wiped them away and huffed a breath.

That's a start.

I glanced around my shabby little place with its second-hand, mismatched furniture, old linoleum floors, cruddy tile countertops and cheap, stained carpet. The bones of the house—as they were always saying on the HGTV shows—were good. It was a classic New Orleans shotgun. It deserved better than this.

I called the bank that owned the house, and set up an appointment for the following day. I didn't call Theo that night and for whatever reason, he didn't call me.

I went into the bank the next day at two p.m, and by five o'clock, I was in escrow.

Outside the bank, I paused to catch my breath, my heart racing for the amount of money I'd just committed myself to paying. $64,000 wasn't a huge mortgage payment but I took out a loan for $75,000 in order to make some renovations. I'd never owed more money in my life. But I wanted roots. A place of my own where I could dig in, stay grounded. I wasn't about to be whisked off on a road tour, or lose myself in the big Los Angeles music industry.

My pounding heart slowed, but inexplicably, it left me left me with that same hollow feeling I'd had before I left for the bank.

What is wrong with me?

I'd settled up with my parents, bought a fucking house for crying out loud, but I still felt like something was missing.

I called Phoebe and told her I was free on Friday, if Matt Porter was still interested. She assured me he was, and she'd give him my number.

I hung up. I waited to feel satisfied.

I felt slightly nauseated instead.

That night I picked at my dinner while sitting on the couch, and then watched *Big Trouble in Little China* until midnight. It was ten in

Vegas, and Theo was out of class.

"Guess what?" I said, my dinner suddenly churning in my gut.

"You finished shooting the music video," he said.

"Yesterday," I said. "Also, I called my parents for the last time. Left a message. If they want to talk, they can call me, but I'm done offering my hand only to have it slapped back."

"Good for you, babe," Theo said.

It was eighty degrees in my house but a shiver slipped up my spine, morphed into a nervous laugh that burst out of me.

"Babe?"

"Ha, sorry. Kace," he said.

"You have too many women to juggle," I said, plucking mercilessly at the couch cushion. "I can see how we all start to blend in."

"Yeah, okay." He coughed, cleared his throat. "So it's good you settled things with your parents. *Kace.*"

"That's not all I settled," I said. "I bought my house. I'm a homeowner. Shoot me now."

"You did?" A short silence. "Wow, that's…great. So I guess you're in New Orleans for good?"

I twirled a lock of hair around my finger. "I guess so. I think so. I think it's what I need to do. To settle somewhere that's mine."

"Permanence."

"Exactly. And it feels right to be here and not in Vegas," I said. "I thought about it. Tried to picture myself back there, and I just can't." I hunched my shoulders. "I hope it doesn't upset Beverly too much."

"She'll understand," he said.

I bit my lip. "In other news…I have a date on Friday."

The silence stretched out taut. I checked my phone to see if we'd been disconnected. "Teddy?"

"I'm here."

"Yeah, I just… I think there might be the tiniest shred of a possibility I'm ready for it." I laughed nervously. "Won't know until I find out."

"Guess not."

He sounded flat. Bored. It didn't seem to faze him, about the house or the date.

Because we're friends.

I yawned loudly. "I'm tired. Buying a house wears a gal out. Talk

to you tomorrow?"
　"I'll be here. 'Night."
　"Goodnight, Teddy," I said, but he'd already hung up.

CHAPTER 22

Theo

Over the next week, I kept up my routine, same as always. The alarm went off, my hand snaked out to shut it off and I had three seconds of peace before reality slammed into me. Only now the first thought was *Kacey's not coming back from New Orleans.*

Followed by: *And she's got a date on Friday.*

I didn't know which was worse.

The date. The date is definitely fucking worse.

I didn't begrudge her any 'Big Somethings.' She needed to do what was best for her, to heal and move on.

But she's going on a fucking date.

I got to work that day in a pissy mood. No one was manning the front desk, so I picked up Vivian's Magic-8 Ball. I shook it hard, silently asking the black-and-white blur: *Will it end with Kacey throwing a drink in his face and never seeing him again?*

I watched intently as the blue triangle righted itself.

Ask again later.

Not what I was hoping for, but I'd take it. I headed back to my station. Zelda and Edgar were already at theirs.

"Hey, guys," I said. "Can I get your opinion on something?"

They gathered around as I opened my portfolio and laid out some ink and watercolor sketches on my tattoo chair. I'd been working on them since the last time I was in New Orleans, trying to keep my mind occupied.

"What's this?" Edgar said, picking up my sketch of an African savannah, spare with only the black silhouettes of two giraffes on the right side, a soaring ibis on the other, with a boiling, heat-wavered sun in reds and orange indistinctly rendered along the back. "This is cool shit, bro."

"I fucking love this," Zelda said, inspecting a black ink sketch of a sugar skull in profile, with bright reds, blues, and yellows shaded through it. She peered up at me. "It looks unfinished. But it is finished, isn't it?"

I rubbed the back of my neck. "Yeah, that's the idea. That the coloring highlights the black ink, but doesn't fill it in or overwhelm it."

"This is killer shit, T," Edgar said, holding a sketch of a woman's eye, with long, dark lashes and an arching brow. The pale blue of the iris was circled with a darker cobalt and the skin tone of the woman's face was only partly hinted at. "You going to show this to *Inked*?"

"Once it's on skin, yeah," I said. "On paper, it's just a drawing."

"I volunteer my services," Edgar said. He slapped his upper arm.

"I appreciate that," I said, "but I'm not trying to pressure you guys. I just wanted your thoughts. See if they might be something."

"Got it," Edgar said. "And my thoughts are, I want one."

"Really? Thanks, man. I'm honored."

Zelda handed the sketches back. "I have a client who would kill for one of these," she said. "I'll send her your way. For a small finder's fee," she added with a smirk, and returned to her station.

"You gone shy on us, Rossi?" Edgar called after her. "The idea of the Theo's manly man hands on your bare skin too much for ya?"

"Bite me," Zelda said, busying herself with her inks.

"Be cool, man," I said to Edgar in a low voice.

He slapped me on the back. "Just playing, bro." He tapped the sketch of the sugar skull. "Can you give me this with more reds and orange?"

"Sure. We can start tomorrow." We clasped hands. "I really appreciate it."

"Dude. It's rad. *Inked* is going to be all over this."

I hoped so. The idea for the unfinished tattoos came to me the night before, right as I was falling asleep. I'd spent the most of the night making the sketches to keep the idea from slipping into the abyss of forgotten good ideas.

A small smile played around my mouth as I packed the sketches up. If this idea took off, it'd make me feel a hell of a lot better about buying my own place. Maybe I'd have a little bit of a name for myself to stave off the fear of utter and total failure.

Ideas for other sketches came to me as I readied my station: Tarot cards and jazz halls, cemeteries and voodoo dolls. Vegas was overflowing with tattoo shops. The New Orleans market was much wider. I knew this because I'd researched the city last night. Maybe Kacey buying a house in the Big Easy wasn't such a terrible tragedy after all. Or a closed door. Maybe it was a door opening. For both of us.

My cell phone rang as I finished with my first client. I frowned at the number.

"What's up, Ma?"

"Theo?" Her voice sounded weak and shaky. "I hate to bother you but…"

"What is it?" I asked, my heart thudding. "You okay?"

"Oh, I'm…having a bad day," she said. "I was going through some old boxes and found some photos." She sniffed and forced a small laugh. "I'm a bit of a mess but I promised Lois I'd bake eggplant parmesan for our cribbage tomorrow. I just…I can't seem to muster the energy to clean up and make myself presentable for the grocery store."

"I get it, Ma," I said, gently. "What do you need me to do?"

"Would you run to the store for me? I'm sure I'll be fine by tomorrow, but if I don't get started tonight…"

"Where's Dad?" I asked, trying to keep my tone even.

"Oh, you know him. He's at the office. Says he can't get away."

I closed my eyes for a moment, then glanced at the entrance where a couple of clients were waiting.

"Are you busy?" she asked. "I'm so sorry, dear. I feel so useless."

"No, Ma, it's fine," I said. "Give me a list of what you need. I'll go now."

"You're so good to me," she said, tears thickening her words. "I was blessed with two wonderful sons, wasn't I?"

Pain squeezed my heart. I got the grocery list from her, then gathered my stuff.

"Where are you going?" Vivian asked from the front desk. "You have a client coming in twenty minutes."

"Call them back, would you? See if you can push it to forty."

She shook her head but took up the receiver. "You're lucky you're so damn cute," she muttered.

"Thanks, Viv. You're the best."

I stopped, grabbed her Magic 8-Ball and gave it a shake.

"You asking if Gus is going to fire your ass?" she muttered, her hand over the phone's mouthpiece. "Spoiler alert: *It is certain.*" She turned aside. "Yes, hi, is this Brittany? This is Vivian from Vegas Ink…"

I didn't ask the toy if Gus was going to fire me, but the same question I had this morning. It was later, so I was asking again later.

I swear the fucking triangle looked smug as it floated its answer: *Outlook not so good.*

After I tore through the grocery store with Mom's list, I screeched my truck into the drive. My forty minutes was up; I was nearly an hour out of the shop. But my hopes for dropping off the food here and heading back out were smashed to pieces when I found my mother sitting on the living room floor, a hundred photos spread out around her on all sides, and one held slack in her hand as she cried.

"Christ." I dropped the grocery bags and hurried to kneel beside her. "Come on, Ma. Let's get you to the couch."

"He was so handsome," she murmured, staring at the photo in her hand of Jonah at UNLV graduation, wearing a red gown and red cap. She didn't pull her eyes from the photo as I lifted her off the floor and helped her sit on the couch. Then she looked to me, her eyes red and shadowed. "I miss him so much, Theo."

"I know you do."

She leaned into me, crying softly. "I'm trying to be strong, but some days…"

"I know," I told her, putting my arm around her. "We all have bad days. That's nothing to feel ashamed of. It's okay."

"You're so good to me. I know it's been hard for you, but you're so strong." She sat up, cupped my cheek in her hand. "You're all I have left. I get so scared that something will happen to you too…"

She collapsed back into tears, and I held her together. "I'm right here." I said, my jaw clenched, as if trying not to let the words escape. "I'm not going anywhere."

CHAPTER 23

Kacey

The house was a mess. The drywall had been taken down in some places, my kitchen floor was pulled up, and plastic sheets hung like curtains to keep the dust from flying.

I wanted to do as much of the work as I could, thinking the more I made this place a real home, the more settled I'd finally feel. But holy shit, it was a much bigger job then those HGTV shows make it look.

Thankfully, Yvonne was handy with a sledgehammer and let me pay her in beignets I bought from her favorite bakery. Today she was helping me demolish the old kitchen cabinets. They'd been painted and repainted so many times, the doors stuck together.

"What's with the mopey face, baby," she said, peering at me from behind her safety goggles. "You seem a little down."

"Do I?" I yanked at a cabinet door that hung on one hinge. "Just nervous I guess. I have a date on Friday."

"With Teddy?"

"What?" My head shot up, and I frowned. "No, not Teddy. He's back in Vegas. The date is with a friend of Phoebe's."

"Oh."

"Oh, what?"

"Nothing." Yvonne whacked the sledgehammer into the lower cabinet like a pro golfer, splintering wood and cracking it off the wall.

I don't know why I felt the need to explain myself but the words poured out anyway. "Teddy's only a friend. He's my best friend."

Yvonne pursed her lips and peered down at me over her goggles.

I laughed and slung my arm around her. "I mean best friend from my old life. You're my BFF from my new life."

"That's better." She took aim at another cabinet. "And does your other best friend also go out on dates?"

"He says he's not seeing anyone serious, but I'm sure he must go out. You've seen him, right?"

"I have. He's sex on a stick."

I nearly lost my balance, and a flush of heat swept over my face. "Yvonne!"

"Isn't he?"

"He's…handsome."

Yvonne snorted. "My grandfather was 'handsome.' My grandmother too, come to think of it."

"I admit, he's sexy," I said. "He probably has many manly urges to satisfy and many women to help him."

"There it is again."

"What?"

"That sad look on your face is back."

"What? Stop. It's…probably jealousy. I have urges too, you know. I haven't had sex in forever. But I'm not sure this date with Matt is a good idea."

"Why not?"

"A date with an unknown guy makes me feel like everything I had with Jonah was…disposable. As if all I have to do is wait until enough time goes by and *boom.* I'm back in the saddle."

"What more is there?" Yvonne asked.

"I don't know," I said. "But I feel like… I can't follow up being with Jonah by doing something as superficial as *dating.* Trying out different guys to see if they fit. Kissing them, maybe even sleeping with them, only to break up a week later because it turns out he's still not over his ex, or he's not into 'getting serious,' or he hates dogs."

Yvonne quirked her brow. "Hates dogs?"

"You know what I mean," I said. "All the bullshit that comes with dating. I can't do it. Not after Jonah. What we had was beyond special. What comes next needs to be special too. Going on one date already feels like a betrayal. It would be a million times worse if I did it over and over again, one stranger after another."

"Theo's no stranger."

I stopped what I was doing and gave her a look.

Yvonne held up her hands. "He's cute. He's tatted up, like you. He's obviously a good man for flying out here to help you like he did. And you two are close. You share a common pain."

"Yes, because he's Jonah's brother," I said quietly.

"So?"

"So?" My eyebrows shot up. "So that's...I mean, he's..."

Yvonne leaned on her hammer. "Yessss? Have you thought about it? Maybe just a little?"

I shook my head. "No. Well, maybe."

She pursed her lips.

"Okay, yes. Fine, I think about it. I think about him constantly. My favorite part of the day—besides talking to you—is my phone calls with him. But I can't tell if our friendship is really strong or if I'm just clinging to him for comfort."

"Maybe," Yvonne said, "you should try to find out."

I sighed. "I don't know. I don't know that I'm ready. I can't dump all that confusion and guilt on Teddy. He's precious to me. So precious, in fact..." I spread my arms out to indicate the house. "I buy a house fifteen hundred miles away from him."

"You want to know what I think?"

"In the worst way possible."

"I think something's happening between you and Theo, and it scares you to pieces."

A thousand reasons why that was wrong piled up on my lips. I swallowed them all down.

"I think you might be right," I said softly, and all at once I felt something shift in me. A settling. A Big Something I might have been waiting for.

Yvonne's smile was gentle. "Keep going, baby. Tell me."

"It's been a long time since I've been able to imagine a life after Jonah," I said. "A future like other people have, with marriage and kids, and careers we help each other to build. It's been almost impossible to imagine loving someone else. But when I let myself have that kind of hopeful vision, the only person I see is Teddy."

Yvonne nodded. "And now the *but...*"

"But the guilt. And how Beverly would react. And what Oscar and Dena would think. And the worry that I'd mess it up. And the fact that I'm... I'm terrified something will happen to Theo like it did to Jonah." My eyes stung with sudden tears. "I've lost too much already."

"I know." Yvonne dropped her sledgehammer and embraced me in a dusty hug. "I know you have."

"I had Jonah. For a few, short moments that beautiful man was mine and I was his. I'll never have anything that real or good again, will I? Who gets a second chance like that?"

"The ones who step back up to the table and lay it all out there." Yvonne pulled away, pushed the hair from my eyes. "You're not done, Kacey. I know you aren't. You have more cards to play."

I smiled through the tears. "I am a universe."

Yvonne's eyes widened. "I like that. Yes, you are a universe, right here in this room, and you are *not done*."

She put her arm around me, and we surveyed the demolished kitchen.

"You're starting over again. New life, new place. It's brave, putting one foot in front of the other. You don't have to figure it all out at once. Don't force it, and if something good and real is waiting for you around the corner, it'll still be there when you're ready."

The cabinets were all down, and we were up to our ankles in splintered wood. Dust motes danced in the afternoon light streaming in through the window.

Yvonne gave me a squeeze. "Can you see it yet? Your new home?"

"Not yet."

"You will, baby. You will."

CHAPTER 24

Theo

Friday afternoon was dead at the shop. I'd been hoping for a hard job—a client who wanted something intricate to keep my mind off Kacey's date. Instead, all I got was a young, nervous-looking girl, about twenty years old, who wanted a semicolon on the inside of her right wrist.

Great, I thought. *That'll take me all of ten minutes.*

"What's it mean?" I asked her, loading black ink and a liner needled in my tattoo machine.

"A semicolon is where a writer can choose to end the sentence," she said, tucking a lock of brown hair behind her ear. "But they don't. The story goes on. It's a symbol of hope. To keep going." She smiled tremulously. "Sometimes I need that reminder."

I stared at the girl a moment, nodded, this job suddenly taking on a whole new meaning. *This is why I do this.*

I inked the semicolon onto the young woman's wrist and when she was done, I thanked her instead of the other way around.

Time crawled.

A glance at the clock said it was just after six. Eight, Kacey's time.

She was probably on her date right about now.

A new emotion erupted in me to add to the already noxious mix churning in my gut: Pure, old-fashioned jealousy, straight up. No chaser.

The story goes on. Kacey's story was going on in New Orleans. It wasn't the same gravitas as the semicolon symbolism, but the idea stuck with me anyway. She was going on. I was stuck. Period.

"Zelda," I called over the buzzing of Edgar's gun and the pounding metal music.

She looked up, her hair falling like black silk around her

shoulders. Her impossibly large eyes were the greenest I'd ever seen.

"Yessss?" she drawled, when I just stared at her. "Something on your mind?"

"You want to grab a late dinner tonight? A new place opened at the Paris. We could give it a shot."

Zelda blinked twice, her face expressionless. Then she shrugged. "I could eat."

"Cool," I said. *Then it's a date,* I thought, but couldn't bring myself to say it aloud. Guilt assailed me. The guilt of a guy cheating on his woman.

Kacey is not your woman. She never has been and she probably never will be.

What was she doing right now? Was she having the time of her life? Was her date keeping his goddamn hands to himself or did she want him to touch her? Were they kissing? Or going to bed? Was she letting him take her dress off, letting him put his mouth on her…

Fuck me.

I leaned over and mucked around in a drawer, surreptitiously adjusted my crotch.

Now, that's a date, Fletcher, a voice like Oscar's cackled in my mind. *Dinner with one girl. A hard-on for another.*

We closed up shop at seven. Fortunately, Edgar and Vivian said goodnight and split, leaving Zelda and I to make plans without merciless teasing or speculation.

Zelda waited as I locked up, her small frame hunched into her black leather jacket.

"You like Italian?" I asked.

"My last name is Rossi," she said. "What do you think?"

"Martorano's is the new place in the Paris. Supposed to be good."

"Works for me." Her large eyes widened when I opened the passenger door for her. "Thanks. And here I thought chivalry was dead."

I got behind the wheel and immediately, it felt like *a date*—a girl in my truck, filling the small cab with her perfume and presence, on our way to a slightly more than casual restaurant.

This is good, I thought. *I can do this.*

Over dinner, I learned Zelda was a comic book junkie. She was trying to put together a graphic novel. "Eventually, I hope to pitch it to the big ones. Dark Horse or DC."

"So tattooing is just your day job?"

"It's the only way to make any consistent money drawing little pictures," she said with a dry smile.

I nodded and as we talked, I tried to force myself to feel something, *anything*, for Zelda. She was beautiful. Smart. Sharp sense of humor and a crazy-talented artist to boot. I ran a play-by-play commentary of every observation and feeling. Examining and cross-examining impressions, looking for something more, convincing myself it was there, even though I knew damn well it wasn't. This wasn't a date. It was a distraction. Beyond a possible friendship, I didn't feel one damn thing for her.

It's not fair. Time to call it.

"Listen, Zelda," I said, but then my phone buzzed a text. I pulled it out of my jacket pocket. "Sorry, I thought I shut this off."

It was Kacey.

Terrible date. Awful. Are u free? Need to vent.

A bomb of happiness exploded in my chest. I'd have a few things to say to Viv's Magic 8 Ball tomorrow. *Who's got your outlook now, bitch?*

Zelda cleared her throat pointedly. "Good news?" she asked.

"No, it's…"

She sighed. "Spill it, T."

"Spill what?"

"Seriously?" She rolled her eyes. "I'm not stupid, you know. This isn't a date. Or if it is, it's the worst date in the history of dates."

I sat back in my chair. "I'm sorry."

"Don't be," she said, waving her hand. "I just ate a twenty-eight dollar ziti and this wine definitely didn't come from the rack at the grocery store. The food makes up for what I already knew was a sham."

"You did?"

She nodded. "Right before you visit She Who Shall Not Be Named, you get ridiculously happy. And when you come back, you're a goopy puddle of misery."

"It's that obvious?"

"Yeah." Zelda reached for a long, crackery breadstick from the cup between us and took a bite. "So what's Miss Kacey up to tonight?" She batted her eyelashes, still chewing.

"She went on a date and it wasn't good."

"Not good for her is good for you. I mean, you *do* like her."

"I do," I said. "And it's completely fucked because she's Jonah's girlfriend."

"*Was* Jonah's girlfriend," Zelda's sharp voice turned soft around my brother's name. "She is no longer Jonah's girlfriend. It's been almost a year since she's been *anyone's* girlfriend. The statute of limitations has run out on self-imposed celibacy. How old is she?"

"Twenty-four."

"She's a twenty-four year old woman. So let's say she lives to be…seventy-five. What, she's supposed to stay celibate for fifty years? Never love anyone again? Be alone forever?"

"No, but…" I drummed my fingers on the linen tablecloth. "If she's going to be with someone else, it probably shouldn't be me."

"Why not?" Zelda asked.

"Where do I start? I danced with her at a wedding and Jonah's best friend looked like he wanted to murder me. Worse, my mother takes a lot of comfort from her. Kacey dropped out of nowhere and made Jonah really fucking happy at the end of his life. It's a huge deal to Mom. And to our friends. And to me, too. She loved him right up to the end." I rubbed my hands over my eyes. "How do I take that away from my mother? Why would I even try?"

Zelda's expression became pinched. "Why would that take away something from your mom? Don't you think it would make her happy to know you're loved too?"

"We're not talking love anyway," I said, shaking my head. "My last visit to New Orleans, Kacey friend-zoned me hard. Or maybe I friend-zoned her. Whichever the case, she needs the space to figure her shit out."

"Yeah, you're giving her space all right," Zelda laughed. "She lives four states away. No one can say you're being too needy." She leaned forward on her arms, pointed the breadstick at me. "You know what I think your problem is?"

"Enlighten me."

"You want to be with her, but you've never had a serious relationship and you're afraid of fucking it up. Right so far?"

"Maybe."

"You want to give her space, let her recover on her own terms, without looking like you've been dry-humping her leg for the last year."

A laugh barked out of me. "Something like that."

Zelda narrowed her large green eyes at me. "Have you two ever…?" She sawed the bread stick in and out of the O of her thumb and index finger.

"Jesus, Zelda."

"Well?"

"No. We haven't even kissed. And I feel like a junior high school dork talking about this."

"You *should* talk about this. With her. If you want her, tell her. Fly to wherever she is tonight, and tell her."

"Tell her what? I don't have the words," I said. "Jonah did. He could say all the right things to make her feel special, or at least tell her how he felt. I don't know what the fuck I'm doing. I'm not good at romance and shit."

"Not calling it 'romance and shit' is probably a good place to start."

I shrugged. "Straight sex is easier for me."

"Fantastic." Zelda rolled her eyes. "I'm on a non-date with the last nice guy in Vegas, who's probably a beast in the sack and happens to be in love with someone else. Who's luckier than me?"

"I'm not in love with her."

Zelda rested her cheek in her hand, stirred her beleaguered breadstick in her water glass. "Liar."

"I don't know what I feel. I'm fucking frustrated. Is that what love is? Trying to do right by everyone while feeling like my guts are inside out? I can't think about, sleep with or even touch another woman."

Zelda's eyebrows shot up. "You haven't slept with anyone else? Since when?"

"Dude, I haven't so much as jerked off in year."

Zelda stared at me for a moment, then blinked and shook her head. "I feel like I should drink some water and have you tell me that again so I can do a spit-take."

"Yeah, well…"

"What about all those dates Edgar is always teasing you about? The blonde and her party? The redhead with the snake on her ankle?"

I shrugged. "Lies."

"I've heard you blow off Edgar a hundred times, saying you had a woman waiting. Where do you really go?"

"Church."

ALL IN

"Say that again," she said, taking a sip of water.

I smiled into my own water glass. "I go see Jonah's installation. It's still at the Wynn. I just sit there and think. I don't pray or anything, but it's like…sitting in a cathedral."

Zelda shifted in her chair. I looked up and her green eyes were heavy and soft. The sharp edge of sarcasm fell away, revealing a soft vulnerability underneath. "I see."

"It's stupid."

"It's *not* stupid. Jesus, why do you dismiss or belittle every single emotion that crosses your heart?"

I stared. "I don't…" I thought of Kacey in the cemetery in New Orleans, how I'd kept my mouth shut at maybe the worst time.

"We're just friends, right?" Kacey asked.

Zelda leaned on her hand, smiled. "Tell me."

"Fucking hell. Okay, here it is. Jonah knew I cared about Kacey. He saw it, somehow. And he told me, right before he died, he wanted me to take care of her and…"

"And?" Zelda asked softly.

"He wanted me to be with her."

I let out a long breath. A sigh over a year old. Across the table, Zelda's eyes were wide, but no judgment was in them. No shock, no disgust, no opinion. Only a thoughtful, considering gaze.

"I haven't told anyone about this," I said. "I mean, *no one.*"

She nodded slowly. "Least of all Kacey."

"I'll never tell her," I said. "It's impossible. First of all, she'd think I was making it up. Manipulating or guilt-tripping her into feeling something. Second, I don't *want* to. If she and I are going to happen, it has to be honest. It has to come from her heart. On its own. Otherwise, how would I know it was real?"

Zelda nodded. "Yeah, I get that." She tossed a lock of straight black hair over her shoulder. "So what are you going to do?"

"I have no fucking clue," I said, scrubbing my hands over my face. "I'm stuck. Suspended. Like the Hanged Man." I looked up. "It's a Tarot card…"

"I know what it is," Zelda said, putting her chin on her hand. "Why don't you just say fuck it, and move to New Orleans? Open a shop. Be closer to her. Let it play out."

"My mother needs me. I can't move away. And Kacey just bought a damn house. She's never moving back here. Vegas is too full of memories of Jonah. She wants a new life. It's better she finds someone with no connection to Vegas or to Jonah, and I'm both."

"What about you, then? You going to become a monk?"

I shrugged. "I'll get over it. Move on."

"There you go dismissing again."

"Forget I said anything," I said, my hands making fists under the table. "See, this is why I don't talk about shit. It just doesn't do any fucking good and it just…"

"Hurts," Zelda said. "It hurts, right? It's messy and complicated and it's like a tattoo that never ends. A million needles inking something on your heart that isn't even beautiful."

"Something like that." *Something exactly like that.*

"You can't let it all stay buried, T. I mean, I'm no expert at throwing it all out there, believe me. But you're a good guy. You deserve some happiness, too. What the hell happened to convince you you're worthy of *nothing?*"

I sucked in a deep breath to cool my blood, and took a sip of ice water. Zelda watched me for a moment, then scooted her chair around the table to sit beside me.

"You need to answer Kacey's text," she said. "Tell her you're on a date too. The worst date of your life."

I stared at her incredulously. "What for?"

"So she won't feel guilty. You both tried out other people, you both failed. Tell her that. Tell her I suck. Tell her I had spinach in my teeth and talked nonstop about my ex."

"I'm not telling her that." But suddenly I was laughing and irritated at the same time; like the way you get with a sibling. *Like how I'd get with Jonah.*

"Fine, then I'll tell her." She snatched the phone from my hand and started tapping.

I lunged. "Wait. Don't."

She contorted out of my reach, thumbs flying. "Aaaand, sent. There you go."

She turned the phone back to me, showing her text: **My date was the WORST. Call you later?**

I grabbed it back. "You little punk."

Already the dots of a reply were rolling under the message. Zelda put her chin on my shoulder and squeezed my arm. "This is so exciting."

"Get off me, I'm not speaking to you."

The rolling dots appeared, then disappeared, then started up again.

"Type, delete, type," Zelda said. "She's second-guessing her message."

"Jesus, I hate this."

"You love it."

With a cheerful bloop, Kacey's message bubbled up: **Is it wrong I'm glad about that?**

I looked back at Zelda, whose expression was triumphant. "Tell her the truth," she said.

No, I typed back, my heart thudding in my chest. **I'm glad too. Call me soon, OK? I miss you.**

Zelda signaled a passing waiter. "Check, please."

Zelda lived on the northeast side of town. Her apartment building was a shabby cement block, similar to mine, with lights and loud music spilling out of a corner window.

"That would be my roommates," Zelda said with a sigh. "Always a party at my place. Thanks for the dinner, T."

"Thanks for being cool about everything, Z. More than that. For being…well, shit, for being like a sister to me."

"Just what I always wanted." She smirked and reached for the door handle, then stopped, her smile softening. "I don't think I ever said it when Jonah passed but…I'm sorry for your loss."

"Thanks."

She sighed and climbed out the truck. "You know what you have to do, right?"

"Remind me."

"Either tell Kacey how you feel about her…" She shrugged. "Or just throw her on the nearest flat surface and fuck her senseless. God knows you both need it."

"Those are my two choices?"

"Yup." She sighed dramatically. "You know I'll miss you when you move to New Orleans."

"I'm not moving to New Orleans."

She grinned and shut the door. "Yeah, right."

CHAPTER 25

Kacey

I paced my living room, circling the coffee table and my cell phone lying there. Taunting me.

Are you seriously this pathetic?

I'd lied to Theo in my text. My date hadn't been terrible. Matthew Porter was sweet, considerate, and easy on the eyes. He didn't chew with his mouth open, he was polite to the waiter, our conversation flowed back and forth. He was a perfect gentleman at the end of the night, kissing me on the cheek and asking if he could see me again.

I said no because the only thing I could think of when Matthew leaned in to kiss me was that I wished it had been someone else.

The phone rang.

My someone else…

"Hey."

"Hey."

"So you had a date tonight?" I blurted. *Oh, very smooth.*

"Yeah, I did. It sucked."

A smile burst over my face. "That's too bad."

"And your date was shitty too?"

"Yes, he was." I frowned. "Well. No. He wasn't that bad actually, but…"

"What?"

He wasn't you.

"I don't know," I said. "I didn't feel a connection, I guess."

"Was he a good kisser?"

"I didn't kiss him," I said, wondering why a ball of warmth bloomed low in my belly at Theo's tone. It sounded like jealousy. "He tried, but I turned the other cheek."

"You did?"

"Yeah. What about you? Did you get any action?" I asked,

bracing myself for the answer.

"No kiss," he said. "No connection."

I eased a breath as quietly as I could. "Bummer. We both struck out."

"Kace?"

"Yes?"

"What are you doing this week?"

"Finishing reno on the house. Waiting for final edit of the video. You?"

"I was thinking I'd fly out to visit you."

I dropped onto the couch, my heart pounding ridiculously hard. "You are? I mean, you would? Why?"

"No reason," he said slowly. "Except I want to."

"You can take off work? And school?"

"I actually have one whole vacation day accrued. How about I get there Friday, leave Sunday?"

"I'll take it. Oh my God, I'm so happy. I mean, I miss you."

"I miss you too."

"We say that a lot, don't we?"

A silence fell, filled with unspoken words. I twirled my hair so tightly, the tip of my finger lost circulation.

"Kace?"

"Yeah?"

"I'll kiss you goodnight."

A warm-water heat swept through my entire body. His voice... God, his voice. Deep and gruff and sexy as hell. *I'll kiss you...*

I wanted him to say it again.

"Okay." I laid down, stretched out on the couch. "Tell me when."

"Shhh. I'm touching your cheek now."

I raised my hand to my cheek. "Feels nice."

"Close your eyes."

"I did," I whispered.

"Open your mouth, just a little..."

I sucked in a breath. With my eyes shut, the power of his words was amplified. Every nerve ending stretched out to listen. To translate sound into touch.

"I'm going to kiss you goodnight now."

"On the lips?"

A pause. "Yeah."

ALL IN

I gripped the phone tighter. "Okay."

"Goodnight, Kacey," he said softly.

I ran my tongue over my bottom lip, but in the dark—with Theo's deep voice like a purr in my ear—it was *his* mouth I felt and *his* lips that brushed mine softly.

A sigh eased out of me, leaving me heavy and content.

"Did you feel it?" he asked.

I nodded against the phone, snuggling into couch cushions. "I felt it. So nice. Made me sleepy."

"It did?"

"Mmhm. I feel warm all over. And safe. How did you do that from so far away?"

"I don't know," he whispered. "Get some sleep now."

"I will. Goodnight, Teddy."

I usually hung up then, but I hesitated. I heard his intake of breath, like he was about to say more.

"Teddy?"

"Nothing. Just... I'll see you soon."

CHAPTER 26

Theo

Friday afternoon, Kacey greeted me outside the Louis Armstrong Airport by flying at me and throwing her arms around my neck.

"You're here!" she cried.

"I'm here." I hugged her back as long as I dared. She smelled so good. Like fresh flowers, fresh paint, and the green heat of New Orleans. It permeated her skin now, the scent of the Nevada deserts long gone.

At her place, I noticed the green and magenta paint outside had been freshened up. Jonah's whiskey lights hung over a porch that looked sharp and sturdy, and Kacey fitted a key into a brand-new front door.

"Ready?" she said. "Prepare to be amazed."

"Holy shit," I said, stepping inside and setting my bag down on the new hardwood floors. "It hardly looks the same."

She snorted. "After fifteen grand, I hope not."

The hardwood planks were gray with shades of beige running through the grain. New travertine tile in the kitchen picked up the light browns. The cabinets were new, pale gray, the countertops beneath a shiny white quartz. Gone was the fridge, and the stove that had seen its heyday in the seventies. Stainless steel appliances gleamed in their place.

"It looks amazing," I said. "You did good."

She beamed, buffing a smudge on one of the refrigerator doors. "I had help. Yvonne worked her butt off and then I hired some guys for the floor. But the tile work in the bathroom? All me. Check it out."

I chuckled as she planted two hands on my back and pushed me toward the bathroom. The tile was dark gray, smattered with graphite and glittering under the light of a small chandelier. Its light sparkled off chrome fixtures and a claw-foot bathtub with a rainfall showerhead.

Kacey planted her hands on her hips, surveying her handiwork. "What do you think?"

"It looks amazing."

"You said that already," she said, her smile brilliant. She took me down the last little stretch of her shotgun house to the bedroom. "I didn't do much. Just the floors and some new furniture."

"Looks good," I said, my eyes on the glass ball Jonah had made for her. It was no longer in the center of her bed, but on a stand on the dresser. "Looks real good."

Back in the living room I sat on the couch.

"Tell me everything. How are things back home?" Kacey asked, curling up in her new high-backed chair.

"Did you just call Vegas home?" I asked as casually as humanly possible.

"Well, shit," she said, laughing. "I did."

"Graduation is coming up," I said. "My dad's being a dick about my tattoo shop idea, as usual. He's pushing me to use my degree for something else, for the business side of dealing art, or maybe curating. And he still hasn't given up on me using my art as a graphic designer. Shoot me now."

Kacey frowned. "No offense to Henry, but fuck that. You're crazy-talented at what you do. Born for it."

"Thanks."

"I can't wait to see you in your cap and gown, accepting your diploma."

"You're coming?"

Kacey cocked her head and fixed me with a look. "Theodore James Fletcher…"

I laughed and waved my hands. "Okay, okay. You're coming. But fair warning, it'll be boring as hell."

"Wouldn't miss it for anything."

A short silence fell but it was a good one. A silence where two people who hadn't seen each other in a long time basked in each other's presence, getting re-acclimated. Settling in. Zelda's advice to me to talk to Kacey rattled in my head.

How do I start? 'So I came all this way to fuck up our friendship forever…'

"That couch folds out," Kacey said.

I blinked at her, wondering if she'd just cut to the chase and I'd be taking Zelda's second piece of advice. "What?"

"So you can sleep here," she said.

"Oh. Right. No, I got a hotel room," I said.

"Cancel it. This is super comfy, I promise. Save your money."

"Okay," I said slowly. The back of my neck reddened. God, I wanted to take her to bed. Screw this small-talk and just *show* her how I felt.

Her phone chimed a text.

"Oh damn, it's Grant," she said. "The music video is done." She dumped her phone and picked up her laptop from the coffee table. "He just sent me the file. I think I'm going to throw up." She sat beside me on the couch and dumped the Mac onto my lap. "You click it. I can't."

"Chicken."

"The Drowned Chicken."

"Shh."

I leaned into her a little, pressing against her shoulder and hip as the opening riff of "The Lighthouse" began to play against a watery background. A hand emerged. A tattooed arm. The curve of a shoulder into a long, white throat. Long strands of brass-colored hair undulating across pale lips. Closed eyes that slowly opened with a flash of blue.

"Holy shit," I whispered.

Like a mermaid, Kacey moved underwater. Her blonde hair and billowing white dress became a screen, superimposed with scenes: a club, a street, an apartment. Discovering her man in bed with another woman.

Beside me, Kacey made little cringes and flinches, occasionally hiding her face against my arm. I hardly moved. I was rapt. Enthralled. I could feel cool air moving in and out of my open mouth. I breathed in her voice, her luminous, amber-lit face. The pain and loss in her eyes shimmered through the water and found me. The Drowned Girl.

The video ended and we both exhaled.

"What do you think?" she asked against my shoulder.

"I think…" I stared at the black screen. "I think you're so fucking beautiful."

She raised her head and I turned mine. To look at me as I realized I'd spoken my thoughts out loud. They'd fallen out of my slack-jawed mouth before I could catch them back.

"Oh," she said softly, her face inches away; I could feel the whisper of her breath on my lips. "Thank you, Teddy."

Our eyes met. She glanced at my mouth, then back at my eyes. Light-headed, I looked at her lips, wondering if it was time. Now. I could kiss her. Kiss her and see what happened.

Would her lips part for me, take my kiss deep inside her mouth and give it back?

Or would she recoil because I wasn't the brother she wanted?

My fucking hesitation cost me. Kacey pulled back and tucked her hair behind her ear self-consciously. "So, it's pretty good, isn't it?"

I handed her laptop back to her. "It's a great video. People are going to go crazy for it."

"I guess I'd better tell Grant I've watched it and feel it's suitable for public consumption."

You do that while I go dunk my head in the fucking sink.

Kacey made lunch for us—crabmeat po'boys with potato chips and soda. We ate and talked and later, we watched one of her damned 80's movies. She curled up close to me, but not close enough, laughing easily, smiling and talking, but I was tired of playing the part of the best friend. I wanted to ask her what those smiles meant, and if they were for me. But I couldn't ask, couldn't push it. It was such a fragile energy, simmering in the heat between us. Too much pressure and it would dissolve away.

But goddammit, I want this life, I thought. *This is what I want.*

To live in her space, my razor sharing the same shelf as her toothbrush. Our clothes tangling in the bedroom. Making breakfast together, then letting the food burn as I took her on the kitchen floor…

Tell me what you want, I thought, glancing at her from the corner of my eye. *Because I want everything.*

CHAPTER 27

Kacey

The next day, I took Theo to Magazine Street, where we wandered in and out of antique stores, pastry shops and vintage clothing stores. We hit a few art galleries, where Theo pointed out works by artists I'd never heard of—Katherine Bradford and Ted Gahl. The depth of his knowledge surprised me, stirred up fresh anger at Henry for not appreciating his son's talents. A fierce conviction swept through me. More than ever, I wanted to see Theo achieve his dream of owning his own place. I vowed to help him, support him however I could.

He doesn't need money, I thought. *He'd sooner chop off his hand than take any. Maybe a grand opening party? I could play...*

It sounded arrogant, but I had to admit, the video for "The Lighthouse" didn't suck and my songs were selling like mad on the digital sites. Maybe I'd have something of a name by the time he was ready to open his own place. A name with pull.

"What are you smiling about?" he asked.

"I was thinking about your future shop." I nudged his elbow. "When did you know you wanted to become a tattoo artist, anyway?"

He shrugged. "I don't know. Long time."

"Come on, Teddy."

Theo frowned. "I usually don't talk about this stuff."

"I want to know. For real." We came to an old-fashioned bench in front of an antique store with a gramophone and Victorian-era dresses in the window. "Here, sit," I said. "Tell me."

He sat, glanced once at me sideways. "I got my first tattoo when I was sixteen. This one."

He turned the inside of his wrist to me. A black and red scorpion perched on its tail. *Helen* was inked below it in beautiful script, cleverly at an angle, so the name looked like the scorpion's shadow.

"Helen the Scorpion?"

Theo gave me a strange smile. "I'll get to that," he said. "I thought a scorpion was badass at the time. I knew my dad would shit his pants—it's illegal to get inked in Nevada when you're under eighteen. But I knew a guy who knew a guy."

I laughed. "I knew a guy who knew a guy too," I said, showing him the stars on my middle finger.

"They're out there, they work cheap, and they piss parents off. Anyway, it took four hours, and while I was there, another artist was working on a client. Middle–aged woman. She'd just lost her daughter in a car accident. She was getting a tattoo of an angel with the girl's face and her birthdate."

"Oh God, that's so sad."

"I couldn't see it from where I sat but I heard the whole story. Sat and listened as the woman told her artist everything. I was a sixteen-year-old punk kid. I couldn't get why some woman would pour out her most personal tragedy to a total stranger. But she talked about her daughter the entire time, sometimes crying, sometimes laughing. She even talked about the moment she learned her kid was gone. And the whole time I'm thinking, *That poor guy inking her. He's gotta be wishing he were anywhere else.*"

I nodded, but said nothing. Theo's eyes were fixed on the street but in the past too. I didn't want him to stop talking.

"The lady's tattoo was done before mine. She checked it out in the mirror, crying. Her artist looked like Chester from the band Linkin Park, but he was hugging her, and she patted his cheek like he was her son. She told him he gave her the greatest gift: her daughter as she wants to remember her, any time she wants. She just has to look down on her arm, and there she is."

He stared straight ahead, beyond the passersby and the streets and the sky. I thought he'd come to the end of the story, but then he leaned over, rested his forearms on his knees. His fingertips traced the lines of the scorpion on his arm.

"Her name was Helen. And I never forgot her. When it was time to start college, everyone was on my ass to become a graphic artist. Computers, tech, websites—*that's where the money is, T.* If I had a dollar for every time my dad tried to steer me toward graphic design…" He shook his head. "I wanted to *draw*, not work on computers. I wanted the response between the art and the audience to be immediate. As visceral as it could be. Up close and personal.

Except I'm not an up-close-and-personal guy. I'm not a big talker…" His eyes flicked toward me. "Except with you."

I smiled. "Go on. Please."

"I thought of that woman telling her tattoo artist about her daughter. How the artist listened like a priest or a bartender. All the while he's using his talents to give her a piece of art everyone can see on her body, yet it's for her alone at the same time. Art on display, but utterly personal. It became what I wanted to do. It is what I do. A client comes in and I listen. Not just to what kind of tattoo they want. I listen to their stories. I listen and do my best to render what they've envisioned." He turned over his wrist, traced the name under the scorpion once more, then sat back on the bench and tucked his hands in his pockets. "So there you go."

I rested my cheek on Theo's shoulder. "Have you ever had a Helen?"

"Some. I've had a couple of Iraq War vets. They come in for tattoos of important dates, like deployments. Or they want their company insignia, to honor the guys they served with. Friends who've fallen. They tell me their stories. Or I'll get a young woman and she'll be kind of nervous about getting a tattoo on her stomach or hip because she thinks she's fat or whatever. At first, they joke around and say they'll need to lose weight if they're going to show it off. But after it's done, they're proud of the tattoo. They want to show it off, just as they are. Those are good ones."

Theo was quiet for a minute then looked over at me, caught my rapt expression and shifted on the bench. "Okay, story time's over. I'm ready for that drink now."

We strolled along the street in search of a café. My eyes kept stealing glances at this man beside me. Realizing Theo wasn't only there for Jonah during the worst moments of his life. He was there for a lot of other people too. Taking their pain, listening to it, deconstructing it. Turning it around and giving it back to them as a piece of art. Uniquely their own, just as pain is unique to the person who bears it.

"Have you ever told Helen's story to your dad?" I asked.

Theo shook his head. "Why bother? He's made up his mind."

I linked my arm in his. "I can't wait to get my tattoo from you. Now, more than ever."

"You know what you want?"

"Nope," I said, smiling up at him. "Don't know yet which story of mine I want you to tell."

Theo's brow furrowed and a funny smile came over his lips. His expression was amused, but I'd come to see that Theo's feelings were all in his eyes. And right now he was touched.

We stopped at a small café where Theo had a beer and I had a strawberry lemonade.

"You don't mind I have this?" he said, raising his bottle.

"If I were to ask people not to drink around me, I'd stop being invited to parties."

Theo snorted a laugh. "I need some fries or something. You want anything else?"

"I want that dress," I said, pointing at the window of a vintage clothing store across the street. In its window was a housedress. Something out of the 1940's, with hundreds of tiny green apples on it and red buttons down the front.

"Perfect for tonight," I said, grinning at Teddy. "We're gonna do it up in real New Orleans style."

We started getting ready around seven. I put on the retro housedress and instead of heels, I went for black, high-heeled Mary Janes. They complimented the black of my tattoos while bright red matte lipstick and black cat-eye liner completed the look.

I emerged from the bedroom to find Theo wearing his simple black-shirt and jeans, his tattoos snaking down his arms. *He needs a watch,* I thought. A watch would draw attention to his muscle definition, and contrast the ink.

We drove out to Louie's Louisiana Kitchen, a Cajun restaurant near the river that also hosted nightly musical acts. It was an older, more classic New Orleans joint, with no air conditioning, no fancy décor, and no world-class chef. Just real, authentic Cajun food and jazz music by local artists.

I remembered the night I first met Dena and Oscar, we'd eaten at the Cajun restaurant in the MGM Grand. Theo had a thing for ultra-spicy food.

"If you want spicy, this place is it," I shouted to him in the crowded line waiting to see the hostess. "Hottest jambalaya in New Orleans."

He narrowed his eyes at the challenge. "We'll see about that."

The place was packed. Apparently, the band playing tonight was hugely popular—a bluesy quartet with a young, sultry female singer. I'd made reservations, but even the front entry was crammed like a dance club and stifling hot, the last vestiges of summer. Sweat beaded on my brow, threatening my makeup. Theo stood just ahead of me as we waited, while a cocktail waitress came around handing out free short glasses of beer to help ease the wait.

The guy behind me—a skinny, pale man in his early twenties with red-rimmed eyes and a rumpled shirt, took two glasses and downed them quick. Judging by his look—and the smell of hard liquor that wafted off of him—those beers weren't his first of the night.

"Hey," he said, nudging me. "You a sweet little thing, ain't you?"

I rolled my eyes and turned away, to face Theo's broad back. Sweat glistened on the back of his neck, turning the hair there into little barbs.

"Hey." The guy nudged me again. He leaned in close enough that the stringent smell of booze on his breath was actually a mist on my cheek. "I'll bet you taste sweet. Like candy." He chuckled. "Can I have a lick?"

Unfortunately for him, a lull in the music came at that exact instant. Theo spun around, his eyes boring into the drunk guy with a dangerous intensity.

"What the fuck did you just say to her?"

The drunk guy held up his hands. "Sorry, man. Didn't realize she was yours."

"Don't apologize to me," Theo said. He wasn't a super tall guy, but he had at least fifty pounds more muscle on him. He jerked his thumb at me. "Apologize to her."

The guy thought about it for a moment, then snorted a wet laugh and staggered a little, jostling me again.

A muscle in Theo's jaw twitched. "You're standing too close to her." He laid his hand calmly on the guy's chest. "Fuck." He gave a small shove. "Off."

The guy staggered a step or two back, and held up his hands again, his laughter gone. "All right, man. Be cool."

Theo's eyes remained locked on his in warning for another second, then he put his arm around me and pulled me in front of him, keeping me in the protective circle for the rest of our slow migration to the hostess stand.

"Reservation?" the hostess asked, and it took me a second to realize she was talking to me.

"Two," I said. "Dawson." My heart was still thumping loudly in my chest and the heat flushing my cheeks had nothing to do with the lack of air conditioning.

The way Theo had handled that guy…

I wasn't a fan of violence, but some strange, primal urge in me almost hoped the guy had pushed Theo back, just so I could watch Theo defend me again. Protect me because I was his to protect.

Oh my God, get a grip. You're setting the feminist movement back fifty years.

The hostess sat us at a tiny table. I fanned myself with the menu while Theo studied his intently, totally oblivious to my reaction. It took an eternity for the waiter to show up, then another eternity to bring the food. When it finally arrived—chicken fricassee for me, and shrimp jambalaya for Theo—my dinner date took one taste, wrinkled his nose, and started pouring on more hot sauce.

"Are you crazy?" I said, laughing. "My mouth hurts just looking at that."

"It was warmish," Theo said with a grin. "Now it's satisfactory. Barely."

I shook my head, my chin in my hand. "You must've been a fire-eater in a past life."

He laughed and we dug into the hot Louisiana night, and the hotter dinner. The pre-show music hung in the heavy, humid air like pungent smoke. I imagined spirits dancing in the shadows in this city of vampires and voodoo.

We talked easily, and he laughed readily, drinking beer to my lemonade. Still, something in me felt tipsy. High and exhilarated, my thoughts running unchecked down a road I'd never taken before.

Jonah once told me I went up to eleven. Theo went up to one hundred, I mused. Nothing ever halfway. He was the kind of man who, if you wronged him or hurt someone he loved, he'd cut you off without another word. But if he was yours, he was yours for life.

If he was mine…

The thought startled me so badly, I nearly knocked over my lemonade glass.

Theo glanced up from his food. "You okay?"

I nodded, noticing his eyes were watering. I jerked my chin at his plate. "Why do you eat that if it's so hot?"

"I like it."

"It looks painful."

He gave a lopsided grin. "Hurts so good."

"God, you're such a man."

"Last I checked."

I laughed and the other half of his smile widened before he went back to his food. I started into my dish, but my eyes kept straying to Theo. He took a too-big bite of his jambalaya, sweat beading his brow because he'd made it inferno-level hot. On purpose. He washed down the shrimp with a chug of beer, blowing out his cheeks, then hunched over his plate, intent, both inked forearms on the table, gearing up for another huge mouthful.

I wondered if I'd taste the heat on his tongue if he kissed me.

My knee jumped, sending my napkin to the floor. I bent to get it, not coming back up until my face was composed. God, the atmosphere in this place was making me stupid.

Theo took another steaming forkful of spicy food. Another bead of sweat slid down his temple as he licked his lips.

Oh yes, without a doubt, if I kissed him he'd burn me.

"I got something in my teeth?"

I blinked at him. "No, nothing. Just thinking."

"About what?" Theo asked. His eyes stayed on me as his lips wrapped around the beer bottle and took a swig. I watched the swallow go down his throat. All my sordid thoughts visible on my face, or spelled out in neon, flashing above me. A blush inflamed my cheeks as I fought for an answer.

"This place has a lot of atmosphere," I finally said.

God, are you serious?

Theo nodded and another dark look came over him, similar to the one he'd worn confronting the drunk guy in line. Only now it was turned on me. His whiskey-colored eyes igniting another primal urge. Theo, shirtless and sweaty, putting a flat hand on my chest and curling his fingers into the fabric of my dress. Instead of pushing me away, he hauled me roughly to him, intent on taking what was his…

Oh my God.

My eyes were trapped by his stare. My body trapped in the chair by a sweet ache of longing burning between my legs. I didn't blink. He didn't look away.

With loud drum riff and a glissando down the piano keys, the live music began, finally tearing my eyes free. The band was fronted by a young woman with long brown hair wearing a fedora hat, black leather jeans, and a white shirt with a black vest. Three African-American men made up her band of guitar, piano, and bass. They opened with a slow song that permeated the air like fragrant smoke.

I concentrated on the music, pretending to listen and resolutely not looking at Theo. But the damn music was bluesy, sexy… A slow burn of want and longing. It dialed into my already aching body, filling me with a need to be touched.

A shadow fell over me, and I looked up to see Theo standing, his hand outstretched.

"Dance with me."

It wasn't a request, and my traitorous body was already rising to its feet before I could think.

Theo took my hand in his and led me to the small dance floor, where a dozen other couples were swaying to the music. Some, driven by the sultry tones of the song and the singer's smoky voice, were grinding their hips together, thighs intertwined.

Theo slung my arms around his neck, then put his hands on my hips, and began to move.

I'd never stood this close to Theo before. Our bodies pressed tight. Our faces so close, I could smell the sweet heat of his food, the bitterness of beer, the salt of his sweat. His heart beat thick against mine. The ragged exhale of his breath.

"You told me at the wedding you didn't dance," I said, every part of my body conscious of touching every part of his.

His mouth shaped the words, "I lied," but no sound reached me over the music.

I could barely breathe. I was losing myself in him. Our eyes locked. I couldn't look anywhere but at him. The light brown of his eyes fiery, like a shot of whiskey backlit by a white-hot flame. His hips ground a slow circle against mine, his thigh inching between my legs. One arm slid around my waist, the other came up the middle of my back, holding me close. My arms wound around his neck, my fingers burrowed into his damp hair.

"I like this," he murmured. His whole body was flush against mine. I could feel its power, the strength of his muscles holding and moving me with the music. The hollow of his neck glistened. I felt my own sweat slide over my collarbone and between my breasts. My blood was on fire in a way that was entirely separate from the Louisiana summer. A heat Theo was building in me with every roll of his pelvis against mine. I felt the stiffness of his jeans against my skin as his hand slipped down to my ass, pressing me tighter against him. Grinding in a dance that felt more like…

Foreplay.

My breath caught as Theo's forehead came to touch mine, our gazes locked. Deep within, a greedy instinct and a growing need I hadn't felt in a long time. I hooked one leg around his waist.

"Touch me," I breathed.

He made a noise deep in his chest and his hand slid under my dress, up my thigh to my hip, pulling me into him. I bit back a cry as he dipped me back. I let my head fall, arching. He bent with me, his mouth on my throat, his tongue sliding against my skin. Feverish. Burning from the inside out. His touch was scorching, sending trails of fire across my skin in every direction. My nipples hardened. Heat pooled between my thighs where Theo ground against me mercilessly. Slowly his lips dragged up my neck, then my chin, both of us pulling upright until we were face to face again.

The look in Theo's eyes—the almost feral hunger—stole my breath.

"Kace," he whispered.

I expected his kiss. It was right there between us, waiting hungrily. I didn't expect his hands, so rough and hard before, to hold my face gently. I didn't anticipate the furrow of his brows, almost as if he were in pain.

I tilted my chin, wanting this, needing this so badly.

Please.

He laid his lips to mine, kissing me softly, slowly. The world turned around us, blurring and disappearing. I had to hold onto his wrists to keep from slipping away with it, gasping at the sensation that came roaring to life inside me. A match lit in a dark room, flaring with brilliant light. My lips parted with that gasp, and Theo, with a growl of pure want, kissed me again, this time hard and deep.

I wrapped my arms around his neck, clinging to him, opened my mouth to take all of his kiss. The taste of his tongue, the heat of his mouth. We started dancing again, our bodies acting of their own volition, our mouths opening and closing, heads tilting back and forth. Our tongues slid and tangled when the kiss went deep. Teeth and lips bit and sucked when it turned shallow.

On and on, we danced and in the back of my delirium, I knew I'd been right about Theo: if you had him, you had all of him. His kiss was the purest essence of himself: intense, fiery, devoted entirely to the moment. This close, he was my entire world, with no place for anything else. His body pressed to mine, his hands on my body, his sweat, his mouth…

He was so much. My instinct balked, used to thinking it was too much. But no, he was giving me everything and I was taking it. I could take it. And I wanted more.

"Oh, God," I breathed into his mouth. He replied with a groan and I took it in, inhaled him as he kissed me again.

We kissed until the song ended and the applause of the crowd broke the spell. Slowly, the circle we'd been turning in ceased. My feet felt the floor again, our bodies detached. The real world rematerialized. We remained on the dance floor a moment longer, our eyes searching each other for…I didn't know what. Both of us blinking and dazed, as if coming out of a trance.

We walked back to our table—me on shaking legs—and I drank deep from my water glass, trying to quench the swirl of boiling emotions in my body.

"You want to get out of here?" Theo asked, his voice hoarse with desire. I could see it burning in his eyes.

I nodded, my body screaming for his, while the realization of what just happened was seeping into the cracks of my broken heart, and I didn't know if it was harming or healing them.

Outside, the air was cooler, a bracing slug to my slushy mind. I sensed Theo coming down off the high, too. The lust waning, thinking twice and starting to ask questions. The cab ride was too long. I kept my gaze locked on my window, where I could just make out Theo's reflection beside me, his features sharpened into hard angles of frustration.

When the cab finally pulled up in front of my house, Theo tossed some money into the front seat and we climbed out. My hands were shaking as I fumbled the key in the lock, and once in my living room, I froze.

I wanted him to leave. I wanted him to stay.

I wanted to curl up alone on my bed and cry. I wanted to drag him into my bedroom, have him tear my clothes off, take me hard and deep until we both found relief.

I wanted to cry for betraying what I'd had with Jonah. I wanted to cry because kissing Theo felt like nothing I'd known since.

Happiness burned within the fire, a glowing treasure I couldn't reach without getting burned.

My eyes filled with the deluge of swirling emotions. I couldn't hold them back. My shoulders hunched and I hugged myself.

"Oh, God, Kacey," Theo said, moving around to face me. He cupped my cheeks in his hands. "Don't cry, baby. Please…"

I shook my head, fighting for control. "No, it's okay," I heard myself say, trying to explain the unexplainable. "It's just… It's the first kiss since…"

Theo took a step back, his hands falling to his sides. "Fuck. Kace, I'm sorry."

"Don't… I don't know what I'm trying to say. Or what I feel. It's nothing to be sorry for. It's not your fault."

"It's not yours either," he said. "We just…got caught up in the moment."

I looked sharply up at him. "Did we?"

Theo stared at me a moment, his whiskey-colored eyes soft and warm. "Yeah," he said, carving his fingers through his hair. "We got caught up in the moment. The place, the song, the mood. It was like a drug."

I felt a tug in my chest, then a sharp pain. Straight through my heart. "Yeah, I guess so," I said.

"I'm going back to Vegas," Theo said. "Tonight. I think it's best."

No, I thought, even as I nodded my head. "Okay. I think, maybe…you should. I need to think. God, I don't know what I need." I looked at him, so stoic and kind, willing to do anything for me, to do the right thing. "I'm so sorry."

"Don't be sorry," he said, moving to hold me, pressing me to his broad chest. "Do not ever be sorry. Not with me."

As suddenly as his arms closed around me, they then released. He tossed his things in his bag, and in minutes, he was at the door, leaving.

"I'll call you when I land."

"Okay." I said. "Teddy?"

He stopped at the door. "Yeah?"

"Thank you."

A ghost of a smile touched his mouth. Then he was gone.

CHAPTER 28

Kacey

I threw open the kitchen window.

"*Yvonne.*"

From inside her house came a muffled reply. "It's late, baby."

"I kissed Teddy."

"I'll be right over."

Five minutes later, Yvonne busted in the front door, a half-liter of seltzer water tucked under one arm, a bottle of cranberry juice under the other.

"This occasion calls for wine, but seeing as you're on the wagon, this is the best I can do, short notice."

I sank onto my couch, my fingers trailing over my lips, as Yvonne busied herself in my kitchen, scooping ice and pouring drinks. She came back and pressed a cranberry and seltzer into my hand. She dropped into the easy chair, facing me. "Tell me everything."

"Teddy kissed me and I kissed him back. A lot. And it was…magnificent."

"Magnificent? Honey, that's a good thing."

"So good I started crying. So of course he thought he did something wrong and backed off. I couldn't tell him the truth. That I cried because it felt so good. It felt *right*. But then ten seconds later I'm wracked with guilt. I always felt like I had my first kiss with Jonah. Now I'm kissing Teddy and it's the first… The first after the first."

Yvonne let me have a moment before asking, "What did he say about it?"

I took a sip of my drink without tasting it. "That we were caught up in the moment. But I think he was giving me an out. I'm sure I looked stricken with guilt."

"Where is he now?"

"Flying back to Vegas." I read the disapproving downturn of her lips. "No, it's good. He's such a good man, Yvonne. He knew it was too much. If he stayed, we would've slept together, and I am not of sound mind. He knew it, so he left. And as if my feelings aren't fucked up enough, now I wish he hadn't." I looked up at her tearfully. "He's my best friend. I can't lose him."

"You don't have to lose him, honey," Yvonne said. "Maybe what you two have is changing into something else."

"Oh, God, I don't know what I'm doing." I leaned over my knees and held my head in my hands. "Tell me what to do, Yvonne. I'm begging you."

"Sleep on it, baby," Yvonne said. "That's all I got. Sleep, and see how it all looks in the morning. And Kacey?"

I looked up through my hair. "Yeah?"

"The feeling you have in that moment right as you wake up, before your brain mucks it all up with thoughts and words? That very first feeling is where the truth lives."

I sat for a long time after she left, mustering the courage to go to my bedroom. The universe orb on my dresser glowed in the yellow lamplight. I didn't touch it. It didn't feel right to touch it with Theo all over me. I rested my chin on the dresser, and watched the light play over the stars, shine across the red and green surface of the planet.

"I danced with Teddy," I said, my voice shaking. "No, that's not right. We danced like we were fucking and then we kissed. I kissed him and it was…" I swallowed hard. "It was good. It felt so good. But even before that…we went out. We had a good time together. We ate good food and laughed and talked…We lived."

Tears blurred the orb into a dark ball, the stars inside glowing but silent.

"This isn't supposed to happen, is it?" I whispered. "Teddy and me? The idea of being with anyone but you is awful to me, and yet with him… It feels good. It feels…real."

I wanted Theo with me. I hadn't realized until he kissed me how much I missed intimate contact. The nearness of a man, his breath warm on my skin, the presence of him in my space, touching me. I wanted it right now. Wanted him holding me, kissing me again. Kissing me all night. Loving me hard. Heated and sweaty and rough and raw.

"I don't know what I'm doing," I muttered, turning to my bed. I buried my face in the pillow, willing my body to cool down. After being so cold for so long—a bone-chilling loneliness, drowning in icy tears, numb to anyone's touch... Now I couldn't take the heat of a man who wasn't Jonah.

I tossed and turned for hours. Rationalizing. Justifying. I tried to write off the whole incident to plain old-fashioned lust. I got caught up in the moment, just like Theo said. And who wouldn't? Theo was gorgeous. Packed in muscle, tattooed, and sexy as hell. If he moved in bed like he did on the dance floor...

Oh, God, stop.

When I finally started to slip under, it wasn't to feelings of pure lust, or the feel of Theo's body against mine, or even the delicious heat of his kiss. It was his smile. I don't think I'd ever seen Theo smile's so broad and unguarded. Dancing with me, he'd shed the burden of grief and responsibilities. For a few short hours, I'd made him happy.

And when I woke up the next morning, the first feeling in my heart was the desire to make him happy again.

CHAPTER 29

Theo

Sunday dinner with my parents was the last fucking thing I wanted to do, but I couldn't say no. We sat on the patio, and Mom tried to keep up the chatter over plates of roasted chicken and asparagus. Dad shoveled his food in with hardly a word. I kept sneaking glances at my phone and the one text from Kacey: **Wanted to make sure you got in okay.**

I'd replied, **I did, thanks**. But nothing after.

I fucked it all up, I thought for the millionth time.

I was drunk last night. Drunk on the food, the beer and the jazz. Drunk on New Orleans and drunk on Kacey. I'd lost control. The drunk asshole hitting on her awoke something in me: a desire to fight for her, kill anything that threatened her. Followed by the more potent urge to have her afterward. To mark her as mine with my mouth and hands. Strip her bare and fuck her hard until the only thought in her head was me. The only name screaming in her mouth was mine.

She looked at me like I was already naked, her eyes raking me up and down, her lips parted and her tongue running along their seam. *This is it,* I'd thought. The end of my long and agonizing wait.

But no. She wasn't ready. She might never be ready. Worse, we couldn't rewind and put everything back the way it was before. Kissing changed everything.

"So," Mom said, breaking me out my thoughts, "What's the good news this week?" She reached over and patted my hand. "Other than graduation."

I glanced at my dad who kept his head down, intent on his food.

"I do have news, actually. I started a new tattoo series called *Unfinished Ink*."

"Is that so?" My mom smiled and spooned herself more mashed potatoes.

"My co-worker showed the series to *Inked* magazine and they're going to do a feature on me."

"Oh, that's wonderful." Mom leaned toward Dad. "Isn't that wonderful, Henry?"

My dad sipped his cocktail and raised his chin, as if pondering this, lips pursed, inhaling deeply through his nose.

"It could be really good," I said, hating how fucking pathetic this whole scene was, to beg like a dog for a scrap. And yet I couldn't stop myself. "The publicity would give me a boost when I get my own place."

My father's lips drew down farther, which meant he was formulating his thoughts. I hated those few seconds, as my stupid heart always swelled with hope in anticipation that *this* time he would say, "Well done, son. I'm proud of you."

It wasn't this time.

"The market in Vegas is terrible for new business," he said. "For any business. Nick Sullivan over at the commercial real estate office says growth has been slowing. Not to mention Las Vegas already has about a hundred tattoo shops."

"Bit of an exaggeration, don't you think, dear?" Mom asked, her eyes darting between us.

"I can't drive ten feet without passing one," Dad said. "They're as common as the nudie joints."

I bounced my fork onto the table. "I get it. It's a shitty market. You've been saying it for a year—"

"Because it's true. If you've learned anything in your courses, it must be how small businesses fail eighty percent of the time. Never mind those trying to crowd into an already saturated market."

My mother's hand rested on mine. "Henry, I'm sure Theo is aware of the risks. But this is his dream."

"You have a business degree now," Dad said. "It's a wonderful achievement. I'd just like to see you put it toward something worthwhile." He dabbed his mouth with his napkin.

"I intend to," I said through gritted teeth. "I'm going to buy my own place. Goddammit, Dad, it's worthwhile to *me*. Why the fuck don't you get it's what I want to do?"

"Language, please," Dad said with a sigh, as if he'd heard this a thousand times a day.

Mom's fingers squeezed my wrist. "Theo, dear, calm down."

"Yeah, I get the market's crowded," I said. "But Vegas isn't the only city in the country. Maybe I'll buy a place somewhere else."

My mom gasped. "You're going to leave Las Vegas?"

"No. I don't know. It's just an idea." I scrubbed my hands over my face. "Mom, wait."

But she was already pushing her chair back. "Excuse me." She hurried into the house, her hand over her mouth.

My father tossed his napkin down with disgust. "See? Now you've upset your mother."

He got up from the table too, but instead of going after Mom to comfort her, I heard the door to his study slam shut.

"Fuck me," I said to the sky. My eyes found Jonah's glass lights, glowing above the now-empty patio with a table full of half-eaten dinner. The scene of a hasty getaway.

I stared at the lights until they blurred into fuzzy white orbs.

"Now what the fuck do I do, Jonah? She's there. I'm here…"

Of course, I knew what he'd answer.

Love her.

I closed my aching eyes, and rubbed my aching chest.

"I do, Jonah," I whispered, my words swallowed by the night. "I already do."

CHAPTER 30

Kacey

"Are you sitting down?" Grant said, his voice on the speakerphone breathy and high-pitched.

Phoebe shouted from the background, "Sit the hell down. Or you'll fall down, break your throat, and then *Sony motherfucking Music* won't want to sign you!"

"That's how you tell her?" Grant said. "Seriously, Phoebe?"

I sank onto my couch. "I'm sitting," I said. I swallowed over my heart pounding in my throat. "Are you for real? Sony Music?"

"Their office just called," Grant said. "They want a meeting. It's the video, Kacey—closing in on one million views. And sales are still going strong. We've been fielding calls from mid-line labels all week, including the one who has Rapid Confession. But I held out. I knew it was only a matter of time until we reeled in a big one."

"The biggest fucker in the sea," Phoebe yelled. "The Moby Goddamn Dick of labels."

"Oh my god," I said, blowing air out my cheeks. "And they want a meeting? When? *Where?*"

"A week from Monday. Here. Downtown. Dude, they're sending people to *us*. I already said yes. If you have plans, break them."

I laughed, overwhelmed. "No plans next Monday."

"Good," Grant said. "Now get dressed."

"It's six o'clock at night," Phoebe said. "You think she's walking around naked?"

"I meant, get dressed *up* to go *out,* stupid," Grant retorted. "To celebrate."

"I can't go out tonight," I said.

"Why?"

I have to call Teddy. News this big wouldn't feel real until I told him.

"You guys go out and celebrate for me, okay? And hey, listen?"

"Yes, my queen?"

"None of this would be happening if it weren't for you. I'm not going to forget it."

"Thanks, Kacey," Grant said. "This is so—"

"Do you know what this means?" Phoebe shrieked. "Oh my God, we are going to be fucking rich."

"You did *not* just say that. We are about making *art*, not money."

"That's the stupidest thing I've ever heard in my life…"

I busted out laughing and hung up on them, then laughed again as I wondered how long it would take them to notice.

On Wednesdays, Theo had class until ten o'clock his time, midnight mine. Six flipping hours to kill. I could call the Olsens back and go out anyway. No, I'd be too distracted. I'd been distracted for three days, turning over and over again what happened with Theo. Our dance. Our kiss. Three days of radio silence, no calls, no texts, and my feelings were nowhere near sorted out.

Except I miss him. And I want to make him laugh again. And make him happy.

I heated up some leftover ravioli Yvonne made for me, and ate it on the couch while watching *Dirty Dancing*. Which was an idiotic choice. Just watching the dancers grind together in the opening montage brought Theo's and my dance roaring back.

At midnight, I turned off all the lights, climbed into bed, and called him.

"Hey, Kacey," he said.

I leaned back against the pillows with a sigh. I loved his deep voice, and how it settled into my head, sank down to my chest, made me feel warm all over.

"Hi. I wanted to talk about your graduation on Saturday."

A pause. "Are you still coming?"

"Of course I am. But I can only stay until Sunday. Because…"

"Because?"

"Take a guess."

"Tell me or I'll kill you."

"I have meeting with the execs from Sony Music on Monday."

"Are you *kidding* me?"

"They want to sign me. Can you believe that?"

"Hell yeah," he said, his voice growing louder. "Damn, Kace, this is incredible."

"Turns out Grant was right. The video was kind of big."

"Kind of? Last I checked, it kind of had close to a million views."

"You've been checking?"

"Well." A beat of silence. "About a hundred of those views might be mine."

My skin flushed pink as I envisioned him watching the video over and over.

I think you're so fucking beautiful…

"Teddy, after the graduation ceremony…I think we should talk."

"Okay," he said slowly.

"I've wanted to these last couple of days," I said. "Almost started to, but I know you had a lot of work to finish up. And I think it's better if we talk in person."

"Whatever you want, Kace."

"Do you want to talk about what happened?"

"No. I want to kiss you again."

A current of heat swept through me and I curled up in my pillows like a burnt leaf. "Teddy."

"I'm sorry, I shouldn't say that. But I already fucked up our friendship, so I might as well put it out there."

"You didn't fuck anything up, stop. I don't know what's happening, either. One minute I'm torn apart by guilt. Next minute I'm angry about being guilty. And in between all that, I want you to kiss me again too."

"God, Kacey," he said. *"What* is happening?"

"It's commiseration, right? No one gets it but us. No one understands what we went through. We're drawn to each other for comfort. Right?"

"I guess so," he said.

"Well, isn't it? Because you and me…together… is crazy." I exhaled. "Right?"

"Is it?"

I swallowed, a heavy swamp of emotion welling in my chest at those words; a deep warmth that spread out from my heart and a million times more potent than any lust I felt for him. My heart began to pound, for fear or anticipation or…

"We need to talk then," I said, firming my voice. "In person. At your graduation. And no kissing."

"My parents are giving a dinner at their house after the ceremony. We can talk afterward."

"Okay, I'll see you Saturday morning."

"See you then. 'Night, Kace."

"Goodnight, Teddy."

I ended the call, and lay flat on my back, a sigh gusting out of me. My eyes found the universe orb again. It absorbed the wan light of my bedside lamp, turned the yellow to brilliant blue-white. Stars winking like diamonds in the depths of space. Or dark eyes lit with a smile.

CHAPTER 31

Theo

Graduation morning was bleak, the sky stretching flat and grey over Vegas. No storms were predicted, but the air felt tight and tense, full of lightning about to strike. My stomach, on the other hand, was a tornado warning. The day stretched out like an ordeal. First the ceremony to get through. Then dinner and small talk at my parents' place. And *then*…

I scowled at the mirror, tying my tie for the third time. It was amber-colored, to go with my dark gray suit with a vest. I fucking hated suits. What the hell was the point wearing one today, when I'd have the cap and gown over it anyway?

The coil of nerves in my stomach ratcheted up to a full-blown roll when I heard a knock at the front door.

"Don't look beautiful," I mumbled. "Don't look beautiful, don't look…"

I opened the door.

Beautiful.

She wore a silky maroon dress. High neck, puffy sleeves, draping over her lithe body and stopping mid-thigh to reveal the bottom of the sugar skull tattoo. Black platform sandals with high heels and a t-strap made her legs go up to forever. Her lips were painted red, her hair piled on her head. The black silk flower from Dena's wedding tucked behind her ear.

Jesus Christ, I'm a dead man.

"Hi to you too," she said, her eyes sweeping over me. "Wow, Teddy…You look…stunning."

Fine. Wearing a suit once in a while wasn't too bad.

She cocked her head. "Can I come in?"

I stepped aside and the sweet scent of her perfume filled my nose, making my eyes fall shut.

"Are you nervous?" she asked, setting her bag against the kitchen counter.

"Not especially," I said, battling with my tie again. I wasn't nervous at all about being handed a piece of paper by the Dean of the business school. Having Kacey in my presence in front of my parents all day was another story.

"You sure about that?" She laughed.

"Positive."

"Don't fuss with the knot. You're making it crooked."

She turned me toward her and gave my tie a little jerk left, then right. "Perfect." Her hand brushed down my lapel, then rested on my chest for half a heartbeat. I looked down at her. Her eyes widened. She ran the tip of her tongue along her bottom lip, then bit it. I could taste our kiss. It roared into my mouth, the memory of soft lips, a sweet taste and how she moaned softly into my throat…

All I had to do was bend my head a little and we'd kiss again.

She swallowed and quickly moved away. "I got you something. A graduation present."

She rummaged in her a bag and pulled out a small box wrapped in red paper and tied with a purple bow.

"You didn't have to," I said.

"I wanted to. Open it."

I tore off the giftwrap and opened the box. A silver watch gleamed against its gray velvet holder. Clear crystal covered a large face with Roman numerals circling the perimeter. A smaller face was almost camouflaged amid gold and steel gears. It was solid and handsome. Obviously hand-crafted. And expensive.

I stared at it for a moment, touched the thick leather band, then shook my head. "I can't. It's too much."

"Too much what?" she said, smiling as she took it out of the box. "It's a manly watch to fit your manly muscles." She laid it over my left wrist and buckled it, her fingers brushing the inside of my wrist like feathers. "Do you see how it has two faces?"

"Yeah," I said, looking down at her head that was bent over my wrist.

"I had the small face set to New Orleans time." She touched her chin to her shoulder and smiled, not quite looking at me. "It's only a two-hour difference. But you'll always know what time it is where I am."

She looked up at me, and I saw my reflection in the strange blue of her eyes: a dumbstruck idiot wanting to kiss her again. Fuck the consequences.

"Do you like it?" she asked, almost a whisper.

"I love it."

"I'm glad."

Her chin tilted up higher, her lips parting for me. "Teddy…"

"My parents will be here any minute," I said, my head sinking toward hers.

"And we haven't talked yet." Her eyes were on my mouth. "We're talking, not kissing. Remember?"

I moved in. "Fuck talking."

She gasped a little as my lips brushed hers. I pressed in, hard and demanding, groaning at the sweet taste of her on my tongue. She let loose a little cry into my mouth, and fell back against the front door, her hands carving through my hair. I kissed her deep, the fire between us flaring up fast. I whispered her name as my hands slid down her back, over the silky material of her dress, down to the hem. One hand pinning her to the door, the other gliding up her thigh until my fingers brushed the lacy edge of her panties. She tilted her hips toward me, like an offering, her hands clutching my ass, keeping me tight to her.

The doorbell rang.

"Knock, knock," my mother called from outside. "Theo, dear? We'll be late."

Kacey jerked away from me, cheeks flushed and eyes bright as she smoothed her dress back into place. Murmuring, "Shit, shit, shit," and re-pinned the flower that was hanging by her chin.

My erection had fled at the sound of my mother's voice. I tugged trousers and jacket and put my hair back where it belonged.

"Your lipstick is smeared," I said.

She swiped the back of her hand beneath her lower lip. "Gone?"

"Gone."

"You have some too."

I brushed the back of my head over my mouth as my mother knocked. "Theo? Are you there?"

"Let me get it," Kacey said, smoothing her skirt down and taking a deep breath. She squared her shoulders and opened the front door. "Beverly. Hi."

"Kacey, dear." My mom's smile was tilted with surprise and

confusion. "I wasn't expecting to see you here."

Kacey gave her a big hug. "I just arrived. Literally five minutes ago. I thought I could catch a ride with you guys, if that's okay."

"Of course it's okay," Dad said, stepping inside. He bent to give Kacey a hug. "Good to see you, sweetheart. How are things in the Big Easy?"

Kacey chatted with Dad while my mom came over to kiss my cheek.

"Wonderful she's here, isn't it?" she said, her expression still dazed. "She's part of the family, after all."

"She is," I muttered.

"Masters in Business." My mom sighed, shaking her head. "I'm so proud of you." She patted my cheek. "And I know Jonah would be too."

I coughed to loosen the sudden tightness in my chest. "Thanks, Ma."

Mom's brows came together. "You have a little something..." She reached toward my chin. I reared back, swiping thumb and index finger down the corners of my mouth, then jamming that hand in my pocket.

"We should get going."

My mother's eyes widened, flicked to Kacey's painted mouth, then back to me. "Yes," she said, smiling brightly and looking around as if she'd lost her purse, which was on her shoulder. "Yes, let's go before the parking gets too bad."

My phone chimed a text and I grabbed it from my pocket. "It's Oscar," I said too loudly. "He and Dena will meet us at the T & M."

"Wonderful." My mother tucked her arm in Kacey's. "Shall we?"

She kept Kacey close as we walked down to the parking lot. "Let's all drive together," she said. "Men up front, girls in the back. I haven't seen Kacey in so long."

Kacey's eyes met mine as she slid into the back seat of Dad's Chrysler sedan. The electric blue of her eyes when I kissed her was gone, replaced by a wide-eyed panic. A 'what are we doing?' kind of look that echoed my feelings exactly.

Fuck. What are we doing? What am I doing? Tearing apart my mother's memories so I can have what I want?

The UNLV Thomas & Mack Center was a small, enclosed stadium that looked better suited to hosting rowdy basketball games than sedate ceremonies. The parking lot was little less than halfway full. My mother kept her arm locked with Kacey's the entire time.

I got the subtext: Kacey had been Jonah's, and now she was hers. Not mine. *Her* daughter-in-law, even if there was never going to be a wedding.

Pain compressed my chest as I walked ahead of the three of them, not in line with them. It was all well and good to steal a kiss in New Orleans or behind closed doors, but the reality of what it would mean for Kacey and I—if there was such a thing—crashed in hard. My mother would probably never accept it and how could I blame her? Who the hell was I to think it would be okay to go after my dead brother's girlfriend? The love of his life. Never mind that he fucking told me to.

Jonah hadn't seen how impossible it was on every angle. No matter how I looked at it, from anyone's perspective, it was selfish and wrong.

Isn't it?

I looked back over at Kacey, looking stunning and vibrant, wedged between my parents, and a pathetic fantasy tried to take root in my mind. She *was* their daughter-in-law. Because of me. And when I bent to kiss my wife, my mother wiped the smudge of Kacey's lipstick off for me, her eyes filled with teasing affection, not tears.

CHAPTER 32

Kacey

The ceremony was a snore, the only highlight was watching Theo walk across the stage to take his diploma and shake the Dean's hand. Oscar put two fingers in his mouth and whistled, while I hollered as loud as I dared for a singer two days away from a meeting with Sony Music.

After, I watched Theo talk with Oscar, Dena, and some friends of his from UNLV. His cap was gone: after the toss, he'd made no effort to retrieve it. He tore the gown off too, and left it crumpled on his auditorium seat. Underneath he wore a vest instead of a jacket, with his sleeves rolled up. The contrast between his tattoos and the sleek cut of his dress shirt made my heart flutter.

That gorgeous man kissed me.
Twice.

Beverly's grip on my arm tightened as she followed my eyes to Theo.

"He was never one for ceremony," she said, smiling a little. "Jonah would've neatly folded it and tucked it under his arm. Funny how different my sons are."

"Mm."

"You and Theo have grown quite close, haven't you?" Beverly said, and continued before I could answer. "I believe it's natural to bond when tragedy strikes. We lift each other up, don't we? Theo's lifted me up this last year. I don't know what I would do without him."

I nodded and forced a smile. I heard nothing harsh or rebuking in Beverly's tone, but in her eyes I saw the fear. A pleading look, echoing, *Don't take him away from me.*

Theo finished up his conversations and joined us. "Ready to head out?"

Our group moved toward the door, and Theo fell in step beside me. While on my other side, Beverly clutched my arm, linking me firmly to her and to the past.

At the Fletchers', we had a dinner of lasagna, warm bread, and salad. Beverly and Henry sat at the heads of the table. Oscar and Dena on one side, Theo and I on the other. Under the glow of Jonah's lights, we ate and talked, celebrating another major milestone he wasn't here for.

The mood started to stagger under the old weight of grief, and stumble over a current of nervous energy. Beverly was unsettled and the normally jovial Oscar seemed subdued, his lips pursing as his dark eyes volleyed between Theo and me.

Dena lifted her glass. "Shall we have a toast?"

"A toast, or an excuse to recite more Rumi?" Oscar said affectionately.

"The best poet's words suit every occasion." Dena raised her wine glass higher, as if insisting the mood do the same. "Rumi said, *Everyone has been made for some particular work, and the desire for that work has been put in every heart*. This is never more evident than in Theo, who's been rendering life through his incredible drawing for years. Much success to you, my friend, in this next chapter of your life."

The table murmured assents, and then the table fell silent. Beverly shot her husband a pointed look from her end.

"Yes, yes," Henry said, proposing a toast from his chair. "To Theo, for taking initiative and seeing this venture through. Well done."

Another round of murmurs, these deflated and limp. Theo nodded thanks to Henry, but I knew the little compliment was like a tiny bite of food to starving man. It was the shittiest toast in the history of shitty toasts. I stood up, Diet Coke glass raised.

"I'll propose a toast," I said loudly. "To Theodore Fletcher, an extraordinary artist who now holds a Master's Degree in business administration. I've never seen anyone devote so much time and energy to their craft as you have. And with that kind of dedication and responsibility, your own business can't help but be a huge success. Cheers."

That's better.

I sat back down, satisfied with the louder assents and clink of glasses. Theo leaned in and murmured, "Thank you."

I smiled back, my head inclining toward his. "No thanks allowed, remember?"

It was a moment between us, small and private, until Oscar's hard stare wormed its way in, and we both sat up straight again.

"Theo, have you been scouting for a location for your new business?" Dena asked.

"He's looking for something close to the Strip," Beverly said.

"I'm not looking at all actually," Theo said. His glance slid to Henry. "Market's not great right now."

"Indeed," Henry said.

"It'll turn around," Beverly said brightly. "They always do, back and forth. Wait a month or two and you'll see."

An itchy silence fell. Dena turned to me. She reminded me of one of those plate spinners at a carnival, trying to keep the momentum going but seeing plates wobble at every turn. "Speaking of exciting purchases, Kacey, Theo tells us you bought your New Orleans house."

Beverly swung her head around. "Did you?"

"I did," I said. "It's a little shotgun I renovated."

"Now that," Henry said, gesturing at me with his fork, "is a smart investment. I'll bet you've already accrued equity."

"I guess so."

Beverly brightened at this and I heard her release a little sigh. It sounded like relief. She laid her hand on my arm and said, "I guess that settles it as to whether or not you were moving back here. I'm a touch disappointed, but your visits will give me something to look forward to." She patted my hand and turned back to her food with a smile.

"Sure, I can visit," I said, not looking at Theo. "New Orleans isn't very far away."

"Yeah, it's only a four-hour plane ride," Oscar said. "Right, Theo?"

Beverly looked up from her food, her smile vanished.

"I mean, we don't see Theo too much these days," Oscar said, leaning back in his chair. "Since he's going back and forth to New Orleans so often."

I felt cold all over while Theo returned Oscar's gaze with a hard look.

186

"Is that so?" Beverly asked, touching her fingers to her throat. "Do you visit often?"

"Not that often," I said.

"Not that often?" Oscar replied, his laugh sounding a tad sour. He cocked his head at Theo. "I'll bet you've got some serious frequent flyer miles racked up."

"Maybe I do," Theo said, as he and Oscar stared each other down.

"Kacey had a performance for the release of her new album," Dena said into the silence, in a low, calming voice. "We had to miss it, unfortunately, but Theo was able to attend and lend support."

"Oh," Beverly said. "How wonderful."

"It is," Theo said. "Kacey's becoming a huge success."

I waved my hands. "Hardly."

Theo glanced at me. "Sony Records wants to sign her."

Dena gasped. "Really? Oh my God, Kacey, that's huge."

"That is quite something," Henry said.

"They just want a meeting on Monday," I said. "Nothing is finalized."

"This Monday?" Beverly asked. "Oh, you'll have to leave so soon then. But it's wonderful."

I felt a split in my heart—sadness at Beverly's obvious relief and anger at Oscar's catty remarks. Clearly neither of them had any confusion about what I was supposed to be to Theo.

Nothing.

CHAPTER 33

Theo

Over the course of the dinner, I watched the light dim in Kacey's eyes under the shadow of my mother and Oscar's comments. My mother had her reasons for being protective about Kacey and Jonah—I wasn't about to call her out on them. But Oscar was being a dick and I had no clue why, except that it hurt Kacey.

Just Kacey?

I shrugged that off.

After dessert, Oscar didn't wait around, but muttered something about waiting outside for Dena. Kacey was saying goodbye to my parents, so I followed him to the street.

"What the hell is your problem, man?"

He jerked around to glare back at me by the light of the lone streetlamp above us. "You really have to ask? No, wait. Me first. I've got a question I've wanted to ask for *weeks*."

I crossed my arms over my chest. "By all means."

"What the fuck is going on with you and Kacey?"

"Nothing's going on. We're friends."

"Oh yeah. Just friends." His gaze flickered to the silver watch on my wrist. "Hey, you got the time, by any chance?"

I nodded slowly. "Yeah, I do."

"I'll bet you do. It's a sweet watch, man." Oscar's eyes were challenging. "Where'd you get it? Let me guess. Your *friend* Kacey gave it to you."

"You got something to say to me, Oscar, then go ahead and say it."

Oscar shook his head, a short, disgusted laugh gusting out of him. "You know, I thought it was strange you kept flying back and forth to see her, but I was willing to give you the benefit of the doubt. I told myself you were just friends too. And then I saw you today. We *all* saw you. Including your mother, I might add."

"Saw what, exactly?"

"Don't play stupid. Neither of you could stop looking at each other all fucking night." Before I could reply, he took a step closer, dropped his voice. He had the look of a man itching for a fight. "Are you sleeping with her?"

My jaw clenched and I spat the words through gritted teeth. "None of your fucking business."

"It is my business. Jonah was my best friend and I *know* how you operate."

"The fuck is that supposed to mean?"

"Why her, man? You can *fuck* any woman you want. And you do. So why Kacey?" His jaw worked and it seemed like he was trying to keep his fists from flying. "Why do you have to go after Jonah's girl?"

I took a step back. "It's not like that."

"No? You trying to tell me this time, after *years* of chasing after anything in a skirt, it's now *different* with her? *Special*?"

I fought to keep my voice even, while inside I was ready to combust. "What the hell is wrong with you? You spend one day with us and you think you know the story?"

"I know *your* story," Oscar said. "I've heard it before. Holly. Rachel. Lana. Brandi… Shit, those are only the ones I can name. You got at least a hundred more in your phone. Different names, same fucking story. But not Kacey, man. She's not like the rest. She's not some chick you can bang and then never call again."

The blood drained from my face. "I'm aware of that."

"Are you?" He leaned close, his words hissing at me while his finger jabbed my chest. "Because it looks to me like it's business as usual with you, only this time it's your dead brother's girlf—"

My hand shot out and gripped Oscar by the front of his shirt, and I yanked him to me until we were nose to nose. "Shut. The fuck. Up. You don't know *shit* about it."

"I know what I see." Oscar tore away from me. "I know what you do with women, and I'm warning you, you can't do that with Kacey."

"Oh, you're warning me?"

Kacey and Dena were on the front walk and both stopped, staring. The air thickened so I could hardly breathe.

"What's going on?" Dena asked.

"Nothing. Let's go." Oscar headed for their SUV. He opened the driver door and put one foot in.

"Bye, Oscar," Kacey said in a small voice.

"It's a really nice watch, Kace," Oscar said in return, his eyes hard on me. "I hope you kept the receipt. Dena, let's *go*."

I caught Dena's eye and managed a smile. "It's okay," I said. "Go ahead. I'll talk to you later."

Dena nodded and slid into the passenger seat. I drew some comfort from the probability of Oscar getting an earful from his wife the second the door shut.

Or maybe Oscar will tell her I'm just using Kacey for sex. Another conquest.

They drove away, leaving Kacey and me to stare after.

"What was that about?" she said.

"Nothing. Let's get you back to your hotel."

"Tell me."

"It's cold out, Kace," I said, softening my voice. "Come on, you're shivering. Get in the car."

I started the engine and cranked up the heat, pulling slowly out of the cul de sac when I only wanted to peel out and leave a scar of rubber a mile long.

"It was about us, wasn't it?" Kacey asked.

"It's not important." My hands clenched the steering wheel.

"I heard enough," she said. "And your mom. Jesus."

"I know."

"We haven't even figured anything out between us but they've already made up their minds."

"Yeah, they have."

"Where are you going?" she asked, frowning at the streets outside her window.

"Your hotel. You have an early flight tomorrow."

"Teddy..."

"Let's just call it a night, Kace."

"Why? I thought we were going to talk?"

My gaze slid over to her, to the smooth skin of her thighs and the curve of her breasts beneath her dress. What if Oscar was right? What the hell did I know about getting serious with someone? I knew brute, emotionless sex. I could barely put together two words to tell Kacey how I felt.

I walked her to her hotel room door, where she hesitated with the key card in her hand.

"Teddy..."

"Look, it's been a monumentally shitty night," I said. "You have the most important meeting of your life on Monday. You should get some sleep, get back to New Orleans, and prepare for it."

"Is that what you want?" she asked softly.

My hand itched to reach out and touch her face, but I didn't dare. "I want you to be happy, Kace. Your whole life is about to change. Now isn't the time for all this unnecessary headache in your life. My mom and Oscar and all the rest of it."

She nodded slowly. "I'm sorry today wasn't what it should've been for you. You deserve better."

I bent and kissed her temple. "Have a safe flight."

At home, I changed out of the suit into flannel pants and a wife-beater. I shut off all the lights and put SportsCenter on the TV, but I wasn't watching. It was all mindless chatter.

The part of me feeling like I'd done the right thing was getting its ass kicked by the part of me worrying I was letting Kacey go without a fight.

"Just talk," I said. "Talk to her. On the phone. No kissing. No sex."

I picked up my phone and pushed her number. It went to voicemail. I checked the time—a little after eleven. Maybe she was sleeping.

I sent her a text.

You there?
I'm here.

Then I heard the knock on my front door.

My phone slipped out of my hands and my heart clanged against my ribcage like an animal trying to get out. I strode into the kitchen, flipped the light on and opened the door.

She came in, breathless and beautiful. Pushed the door shut and leaned against it. Her eyes raked up and down my skin.

"You want to talk?" I said.

ALL IN

Kacey reached and turned the light off, plunging the kitchen into darkness. "Fuck talking."

CHAPTER 34

Kacey

As the dark enveloped us in soft blackness, I reached for Theo, my hands slipping around his neck. He froze for a moment, then brought his mouth to mine in a crushing kiss.

In the dark, in the silence, we were alone in the world. No prying eyes, no judgment, no words to break the spell, no names spoken. We had the wrong names, he and I. I was wrong for being here and he was the wrong brother.

But not tonight.

We fell back against the wall, writhing, grasping, and yanking at clothes. Desperate to expose more skin, to touch more, to kiss harder, to finally take what we wanted.

We kissed until kissing wasn't enough.

Theo's hands roamed my back, found the zipper of my dress. He flipped me around, and I braced myself on the kitchen counter as he slid it down, exposing my back to the air. He made a growling sound of want as my dress slipped into a silky puddle at my feet, leaving me in my bra, panties, and heels. Theo's hand made a fist in my hair, pulling it aside, exposing the skin. His mouth worked along my shoulder. Voraciously, like a starving man. I gasped as he trailed open-mouthed kisses up to my ear. My skin turned to fire under his grazing teeth. His tongue was hot and wet, tasting me, sucking my skin, biting and then licking again.

My legs trembled as I pressed back into him. His hands slipped up to my bra-clad breasts, kneading me while his mouth continued its assault on my neck. I arched until my head rested on his shoulder, as my hand slid between our bodies to find the length of him—huge and iron hard—straining against his pants. I stroked him through the material, then slipped my hand inside, wrapped my fingers around him.

ALL IN

"Jesus…" I breathed.

He let out a small grunt, and bit down on my neck, sending fresh licks of fire down my back.

"Want you," he growled, his right hand sliding down between my breasts, down my stomach, to the top of my panties. "Wanted you for so long…"

His fingers slipped inside my panties, and my thoughts broke into the air. "Oh God yes," I whispered. "Touch me."

Two fingers slid inside me and with a cry, I arched harder against him. His mouth worked against my neck, my ear, sending currents of heat down to where his fingers pressed deliciously hard, until I unraveled from top to bottom. I writhed against him, my hand still stroking him but hands and fingers weren't enough.

"More," I whispered. "Please, more."

Theo withdrew his hand and spun me around. Our mouths crashed together, all teeth and tongues and our breaths rasping in our noses. His hands cupped the back of my neck and the curve of my waist as we mauled each other's mouths, raw and frenzied. He groaned into my mouth and I took it, gave it back as a whimper—a silent cry as my entire body screamed for his.

My hands tore across his broad back, the muscles of his shoulders, into his hair, down to his tight ass. His kisses overwhelmed me. *He* overwhelmed me with his relentless presence, the solidity of him, his scent, the taste of his tongue dueling with mine, the feel of his strong body mashed against me. In his grip, I was small and fragile yet utterly desired and powerful. I'd never seen a man want me this badly. Ever.

He lifted me and sat me down on the counter. My legs instantly wrapped around his waist, my arms around his neck, still kissing, biting, sucking until I tasted the tang of blood—his or mine, I didn't know. I was lost. Delirious with him. Blindly we tore at each other's clothing. His large hands went to the front of my bra, found the clasp and tore it open.

"*Yes,*" I cried, as his hands sought my breasts. I wanted to scream *Yes* to everything he was doing to me, but I swallowed the sound and kissed him harder, my own hands finding the bottom of his shirt and hauling it off.

It was too dark to see each other. Our hands and mouths did all the looking. My fingers trailed up the hard cut of his abs, up over his broad chest, to his right nipple where I found a hard glint of metal. A tiny barbell piercing. I hadn't known it was there. I'd never seen him without a shirt. I bent to put my mouth on that piercing, nipping at it with my teeth and tugging it gently.

Theo hissed a breath and let me work over his nipple with my tongue, then drew me back to his mouth for another bruising kiss. His hands slid up my thighs, his fingers hooked my panties and slid them down. My hands tore at the ties on his pants, pushing them off his hips. He was huge and hard, soft velvet over steel.

"Wait," I whispered.

"I got it," he said. He pulled a condom from his wallet on the counter and rolled it down, his mouth on mine again. With delicious roughness, he thrust my thighs apart.

I thought he'd drive straight into me but he was slow—for the first and last time all night he was slow—pushing into me, gripping my hips until his touched mine, joined completely.

"God, yes," I hissed, then bit his shoulder. The feel of him inside me, the heavy pressure, the heat and hardness of him. He was so much, stretching and filling me.

A few slow, deep thrusts, and then Theo began to move.

He braced himself with both hands on the counter and I wrapped myself around him, my legs tight to his waist, my high heels digging into the small of his back. I clung to his neck, our mouths trying to form something like a kiss but merely touching, teeth clacking together, tongues stroking one another. I held him tighter as he drove into me, fast and hard, and his mouth moved to latch onto my neck, biting and sucking. My fingernails answered, clawing at the ropes of muscles along his back, until finally the sensation building in me stole every bit of energy.

"Come for me," he growled.

His hand gripped a fistful of my hair and he brought my mouth to his, hard and deep. I came then, pain and pleasure driving me over the edge. Theo showed no signs of being close or tiring. His body was powerful with lust while mine felt limp from the climax that ripped through it. I clung to him, content to let him take me however he wanted, to stay inside me as long as it took to find his own release. But another orgasm, stoked on the fires of the first, began to build in me.

"Again," he grunted against my lips. "Come for me again."

I arched back and he held me with one arm tight around my waist, driving into me over and over. Until the second climax—a thousand times stronger than the first—tore through me.

I cried out as my body tensed, every muscle and sinew threaded tight, bound together in an ecstasy I'd never experienced. His hands were locked on my hips, hauling me to him as he thrust and just as my second orgasm began to wane, he came.

He shuddered and bit back a cry through gritted teeth, turning the cry into a low rumbling growl. His thrusts slowed, deepened, but were just as hard. God he was so deep in me, and I held him there, my legs still wrapped around him until he had emptied himself into me completely.

I slumped against him. Theo rested his head against my shoulder, his breath gusting over my skin. I stroked the broad muscles of his back, up to the base of his neck, and threaded my fingers through his thick, silken hair. I held him to me, our sweat mingling, our breaths slowing together.

He pulled away enough to look at me. His whiskey-colored eyes glinted and I could feel him searching me, trying to find me in the relentless dark. Forehead to forehead, we held on to each other, and the hunger began to build again. We weren't done yet. Our lips met—a small touch—and then again. And again. And again until the fire was stoked and rising once more. I parted my lips wide to take him deeply, to kiss away any doubt that I was satiated. I wanted more. I wanted all night.

He pulled out and I let out a small cry at the loss of him. He disposed of the condom and then came back to me, and lifted me up off the counter. Under my knees and around my back, he carried me to his bedroom.

I'd never been in his space like this before. In the dark, there were no colors and only sparse furniture: a dresser, nightstand, large bed with dark comforter. The room smelled masculine and sharp, permeated by his cologne, his soap, his shaving cream. I was surrounded by the scent of him, and I inhaled deeply.

He set me down on the bed and I watched his dark shape move to open a nightstand drawer for another condom. I got up on my knees, reaching for him, to pull him down on top of me with a raw urge to let him use my body any way he wanted.

And he did.

All night.

I lost track of how many orgasms I had. Or how many I gave him.

The hours blurred together in a tangled, sweaty mass of aching need and hunger. Finally, as dawn threatened to dispel our safe darkness, we fell heavily into sleep.

CHAPTER 35

Kacey

I woke with the daylight cutting across the bed. My body pulsed in the hundred places where Theo had been. I felt hungover with him, swollen and aching, satiated and deliciously heavy.

I sat up, brushed the tousled mess of hair from my eyes and glanced around. Theo's room was neater than I expected. The comforter on his king-sized bed was dark blue, as were the curtains. Brown furniture, beige rug.

My eyes landed on a picture on the dresser. The sleepy smile slipped from my lips.

Jonah and Theo, the big brother with his arm slung around his little brother, smiling his bright, open smile. Theo's was more of a smirk, but I knew him now. To find Theo's happiness, you had to look in his eyes.

I glanced at the sleeping man beside me. On his stomach, his face half-buried in a pillow. The light fell over the muscles of his back, the smooth skin tattooed along his arms and down his right shoulder blade.

Memories of other men from my past—nameless roadies and faceless musicians with inked skin, swam up at me. Men I'd used for comfort and pleasure, and then discarded.

This isn't the same, I thought. *It's not what I came back for last night. Not why I'm here now.*

My gaze went back to the photo of the brothers, then returned to Theo sleeping. I clutched the sheets to my naked body, waiting to see which feeling was going to hit me first. The one Yvonne said held the truth.

But my eyes landed on the clock radio next to Theo's bedside and a jolt of panic tore through me.

"Teddy! My flight! Shit..."

Theo bolted upright.

"What? Your flight…" He blinked sleepily at the clock, his hair a tousled mess. "What time is your flight?"

"7:45," I said. I glanced around frantically for my clothes. "Oh my god, that meeting. I'm going to miss that meeting…"

"Shit." Theo threw off the bed sheets and drew on a pair of jeans, as I raced out of his room.

In the kitchen I found my clothes lay in a heap on the floor. I dressed quickly as Theo came in, grabbing for his wallet and keys.

"Is there a later flight?" he asked, helping me zip up my dress.

"Yes, but mine is the only one that's direct. All the others have long layovers and wouldn't get me back in Louisiana until tomorrow morning." I stopped, staring at the digital clock on the stove. "I'm going to miss that meeting with Sony."

"No." Theo took my face in his hands. "We'll make it. I'll get you there, Kace. I swear."

We hurried down to his truck and Theo raced us to my hotel where I had only time enough to grab my suitcase. Then on to McCarran where I'd embark on a cross-country Flight of Shame in a wrinkled dress, with Theo all over me. No shower. No time to wash my face. It seemed to like no time at all from waking in his bed to my hurried departure.

On the drive to McCarran, Theo's eyes were intent on the road, driving fast as he dared with cool precision, weaving expertly in and out of the lean Sunday morning traffic. He glanced at me sideways, then did a double-take, his brows coming together. Without taking his eyes off the road, he reached over to touch my lower lip. I felt the little sting of a cut on my bottom.

"Shit, I did that…"

"It's not just you." I reached over to touch the small bruises and bite marks on his neck. "We got a little carried away. God, did we ever." I shook my head, turned to watch the road race by beneath us. "We haven't talked. We haven't figured out…*anything*."

Theo kept silent, his eyes on the road and dropping now and then to glance at the clock, racing the minutes.

I bit my lip. "What are we doing? Is it commiseration? Comfort? No one gets it but us…No one understands what we went through…Is that it?"

Theo's jaw muscles clenched.

"Or was it just an insane sexual attraction we seem to have? Just sex—"

"It wasn't just sex," Theo said, his eyes hard. "What Oscar said was bullshit. I'm not like that. I haven't been with anyone since…" He bit off his words.

"Since when?"

"Since Great Basin."

My head shot up. "Wait… Great Basin?"

He nodded.

I stared. "When? The time that we all went…?"

"Yes."

"You were with Holly…" Memories flooded back. "No, you broke up with Holly. Right in the middle of the trip."

"Yeah, I did."

"Teddy…" I gave my head a little shake. "And that was the last time you were with another woman?"

"I didn't sleep with Holly in Great Basin. The night before, maybe, but not while we were up there."

My heart was thudding in my ears. "Why not?"

"Because of you," Theo said. "You sang, Kacey. And that was it."

"That was it…" I sank back in my seat. "Why…why didn't you tell me?"

He glanced at me sideways. "Tell you when? When you were with my brother?"

"*No,*" I shook my head. "After. Any time after…"

"I couldn't. I can't. It's not up to me."

"What the hell does that mean?"

He started to answer but we'd arrived at McCarran. There was no time for Theo to park. He screeched his truck into the departing flights drop off, and jogged around to my side to help me with my luggage.

On the sidewalk, he pulled me into the strong circle of his arms.

"What do we do? What happens next?" I said into his chest.

"You get on that plane. You take the next step. Sign a contract, make a shit-ton of money."

"You know that's not what I'm asking."

He sighed, shook his head. "You have to get on that plane and make that meeting, Kace. You have to. I can't let you lose this opportunity."

"What about us? You and me?"

You and me. Kacey and Theo.

I swallowed hard. A heavy swamp of emotion suddenly welled in my chest at those words; a deep warmth that spread out from my heart and a million times more potent than the physical pleasure Theo and I had created.

"Please, Kace." Theo said. "You have five minutes." He pulled me to him in a swift, strong embrace. "Get back safe, and call me tomorrow after your meeting. Let me know how it went."

"Then what?"

"Then we'll go from there."

Go where? I wanted to ask. He was in Vegas, I was in New Orleans, and in between us lay not just fifteen hundred miles, but the judgment of our friends and family who didn't want to see Theo and Kacey, but Kacey and Jonah.

Theo pulled away to kiss my mouth—a soft, deep kiss—and then let me go, and the truth I'd been waiting to feel finally rose from the quagmire of emotions.

I'm tired of saying goodbye.

CHAPTER 36

Theo

It was after hours. Vegas Ink was dark. I sat at my station, rolling a little bottle of blue ink over my knuckles. *Inked* magazine lay open on my reclining tattoo chair.

The story on me and my unfinished tattoo series was major. Not the cover story but the second feature. Two and a half pages of text about me and my job at Vegas Ink. Plus three glossy photos of the new tattoos, Edgar and two other clients providing my canvases.

The article had spurred a ton of new business. I had clients booked solid every day. Good money, but I was exhausted.

The ink bottle rolled over my knuckles, under my palm, across my knuckles again.

Weeks had passed since I'd seen Kacey. She'd made her flight, met the execs at Sony, and four days later, they flew her and the Olsens to Los Angeles to sign a contract. Then to New York to do a photo shoot for *Spin*. Then back to L.A. to discuss a tour she wasn't sure she wanted to take. Then the holidays were upon us, and she stayed in New Orleans, no doubt feeling unwelcome at my parents' house now.

Time spun away from us. We were both busy, both tired. Our phone conversations were shorter, less frequent.

We didn't talk about our night together.

The ink bottle rolled, around and around.

A knock on the front door or the shop pulled me from my thoughts.

My heart thudded at the possibility it was Kacey, but it was Dena. I unlocked the door and let her in.

"What are you doing here?" I asked, as she gave me a hug. "Little late for a tattoo. But for you, I can make an exception."

"It's been too long," she said. "And some conversations are too important for the telephone."

She moved through the small shop to my station. She inspected the magazine, a smile spreading over her lips.

"This is magnificent," Dena said flipping the pages. "You're so talented, my friend."

"Thanks," I said. "Have a seat. What's up?"

She sat down, and cocked her head at me, a knowing look in her eyes. I hadn't spoken to Oscar in weeks either; it'd been easy not to. They'd gone back east to visit his family over the holidays.

"He feels terrible, you know," Dena said. "He won't admit it because he's stubborn, but whatever was said between the two of you that night is eating him up."

I crossed my arms over my chest. "Good."

Dena arched a brow, but then sighed and shook her head. "You're right. I can't defend him, except to tell you his ugly words were fueled by pain. He won't talk about Jonah either, but I know he's still hurting."

Take a number, pal.

Dena leaned over her knees, elegant in dark jeans and a white blouse.

"I think he sees Kacey as less of a real human being, and more as the impetus for Jonah's happiness. She came out of the ether to love him those last months. But the reality he saw the night of your graduation, is she's a young human being, with a life ahead of her. With decades to live and love. It took him by surprise. It took us all by surprise. We had no idea something was happening with you and her."

I sighed, ran my hand through my hair. "I don't know what's happening with us. I think we're both hiding out, afraid of what people will think."

She was quiet for a minute. "I know it's been so hard for you since Jonah passed," she said, her voice rich and soothing. "I know Kacey's been a great comfort to you, and you for her. I'm glad for that. You know I worry about you."

"You don't have to worry about me. I'm good."

"Mmm, yes, that's exactly what Oscar says." Dena grinned, but it faded over her next words. "We've all suffered from losing Jonah, but nobody was as close to Jonah as you and Kacey. I hope being together has brought you both some peace."

"It doesn't feel peaceful," I said. "A lot of times it feels like a fucking mess." I met her eyes unblinking, my voice sinking to just above a whisper. "Because he was my brother."

Dena's hand reached out to touch my arm. "I don't see any wrong in this, Theo," she said. "From the depths of grief and pain, something good and joyful growing? Where's the shame?"

"Tell that to my mother. Or your husband."

"Time is the great healer," she said. "But you can't put your life on hold until the rest of the world accepts what you know is true in your heart."

"I know what's true for me," I said. "I don't know what's true for her. I can't...*talk* to her. I try. I want to, and then I get close to her and I'm kissing her instead."

Dena hopped off the chair, and reached up to cup my cheek. "Don't let another moment go by without telling her how you feel, Theo, and ask her how she feels. It's both the simplest and hardest thing you'll ever do, but ask her. Ask her as if no one is watching. Because in the end, it's your life and hers."

I walked her to the front of the store where she hugged me tight.

"Will I become a cliché if I quote my favorite poet one more time?"

"Lay it on me."

"*Where there is ruin, there is hope for treasure.*" She gave me another of her knowing smiles. "It's one of my favorites."

"Yeah," I said, a smile finding its way to my lips. "It sounds pretty fucking good to me too."

CHAPTER 37

Kacey

The rain came down hard, pattering on my roof. I sat curled up on the chair in my living room listening to raindrops hit the gutters with a metallic clang and break open. An addendum to the Sony contract I'd signed sat in my lap, Grant's plain-English translation of the legalese scribbled along the margins. A tour addendum. They wanted me to go on a two-month, fourteen-city tour.

It didn't look so bad on paper, especially with Grant highlighting all the perks and riders in bright yellow. Three different kinds of sparkling water in every dressing room? It sounded like waste, not a perk. Touring meant I'd be cut loose like an astronaut, floating far away from home base. All the fancy bottled water in the world wouldn't keep me from missing my house. And Yvonne.

And Teddy.

I already missed him. We'd both been so busy. His client roster had become a mile long since the *Inked* feature. Soon, the market would turn and he'd buy a place in Vegas, just as I embarked on my career. A tour would only pull us farther apart, and we were already stretched to the breaking point.

I missed him. My chest was hollow with it.

My phone rang, showing the Olsens' number. "Hey," Grant said. "So. Any closer to putting your pen to the dotted line?"

"Sony Records tour," Phoebe drawled in the background. "No dinky little side shows. It's the big time, girlfriend. Big, *big* time. Like Peter Gabriel 'Big Time.'"

"Okay, okay, she gets it," Grant said, and cleared his throat. "So, Kace? What do you think?"

"I don't do well on tours."

"So you keep saying. Is it nerves?" Grant asked.

"Booze," I said. "I'm just starting to have a sense of settling down. I don't want to be uprooted already."

Phoebe snorted. "It's only a two-month tour. Hardly the stuff of uprootage."

"That's not a word," Grant said.

"Yes, it is," Phoebe said. "I just used it."

"Well, shit, can't argue with that logic."

"Guys," I cut in. "I just…give me some more time."

"We can try," Grant said. "But with no new album on the horizon, a tour for *Shattered Glass* is the next big thing. We don't have the clout of a high-end lawyer to negotiate."

"Don't say that," Phoebe hissed at her brother. "She'll replace us with some high-end lawyer."

"Guys, I'm not replacing anyone. Give me a week, okay? I know it's a big deal to you two, I haven't forgotten."

"Sure, sure," Grant said. "One week. No problem. Take your time and think it over."

"Don't think too hard," Phoebe said. "Mardi Gras is in two days. Jump on that tour, and we can pretend the whole city is throwing us a party."

I hung up, feeling shitty for making them wait. As my de facto agents, they stood to make a hefty percentage of a tour's ticket sales. The Olsens had never tasted success like this before. I had. Like any sugary treat, it tasted heavenly at first, but if you gorged on it, you'd be sick. And I was a recovering glutton.

Yvonne was working a graveyard shift that night, and I didn't feel like going out. I put on sweatpants, a t-shirt, ordered a pizza and vegged out on the couch. A cable channel was playing a marathon of the *Vacation* movies.

It was after one a.m. and I was on *Christmas Vacation,* chuckling as Randy Quaid emptied his RV's septic tank into Chevy Chase's sewer, when my phone rang.

Teddy…

"Hey," I said. "It's late."

"Did I wake you?" he said.

"No. I'm sitting around, watching silly movies. Missing you."

"I miss you too," he said. "So much."

A short silence fell and I knew this conversation couldn't be like the others we'd had—rushed and nervous, with neither of us telling the other what we felt.

"God, Teddy... I feel like I've been hiding out here. We haven't really talked, and now the label wants me to do a tour. I'm scared."

"Of what, Kace?"

"When I was with Rapid Confession, all we did was tour. I had no home base, no foundation. I drank all the time..." I shook my head, sucked in a breath. "I'd be gone from my home, and I can't help but feel that it would be the end of us. Whatever us is. More phone calls. More distance. More miles. I can't do it anymore, Teddy. I can't..."

"I can't either, Kace," Theo said. "Fucking hell, I'm tired of living life on the phone."

"God, me too."

"Good. Then can you open the door? I'm getting poured on."

For one heartbeat, I sat frozen. Then the phone slipped out of my hand as I tore off the couch, crossed the living area and opened the front door.

He stood there, rain dripping off his leather jacket, sparkling in his hair like diamond dust.

"Teddy..." I gasped and in the next instant, I was in his arms, his mouth pressed to mine.

We didn't make it to my bedroom. We didn't even make it to the couch. I barely had sense of mind to kick the door shut to keep the rain out. The words we needed to speak were lost in a confusion of aching need. We fell to our knees, stripping clothing and kissing hard, then tumbled to the floor where he slid inside me with one perfect motion.

"Teddy," I cried as he brought me quickly to the threshold, then sent me crashing over. I held him tight as his own climax shuddered through him, warming me from the inside out.

"God, don't let me go, Kace," he said against my neck.

"I won't," I said. "Never again."

CHAPTER 38

Kacey

The rain stopped by ten. Days ago, I'd made plans with Yvonne, Big E, and the Olsens to see the Krewe of Bacchus parade, which started on St. Charles Street and ran through the Garden District. Yvonne had told me the parade was the big daddy, with more than thirty animated floats. Some celebrity always came to New Orleans to represent Bacchus, the Greek God of wine.

I'd bought a gold flapper's dress covered with black tassels, and a matching gold wig that curled under my chin. Yvonne showed up in jeans and a simple shirt but dressed it up with a mask and pink feather boa, and crowed over Theo being here.

"Guess I can retire my Louisville Slugger," she teased, and gave him a hug.

Grant and Phoebe arrived and put us all to shame with their costumes: he was almost unrecognizable as Beetlejuice, in a dusty black suit with white stripes, and Phoebe's long red hair and flawless make-up made her a perfect Sally from *Nightmare Before Christmas*.

Theo and Big E both refused to dress up, the two men clapping hands and patting each other in the back.

"What," I snorted, "you're too old for costumes?" I asked Theo, as we headed out.

"I'm too busy trying to keep my hands off of you in that dress."

"If I show you my boobs, will you throw me some beads?"

"Stop," he said. "You're making me lightheaded."

I laughed and leaned close to whisper in his ear. "Tonight I'll put on all the beads I catch today. And nothing else."

We joined the crowd near the river, where the parade ended. I'd never seen anything like Mardi Gras. Music poured out of businesses and people in every kind of costume danced, drank and gaped at the floats trundling down the street.

I'd only ever seen the Rose Parade as a kid in Orange County. Those floats were sweet little things, covered in pretty flowers. Mardi Gras floats were parties on wheels: huge, elaborate and bursting with color and noise. The first was the King's Float—an enormous white feasting table with huge gold coins. Bunches of purple grapes lay in front of a giant fiberglass Bacchus, raising a wine glass. In front of him, a raised dais held the King of the parade.

"Holy shit, that's Matthew Broderick. Matthew Broderick is King of the Parade." I tugged on Theo's arm excitedly, and screamed, *"Ferris Bueller, you're my hero."*

Matthew Broderick didn't hear me, but some of the krewe did. Teddy and I were immediately showered with ropes of colored beads. He slung a dozen of them over my neck and hauled me to him for a wet kiss.

"Our babies all grown up," Yvonne sniffed dramatically, her arm around Big E.

The big guy wiped a nonexistent tear from his cheek. "I'm so proud."

"I'm going to die of jealousy." Phoebe pouted. She gave her brother a dirty look. "Why do I hang around you so much?"

"Good question," Grant retorted.

I smiled against Teddy's lips, basking in happiness. Such a relief to have friends look at us with only joy and affection.

The parade carried on into the evening. I jostled Teddy's arm as an enormous alligator in bright green made its way down the street. Thousands of strings of brightly colored beads dripped from its open mouth, and its krewe—two dozen people in blue and silver—threw beads and plastic coins at the cheering spectators. Another float called the Bacchawoppa, resembled Moby Dick, if Moby Dick had been kidnapped by drag queens. The giant whale was painted to look as if it were wreathed in colorful seaweed, and its krewe threw beads from within the rolling blue waves surrounding it.

Night fell fast. Big E gave Yvonne a ride home, and Grant and Phoebe took off with other friends. Theo and I watched until the last float passed, then meandered through the Garden District, past groups of revelers in sugar-skull makeup, street musicians playing saxophones and accordions, groups of friends draped in beads and holding sloshing drinks in their hands. The city was intoxicating enough for me, its streets pulsing and breathing. Even the shadows danced.

I felt my pulse quicken, exhilarated by the night and by the man beside me. His eyes met mine, burning with a hunger that made my legs tremble.

Theo took an abrupt turn, heading down an alley between a café and a smoke shop. In the shadows that smelled of sweet cigars, he pressed me against the wall. His body, hard and strong, pinning mine, his hands all over me, his mouth crushing mine.

I moaned into his mouth, my own hands clawing mindlessly at the muscles in his back, crawling up to his soft hair. My legs parted, wanting to wrap around his waist so he could take me right then and there. His hand slipped under the swaying tassels of my flapper dress to cup between my legs. His fingers found the sweet spot through silken material that dampened under his touch. My body undulated against the wall with the force of him, stoking a rising heat. I clung to his neck, astonished at how fast he was driving me to climax.

"God, yes," I hissed through, then nearly cried out in agony as he took his hand away. Then Theo dropped to his knees, lifting my dress.

"Oh God. Oh God, wait. Teddy…"

"You want me to stop?"

I glanced around the deserted alley, realized the passersby on the street couldn't see us. "No."

He went back up my skirt, and tugged my panties aside. Then his mouth was on me and I had to bite back a scream. It took seconds for his tongue to suck and lick me through a titanic wave of pleasure. I flailed against the wall, nothing to hold on to but Theo's shoulders as the ecstasy flooded me. My head fell back against the bricks and I stared at the muted stars above my new city.

Still Theo didn't stop. He delved deeper into me, his tongue and grazing teeth and the deep vibrations of his grunting voice driving me toward another crash. He went at me like he was a starving madman and I was his feast, the only thing that could satiate him.

A second orgasm ripped through me, and I gasped soundlessly, my voice whispering through the alley when I really wanted to scream. I needed to scream. I needed to have Theo naked, in my bed, where I could ride him until he came. And then make him come again.

Theo came up from under my skirt, his face flushed red in the meager light, his lips and chin wet with me.

"Home," I whispered. God, it seemed so far away. Too far.

We looked hopelessly for a cab, standing hand in hand on the street, breathing heavily, my wig askew, my lipstick smeared. By some miracle, a cab pulled up near us and we ran for it, diving into the back almost before its passengers had finished getting out. In the slow crawl of traffic, Theo shifted beside me, restless and impatient. His hand landed on my thigh, over my dress. I looked out the window, bit at my thumbnail and spread my legs ever so slightly.

"God, Kace..." he breathed.

His hand was large and rough and warm on my skin. I shifted again, pressing into his touch, and his hand slid higher up my thigh. I tilted my hips, needy and desperate. I bit back a tiny cry, as his palm slid over me, his fingers pressing down in small circles.

My hand crept across his lap, to the bulge in his jeans. He was hard and hot through the dense cotton and I stroked the length of him.

I bit my lip harder.

The cab ride was maddeningly slow. The keys to my front door wouldn't cooperate. Too many steps from the door to the couch, where I pushed him down. Just enough light came from the kitchen to see Theo's eyes dilate with desire. I could tell by the clench of his jaw and the way his eyes raked over me, he wasn't going to wait much longer.

I tore off my wig and hurled it away, then peeled the dress off my body and let it pool at my feet.

"Take your shirt off," I said and reached behind to unclasp my black lace bra. Theo grabbed the back of his collar and hauled his shirt over his head and tossed it aside. I didn't know if I'd ever get used to the sight of him shirtless—lean muscle covered in beautiful ink down one pec. The other side glinted with that piercing that made me lose my mind.

I stripped off my panties, leaving me in a garter belt, heels, and a dozen ropes of colorful beads. Slowly, I knelt in front of him. My hands glided down the tops of his muscular thighs, then back up on the inside. I reached for his buckle as he bent to kiss me—a searing kiss, his tongue brazen in my mouth. I unzipped his pants and freed the hard length of him.

"You're so beautiful," I said. It wasn't the most masculine word, but I meant it that way. His masculine form, every part of him, was perfectly beautiful in my eyes.

"Fuck," he said through gritted teeth as I put my mouth on him and around him, my hand stroking him slowly, then faster. I would have taken him all the way, but he gripped my shoulders.

"Kace," he managed. "I want to be inside you. *Now*."

I rose from kneeling and straddled his lap. Beads hung over my breasts but he roughly brushed them aside to get at my nipple, biting and sucking as I sank down onto him.

We both froze for a heartbeat, feeling him inside me, hard and heavy, buried to the hilt in my wet heat. His hands dug into my hips, driving up into me as I ground down against him.

"So good," he hissed tightly. "God, you feel so good."

"Don't stop…" I cried, almost incoherent now. "Never stop."

My hands found his jaw, held his face and kissed him deeply. Then I let go to grip his shoulders and ride him hard, ride him until the ache in my lower belly unfolded, expanded and then detonated. I could scream now. I yelled his name out, my back arching as his own orgasm erupted inside me.

His arms wrapped around my back and he pressed his forehead to my heart, nuzzling my breasts through beads. I pulled back and held his face in my hands, staring down at him, brushing the damp hair off his forehead. Off of Theo's forehead. My Theo.

My universe.

CHAPTER 39

Kacey

I woke with the morning light creeping over my bed and Theo's warm breath wafting over my neck. I snuggled closer to him, pressing my backside against his lap. Up close, the tattoos covering his arms were mesmerizing. Intricate swirls and whorls of fire, faces and shapes. Each flowed into the other, blending to make a perfect whole.

He stirred behind me, and cinched his arms tight. My skin shivered where he began planting kisses along my neck.

"Morning," I murmured.

"Morning." He kissed the bare skin of my right shoulder blade. "This part," he murmured sleepily, "this is all mine."

I smiled and wiggled against him as a thrill shot along my spine. "All yours."

"Any idea what the tattoo will be?"

"Not yet, but it's going to be the first tattoo in your new place, remember?"

He made a sound deep in his chest. "Don't remind me. I don't want to think about Las Vegas right now."

I rolled over in his arms, traced the hard line of his jaw. "I hate falling asleep at night when you're hundreds of miles away."

"Me too."

"I meant what I said. That I can't do it anymore, Teddy. I can't live over the phone, only seeing you once every few weeks."

"I can't do it either, Kace."

"So I'm going to do what I promised that night in the desert. When we scattered Jonah's ashes. Do you remember?"

Theo's eyes widened, I watched his Adam's apple bob as he swallowed. "I asked you to stay with me," he whispered.

I nodded, tears welling in my eyes. "I will. I'll stay. I won't ever leave you again. No more broken promises."

"But what about your life here? Your friends and your music?"

"I can make music anywhere. I can sign the contract and still be with you. But no touring. I want to stay put and write a new album. New songs about new chapters in my life. Songs about you and me."

"Kacey…" He shook his head.

"Sure, I'll miss my friends," I said, "but I can visit them. I can miss them but I can't miss you anymore."

"It means telling Oscar and my mom."

I nodded. "I know. But I'm not afraid. They love you and they want you to be happy. Are you, Teddy?"

"God, yes. I never thought…"

I grazed the back of my fingers down his cheek. "What, baby?"

"That this was for me. That I'd have something like this. This feeling… I can't explain it."

"You don't have to. We'll go back and tell your mom and dad the truth. We didn't plan this. We've spent too many months living apart. Too much time on the phone. Our first kiss *was on the phone*, Teddy."

He chuckled. "Yeah, it sure was. But it counted."

I laughed as he nuzzled my neck, kissed my throat, then bit my earlobe.

"When do we need to go back?" I asked. "Not soon, I hope. I want you all to myself for a few more days. In this house before I sell it."

"You're really going to move to Las Vegas?"

"Yes. But I won't have anywhere to live. Can I shack up with you until I find a place?"

Theo looked about to say something, then took the words back. A small smile appeared. "You can shack up with me permanently. If you want."

"I want." I ringed his neck with my arms. "I want that a lot."

I kissed him softly, then deeply, my body waking up to him. I fell back into his arms, as we tried to satiate the need that always burned between us. After, we pulled on the bare minimum of clothing and we headed to the kitchen to satisfy our hunger for actual food.

Theo cooked us scrambled eggs and sausage. He ate standing up on the kitchen side of the counter, while I sat on the stool opposite. Outside it was raining again.

"I'll miss that too," I said.

"What?"

"The rain."

Theo looked thoughtful a minute then said slowly, "You sure you want to move back?"

"Yeah, I am," I said.

"You told me Vegas is filled with too many memories."

"It is," I said. "But I love those memories now. They don't haunt me anymore. They remind me of the gift Jonah gave me."

I slid off the stool, went into the kitchen and slipped into his arms. "I didn't know what love was until Jonah. I'd given up on looking for it. I thought the comfort of a man's body was the best I could get. But Jonah saw past all that. He showed me I was worthy of love and that I could love someone in return. I could give all that I had for someone else. He gave me that gift, and then he showed me how to use it."

I reached up to stroke Theo's cheek. "I know what I feel now. I know my heart. It's been forever altered, but it's not broken anymore."

"God, Kace." He shook his head. "Jonah… You know, he…"

"What, baby?" I asked. "You can talk about him. Let's talk about him. For the first time, it feels *okay*."

"It is," he said. "Finally, it is." He looked like he was about to say more when his phone buzzed on the counter, *Eme Takamura - Wynn Galleria* on the display.

Theo frowned as he answered "Hello? Hey, Eme."

"Tell her I said hi," I whispered. My smile faded as Theo's face morphed from concern to shock. His features folding in, his own smile vanishing and his eyes filling with fear.

"Why?" he said, his voice thick. He was pacing the living room now, his hand carving through his hair. "Why didn't you tell me?"

I felt my stomach drop to my feet, biting my lip to keep from interrupting.

"Okay. Okay, fine. When?" He stopped pacing. "Tomor— What do you mean, *tomorrow?*"

Now I was scared. "What is it?"

"Fine," he snapped into the phone. "We'll leave now."

Theo hung up and looked at me. "Eme says the Wynn Galleria is shutting down. They're moving all the exhibits out immediately to make room for more casino space."

"Why?"

"They weren't making enough money."

I leaned against the counter for support. "Where will Jonah's glass go?"

"Pittsburgh," Theo said. "Carnegie Mellon is going to take it permanently."

I closed my eyes as relief gusted out of me. "Oh, Teddy. Thank god. That's a good thing."

"How is that a good thing?"

"Because it means his art isn't going to be shut away in some storage unit," I said. God, just the idea of it made me ill. "It's not going to be taken down and stored in bits and pieces in boxes. His legacy…it's going to go on."

"Yeah, but he's not…" Theo inhaled raggedly. "He's not…home."

I went to him, wrapped my arms around him. "I know," I whispered, thinking of his cathedral. His peace.

He let me hold him a moment, then pulled away, his voice hard again. "If we leave now, we might make it. To see it one more time. Before they dismantle it."

"You pack our clothes," I said. "I'll find us the fastest flight back."

The best flight I could find left Saturday morning and arrived at McCarran at two in the afternoon. We raced to his truck in the long-term parking, then hauled ass down the Strip to the Wynn Galleria.

We were too late.

Wilson, the security guard on duty, shook his head and unlocked the door for us. "You have about an hour," he said. "Then the contractors show up and start tearing down walls."

"Why so fast?" I asked.

"Money, miss," Wilson said. "Why else?"

He let us into the gallery and we walked down its long side. It looked like it had been looted. Nothing on the walls except outlines where paintings had hung. Placards described sculptures no longer there. At the end of the hall, I put my hand in Theo's and we rounded the corner together.

Tears sprung to my eyes. Nothing remained. Only cables and wires, hanging down from the ceiling like stringy hair. Empty hooks and fasteners where a sun had blazed and where water had flowed. The platform where the sea life had lurked was empty except for some sparkling pieces of orange glass.

Theo slowly knelt by the broken glass. His fingers pushed small shards of shattered orange glass around the cement. I worried he'd cut himself. I doubted he'd feel it if he did. His jaw was clenched, his eyes hard and shining, staring at the glass as if he could will it to become whole.

He picked up a shard.

"Careless…clumsy…*assholes*," he seethed, his chest heaving. He turned to me, the tears standing out in his eyes, the pain floating on the surface. "Didn't they know? This is it. This is all that's left of Jonah. If it breaks, it can't be fixed. It can't be replaced. Didn't they *know* that?"

I shook my head.

His voice cracked open. "There *isn't* any more." His face crumpled and he hunched down over his knees. "He'll never make any more. It can't be replaced. He's not here to fix it. He's not *here*. He's…"

He sank his face into his hands. A sob ripped out of him. Then another. I put my arms around his shuddering shoulders as Theo finally let it all go. All the pain he'd kept buried for so long. He buried his face against my neck, and I pulled him to me, kissed his hair, his cheek, his temple. I didn't say a word. I held onto him, same as he'd held onto me when I was drunk and drowning.

"Jesus." He turned away from me to wipe his eyes on his sleeve. He heaved several deep, shaking breaths, then turned his gaze back to the empty gallery.

"It'll be at Carnegie," he said, his voice hoarse. "It'll be there forever."

"It will," I whispered, wiping the tears from his cheeks. "And we can go see it any time."

Theo nodded. He took one more deep breath in and exhaled. "I love you."

It was so simple it almost went straight past me.

I love you.

I looked at him, leaning back a little, stunned. He turned his head to me, his eyes still wet and red-rimmed. "I love you. I'm done keeping it inside. I'm done being afraid to speak what I feel because what I feel for you…" His hands came up to my head, around my cheek and under my hair. His handsome face was no longer chiseled in stone, but open and naked and raw. "I love you. I'm in love with you and I will be for the rest of my life."

Deep in my heart, the answering echo, rising to the surface after being denied so long. Pushed down and ignored out of my own guilt. Dismissed out of worry what others would think. Buried because of my own fear of putting my heart in another's hands, stepping back up to the table and going all in one more time, risking everything.

What if I lose?

I looked at the man next to me and knew that no matter what happened, I'd already won.

"I love you too," I whispered. "I love you, Teddy. I do. I'm in love with you."

His face crumbled even more, and he struggled to take in a breath. "God, I wanted to hear that for so long," he said, pulling my forehead to his. "I've loved you for so long."

"I'll tell you every day of our lives," I said against his mouth. "I'll say it a million times. I love you. I'm so in love…"

My tears were streaming over his fingers now, gathering in the upturned corners of my mouth. We kissed then. Kneeling in the wreck of the stripped gallery amidst shattered glass, we kissed to seal our words, and then rose from the floor to go.

"*Where there is ruin, there is hope for treasure,*" Theo said, staring with wet eyes at the empty space a final time. He looked down at me. "Something Dena told me."

He engulfed my hand in his, his lips brushed mine. "Kace," he whispered. "My treasure."

PART 3

All in (n) (poker): 1. when a player has moved all of their chips into the pot; an all-or-nothing bet.

CHAPTER 40

Theo

Gloria Ng's nail salon was empty. A *FOR LEASE* sign hung askew in the window, the name and number of a realtor's office beneath it.

I cupped my hands to the glass, peering inside. Nothing but vinyl flooring and drywall. Exposed pipes where the pedicure tubs had been. Six hundred square feet sharing an interior wall with Vegas Ink.

I could knock that wall down myself.

A slow grin spread over my face, tempered by a pang of ball-clenching fear. This was it. The solution to my problem of Vegas's market being too shitty and VI being too small.

But if I bought both… If I renovated and redecorated…

"Fuck me," I muttered.

Nah, I'm good, thanks, Jonah answered.

A small laugh erupted out of me. It morphed into an all-out gut-buster and I leaned against the window, laughing like an idiot. Mostly because I could.

In the two weeks since the installation was moved out of Vegas, I could finally think of my brother without a sledgehammer of pain whacking me in the chest. It still hurt. It would always hurt. But I'd purged the poisonous grief and what remained was cleaner. The pain had a peace in it. I could *think* about Jonah now. I had all of him back—his voice, his laugh, his stupid jokes and the way he'd turned globs of colorless glass into fucking masterpieces.

Jonah gave me the money to build a future. He gave me his blessing to build it with Kacey. He took the shapeless glass of my life and blew potential into it. Hope. Now it was my turn to finish the job.

Kacey was selling her house in New Orleans, saying goodbye to friends and coming back to Vegas to be with me. The Sony contract was signed. She'd make more money in a month than I'd see in a year. Money wasn't the point. I couldn't slack off. I had to do right by her by doing right by me.

God, Jonah…This is it, right? Am I standing right in front of it, peering in?

In my mind's eyes, Jonah perfectly raised one eyebrow—his signature move.

Signs point to yes.

Before I could talk myself out of it, I went into Gus's office and offered to relieve him of his job. An hour later, we emerged shaking hands, Gus with visions of Belize's beaches dancing in his eyes. He introduced me to the crew as the de facto owner of Vegas Ink.

The others stared for a minute, then Edgar burst out laughing. "Yeah, right. Good one, boss."

Vivian, standing closer, peered at both of us. "No, they're serious. You're serious? Oh my God." She threw her arms around me. "For real? When? How?" She stopped jumping up and down and smoothed down my shirt. "Sorry, *boss*. I mean, you are my boss now, right? I still work here?"

"You still work here, Viv. I'd be crazy to lose any of you."

I met Zelda's eye. She gave me a nod, her smile cool and knowing.

Edgar slapped my back and said, "Congrats, boss man. You pulled a fast one on us. How long has this been in the works?"

"Roughly an hour," I said. "I'm going to buy the vacant place next door, knock down a few walls and renovate. We can do a big re-opening to get new business and get old clients excited about the new look."

"Genius," Vivian said. "We gotta celebrate. I'm going out for champagne. That cool, Gus?"

He held up his hands. "Hell, I'll buy."

"Boss man," Zelda said, moving to stand next to me. We both leaned against Viv's desk, both crossed our arms. "How's that sound?"

"Doesn't suck."

She quirked a smile. "Good for you. I'm glad I'm not a betting gal. I'd have put money on you moving to New Orleans."

"Kacey's moving here. She's readying her house to sell."

"Smart girl," Zelda said. "You deserve it, you know. Her. This place. All of it. You worked your ass off long enough."

"And what about you? You staying? I'll make you Employee of the Month for texting Kacey for me that night at dinner."

Zelda tucked a lock of her long black hair behind her ear. "Tempting, but no. I'm heading to New York City next week."

"Next week?"

"Already told Gus. I'd have given you better notice if I'd known you were such a business tycoon."

"Well, shit, Zelda. I'd rather not start my business without one of the best artists in the chairs."

She rolled her eyes. "Please. Your *Inked* spread is going to make you famous. You need a huge re-opening though." She tapped her fingers to her chin, brow furrowed. "If only you could get a certain singer/songwriter currently tearing up the indie charts right now to do a show for your grand opening…"

"If only," I said. I nudged her elbow. "I'm going to miss you, Z."

"Yeah, yeah," Zelda said, suddenly pushing off the desk toward her station. "Don't go soft on me, Fletcher. Goodbyes are hard enough."

CHAPTER 41

Kacey

"Boxes, as far as the eye can see," I muttered, standing in the middle of my living room. I puffed a lock of hair that had fallen out of my ponytail. "I hate moving."

But I loved whom I was moving *to*.

After only a week on the market, I'd sold my house for $93,000 dollars to a young woman who worked in the hospitality industry. Teddy's father had been right—even with the minimal renovations I'd done, I'd accrued some serious equity in only a few months.

I smiled and went to my kitchen. I wrinkled my nose as it seemed like my entire kitchen had been drenched in orange juice. In the bowl on the counter was one lone orange that had gone bad—a fuzzy bruise of green and purple on its side.

"Just you making all this stink?"

I chucked the orange in the trash and checked my calendar, taped to the fridge. Only four days left before I flew back to Las Vegas for good. Four days until I had to say goodbye to Yvonne.

That's going to hurt.

Four days and then Theo and I could begin to build life together. I smiled at that and at the gold star marked on another day. Much to the joy and celebration of the Olsens, I signed the Sony contract without a tour addendum. A little thrill—an echo of the first big thrill—shot down my spine to think about it. I was on the brink of having the career I'd always envisioned, without a grueling tour to keep me on the road, or alcohol to make it bearable.

I cocked my head at the calendar, a niggling feeling telling me something was missing. I double-checked what I'd written there.

A reminder to take cable and power services out of my name. The day we'd probably going to close escrow. A going away party with friends at Le Chacal. Nothing out of the ordinary.

Where are my little red X's?

Since I was a teenager, I'd kept track of my period by marking a calendar with red pen. Now, I tore the calendar off the fridge and flipped it back a page. I gaped at what I saw. The last red X was almost a month and a half ago.

I felt the color drain from my face. I'd been so busy and so much had happened I'd completely lost track.

"Oh, shit."

I can smell everything. How long had that been happening?

"Oh. Shit."

I woke up feeling nauseated yesterday but chalked it up to nerves from all these Big Somethings in my life happening one after the other.

This might be a Big Something. The biggest Big Something of all.

I swiveled around and went to the kitchen window and threw it open so hard it slammed in its frame.

"Yvonne!"

"Yeah, honey?"

"I'm late."

"For what?"

"Yvonne," I said, gripping the ledge. "I'm *late*."

My friend appeared at her window like a target at a shooting range. "How late is late?"

"A lot. Three weeks."

"Oh, shit."

I nodded vaguely. "My thoughts exactly."

An hour later, I brought three different brands of pregnancy tests into the bathroom, took all three, and then sat on the couch clutching Yvonne's hands for ten agonizing minutes. The timer I'd set on my phone went off and we both jumped.

"Okay here I go."

I started to get up. Sat back down.

"Almost made it," Yvonne observed.

I gnawed my lower lip. "I'm scared."

"That it might be positive, honey?"

"Yes. And no." I clutched her hands tighter. "I don't know. I hope it's negative, because—*shit*, am I ready? I'm not ready. I don't think I'm ready. I can't even remember to take a damn pill every morning. But then I imagined it's a negative…" I shook my head. "That makes me a little bit sad. Or maybe... a lot sad, actually." I looked up at her. "But how can it be negative? I'm *three weeks late*."

"Breathe, baby, breathe," Yvonne said. "You want me to look?"

I looked up at her. "Would you?"

"I'm a nurse, honey. I give news like this all the time. I'll be extremely professional no matter the results. Okay?"

I nodded and gnawed my thumb as Yvonne went into the bathroom. She came back out holding the three pregnancy tests, their results windows obscured under her hand. Her face was unreadable as stone.

She stood over me. "Kacey Dawson..."

"Oh, god, what...?"

"You..."

Yvonne dropped one test in my lap.

"Are..."

She dropped another.

"Pregnant."

She dropped the last one and then let out a loud cry and began jumping up and down. "Oh my god, girl, you're pregnant!"

"Yvonne," I half cried, half laughed, pregnancy tests rolling around my lap. "That's professional? I *peed* on these."

She crowded onto the couch next to me and we examined the tests: one had a plus sign, the other had two lines, and one flat-out said 'pregnant' on the screen.

"Oh my god." I grabbed at my friend to keep from sliding off the couch from the bizarre concoction of utter fear and complete euphoria that stole my strength. "I'm going to have a baby. I'm going to have Teddy's baby."

"You sure are, sweetheart. How do you think he's going to react?" She made a stern face, laughter in her eyes. "If he's not overjoyed, I can reintroduce him to my baseball bat."

"I don't know, but I think...I think he's going to be exactly that. Overjoyed."

Yvonne gave me a hug. "I think so too."

She and I hugged a little more, cried a little more, and after she went home, I curled up on the couch, running my hand in a circle over my stomach. I thought about Teddy and I, and how our universe just got a little bit bigger.

I said goodbye to everyone two days later. Grant and Phoebe, Big E and Yvonne took me to the airport.

"I feel like Dorothy going back to Oz," I said, pulling the Olsens in close.

"You can't get rid of us that easily," Grant said, his eyes a little misty.

"Yeah, you're contractually bonded to us," Phoebe said, hugging me so tight my nose was squashed against her bony shoulder. "For life. *For life.*"

"God, you make it sound like a prison sentence," Grant muttered at her.

I laughed and fell into Big E's warm embrace. "Thank you," I whispered against his shirt. "I know your manly man pride can't hear that but I'm saying it anyway. None of this…*none* of it would have happened if not for you. No recording contract, no friends, no Teddy…Hell, I might not have made it."

"You'd have made it," Big E said. "You're tougher than you think. Hey." He tipped my chin. "Don't be a stranger now. You or Theo."

I nodded, my tears threatening.

Yvonne.

My tears broke. She held her arms open and I moved in, held her tight, whispering, "I'm going to miss you most of all."

She laughed and rocked me side to side. "Oh, baby. Me too. But I'd move halfway across the country for your Teddy too. Sex on a *stick*."

We laughed, and I knew that's what Yvonne planned all along, to make the goodbye bearable.

"What am I going to do without you?" I said, wiping my nose.

"You take care of that baby," she said. She sniffed and pulled away. "Go on, now, before I change my mind about letting you leave."

ALL IN

I stepped off the plane, and headed out onto the concourse, wishing Theo could've met me at the gate. I used the extra time to rehearse the little speech I'd spent the entire flight preparing, going over and over it in my head, until it was a perfect.

I spotted Theo waiting for me at baggage claim, looking gorgeous in a deep blue henley and jeans. My pulse thundered in my ears.

"Hey, babe," he said, his smile wide and easy. He wrapped me tight in his arms and gave me a deep kiss. "God, I can't believe it. You're here for good. That was our last back and forth flight. How was it?"

"I'm pregnant."

Theo stared.

"Oh, shit," I said. "I had a speech but I saw you and…It's too fast, isn't it? It's too fast and maybe the wrong time, right? I mean, you just bought an entire business, and I'm supposed be working on a new album *for Sony,* for crying out loud, and holy shit, this comes along…"

Theo blinked and looked down at me. "You're pregnant?"

"I am. It's crazy, right? Or…maybe not?" I gnawed my lip, trying to read his face. "Maybe it's…really wonderful?"

He didn't seem to have heard me past my suave opener.

"You're pregnant," he stated, and I saw the words sink in, and spread over his face like a sunrise. His smile…oh god, I'd never seen anything more beautiful.

"You're really…? You're going to have a baby? I'm…going to have a baby?"

I wiped a tear with the cuff of my sweater. "Yeah, honey. We are."

Any doubts about how he might react were tossed to the wind. I let out a little cry as Theo enveloped me in his strong embrace, lifted me, spun me around, and when he kissed me the salt tears I tasted weren't mine.

I insisted that we see his parents immediately. It didn't feel right to spend one more second together and not explain to Beverly about us.

"I'm nervous," I said as we drove to the house. "I think she's afraid her memories of Jonah and I together don't mean what she thought they did. And we're having a baby. She's going to feel ambushed."

Theo nodded, preoccupied with his own thoughts.

I took his hand, pried it off the steering wheel. "Your dad's going to be proud of you. How can he not?"

"He'll find a way."

"You're not thinking about the baby? Maybe that it's too soon or…interfering with your plans…?"

Theo stared at me aghast. "God, Kace, no. I'm so happy that you are…that we are." We'd come to a red light and he turned in his seat. "I love you."

"I love you too, but—"

"No, I mean I love you and that's it. I love you. I love you however you are. No strings or conditions. I love you, and that's it. Okay?"

I bit back a smile. "Okay."

Twilight had just begun to fall when we arrived. Beverly opened the door, a careful, guarded look on her face.

"Hey, Ma," Theo said.

"Theo, dear." She opened the door wider and we stepped inside. "Would you care for something to drink?" she asked, moving through the living room toward the kitchen. "Tea, Kacey? I have chamomile."

"No, thank you."

We took a seat on the couch, Beverly sat in her overstuffed recliner, her hands in her lap.

"Where's Dad?" Theo asked.

Beverly sighed. "He's at the office."

Theo's jaw stiffened. "I told him to meet us here. That we wanted to talk to both of you."

"I know, dear. He heard from someone at the planning commission downtown what you had done. About buying the two shops?"

Theo stood up. "He heard from… He can't even hear it from me?"

"Teddy, sit down," I said softly, even though my heart broke for him. I knew that pain that twisted his features. The futility of it.

"I'm sorry, dear," Beverly said. "He's so stuck in his ways. He thinks you're a tremendous artist, I know he does but—"

"But he hates tattoos and so that's it. My entire life, my career, my fucking *dream* is just something he can walk away from."

Theo sat and covered his eyes with one hand, sucked in a steadying breath. "Sorry, Ma. I shouldn't take it out on you." He looked to me. "You tell her. I have to get outside. Take a walk."

I rose to my feet and held him, kissed him. "Come back soon. Love you."

"Love you too." He turned and walked out, slamming the door behind him. The house rattled from the force. Then Beverly and I sat in the silence that followed.

"You're in love," she said finally. "Is that what you came to tell me?"

I nodded. "Yes."

"I see." She wore a sad, perplexed smiled. "I see, but I don't understand."

"I hate that you feel this way."

"What way is that? I wish you'd tell me because I don't know what to feel. I don't know what's real."

"What do you mean?"

"I'm confused. Instead of feeling happy for you, or him, I just wonder, *How can this be?"* Her eyes filled and her lips pressed together for a moment, trying to remain in control. "My best, happiest memories, the ones that keep me from drowning, are the ones when you made Jonah happy. How you loved him. How he was your everything. Was that true? Or am I a silly old lady clinging to nothing?"

"God, Beverly, I loved Jonah with all I had. It was real. Every moment was real."

"But now you feel the same for Theo?" She shook her head. "I don't see how that's possible. I feel dirty for asking this, but I need to know, Kacey. If Jonah were to walk through that door right now, what would you do?"

"I can't answer that, Beverly," I said softly. "Because Jonah can't walk through that door."

Beverly wilted in her chair, staring at me with wide, frightened eyes. "I know. I *know* that but…"

"But you don't feel it yet," I said softly. "I know. I was the same. For months after Jonah died, I cried for him to come back. I pleaded, and screamed, and prayed, and hoped, and nearly drank myself to death, *begging* for him to come back. I wanted so badly to believe, on some level, it was possible because the alternative was too horrible to contemplate. I jumped at knocks on my door, I flinched when my phone rang. I searched faces in the crowd when I walked, and tricked myself into thinking, sometimes, Jonah was standing right beside me. All I had to do was turn my head and look."

Beverly nodded "I do that too. Every day. But he's never there."

"No," I said. "He's not. The doors never opened, the phone never rang with him on the other end. Eventually, I stopped expecting it. It wasn't a switch that flipped. It was a slow, agonizing journey to the moment I realized he was never coming back. Accepted it. And once I accepted he was gone, I was free. Not free of the love we had. I'll carry that with me forever. I'll love him forever. But free to start again. A new chapter."

"With Theo," she said. "How…?"

"I don't know," I said. "Slowly. Over fifteen hundred miles and a thousand phone calls. Neither expected it. Neither pursued it. I had so many dark days when I thought I'd never love again. But Jonah told me I would. And I have. I just never thought it would be Teddy." I smiled. "Only now, I think it couldn't have been anyone but him."

I pushed off the couch, and knelt in front of her, took her shaking hands in mine.

"I'm the luckiest woman in the world to have known the love of two extraordinary men. And I hope Theo's happiness can bring you the same joy as Jonah's did. He's your son too. And I love him. It's different, but then again, I'm different for knowing Jonah. He showed me what it meant to love someone with your entire being."

Beverly raised her head. "And you love Theo."

"I do," I said. "I'm completely and utterly in love with Theo. He loves me. And…" I swallowed hard. "We're going to have a baby."

She sat back in the chair, staring.

"We didn't plan for that either, but it happened. We're both so happy about it and I hope…" Tears welled in my eyes and spilled over. "I hope you can be too."

Beverly stared a moment more then clapped her hands to her chest, and began to laugh. Big shaking laughs with tears streaming down her cheeks. She wagged her finger at me, then leaned forward and cupped my face in her hand.

"Oh, sweetheart. Sweet girl, yes, of course I'm happy. It's the most wonderful thing I've ever heard."

ALL IN

She gathered me to her and held me tight, crying softly. Stroking my hair in a motherly caress I hadn't felt in years.

A small hope caught flame and flickered in my heart.

My mom might think so too.

CHAPTER 42

Theo

Dena texted me: **I haven't had a pastrami on rye from Sully's in ages. Meet me there at noon?**

I nudged Kacey who was still bundled up in my bed, sleeping.

"Dena wants to meet a Sully's for lunch."

"Sully's?"

"It's a pool hall we used to hang out at in college. They have killer sandwiches. Their pastrami on rye—"

"Stop. I can't even," Kacey said. "I'm so tired for no reason and if you say 'pastrami' one more time I'm going to hurl. But you go. Enjoy."

I noticed a little smile over lips as I bent to kiss her goodbye.

It was a sleepy Sunday afternoon and the pool hall was almost empty. A jukebox played Johnny Cash while half a dozen patrons nursed beers at the bar or shot pool. I found an empty table and took a few shots while waiting for Dena.

I lined up a shot, hunched over, moving the stick between my fingers when someone took hold of it behind me.

"The hell…?"

I turned around.

"I got a text from Dena," Oscar said, eyeing me darkly. "Said she was craving a pastrami sandwich?"

"I got the same text," I said. "Your wife's a mastermind."

Oscar made a sound that might've been a laugh. "You rack, I'll break?"

"Sure."

We played a game of eight-ball, not saying a word but to call our shots, settling in to being around each other again after weeks of silence.

"Haven't been here in awhile," Oscar said toward the end of the game. He twisted a blue cube of chalk over the tip of his cue stick. "Since UNLV, right? Before Jonah went to Carnegie."

"Sounds right," I said. "Beer?"

"Why not?"

I signaled the bartender for two while Oscar bent over the table, lined up his shot, his cue sliding back and forth in the cleft of his thumb. He lanced the stick forward and sunk the yellow two with a powerful crack.

"Nice shot," I said.

"You remember that one night?" Oscar said, lining up his next shot. "Jonah hit the cue ball so hard on his eight ball shot, it jumped to the next table and sank *their* eight?" He chuckled. "That was fucking epic."

"Then he said it counted, because he called it," I said, laughing.

"Yeah, he did." Oscar eyed his next shot, then his eyes flickered to me. He backed off the table with a sigh. "I'm sorry, man. All that shit I said to you. It was uncalled for."

I felt a knot of tension ease in my gut. "It's cool. I know why you said it."

"For Jonah," he said. "I didn't know Kacey all that well, except to see her with him. In my mind…she was it. She was there for him. I know it's unfair to her—and you—but he was so fucking happy, you know." Oscar looked at me. "But now *you're* so fucking happy." He shot me his signature smile. "It's almost embarrassing."

"That so?"

"I'd be an asshole to stay pissed, right?"

"The biggest."

Oscar snorted a laugh and came around the table. We half-hugged, half-clapped each other on the back.

"I love you, man," Oscar said.

"You too," I said, taking a seat at one of the small round tables against the wall.

He went back the table, eyed the eight ball near the right corner pocket. The white cue was in the middle of the table, a clear, easy shot. "I'm going to sink this little bastard for the win."

"So, we're good, man?" I asked.

Oscar leaned over the table, the cue resting on the bridge of his hand. "Yeah, we're good."

He started to take his shot.

"You sure about that?" I said loudly.

He shot me a look. "I said I was. You don't believe me?"

"I believe you."

"Then shut up and let me take this shot."

He drew back the cue stick and just as he let it fly, I said, "Kacey's pregnant."

The stick scraped along the felt and knocked the cue ball sideways, straight into the side pocket.

"Scratch," I said, and sipped my beer to hide my smile. "That's game."

Oscar's eyes widened in shock, then, to my utter amazement, they began to shine with tears.

"Whoa, hey, don't get all soft on me," I said, tossing a cocktail napkin at him.

"You bastard," he said, wiping his eyes, and then laughing. "You want to know if I'm sure? Now *I* know I'm sure. I'm so fucking happy for you, I'm *crying*."

I had to blink my damn eyes to keep from doing the same. "Thanks, man."

He sank into the chair across from me at the table. "How far along is she?"

"Not very. Six weeks, maybe. She has an appointment with a doc in a few days."

Oscar shook his head, whistled low through his teeth. "Do your parents know?"

"Mom's happy. She wasn't thrilled about Kacey and I either, but I think this news helped her accept we're for real."

"What about your dad?"

I shrugged. "Different spin on his usual bullshit. I bought a new business in a shit market and now I've got a kid on the way to support. A responsibility my poor career choices are going to fuck up and I won't be able to support my family." I shook my head. "Holy shit, my family."

Oscar laughed. "Shit just got real."

"It keeps getting realer by the minute."

"You can't worry what your dad thinks. He might come around, he might not. He might need to hold his grandkid in his arms for a kick in the ass."

"Maybe."

"Oh my Christ, the look on your face," Oscar said, shaking his head. "Pitiful. Damn, man, I've never seen you like this. You are so incredibly, amazingly, one hundred percent whipped."

"I saw how whipped you are over Dena and I got jealous."

Oscar tossed back his head, laughing. He clinked his beer bottle to mine. "Welcome to the club."

I came back to my place thinking that the smile on my face must be permanent. I turned the key in the lock, and the smile widened knowing that Kacey was inside.

She sat on the couch, her back to me, though I saw her cell phone sitting limp in her hand.

"Hey, babe," I said, moving to sit beside her. "You okay?"

"Not really," she said, her voice thick with tears.

"Hey." Gently, I turned her to face me, brushed the hair from her eyes. "What is it?"

"I want to see my parents."

"Okay," I said slowly.

"I wasn't going to talk to them ever again. I was done. But now that we're going to have a baby, I feel like it's one more chance to try. To have me in their life. And you. And their grandchild."

She leaned into me and I wrapped my arm around her. "You sure?" I asked.

"No. Part of me thinks it's the worst idea in the world. But the other half can't imagine *not* telling them. Going years and years with them never knowing they're grandparents?" She shook her head. "It doesn't seem right."

They probably wouldn't give a shit about that either.

She sniffed and sat up, her luminous eyes full of hope and fear in equal parts. "Your mom was so wonderful about it. She treated me like I was her own daughter, and I want that from my own mom and dad. I have to do this. The final time. If they still don't want me with a grandchild on the way, then that's it." She exhaled heavily, wilting. "Am I insane risking this again?"

I didn't know how to answer. She wasn't insane, but the last thing

I wanted was for her to be hurt. I wanted to protect her from another rejection by her asshole of a father.

But she's trying, I thought, holding her tight. *She's stepping up one more time, laying her chips on the table. Just like she did with me after Jonah.*

I wiped her tears with the back of my fingers. "It's fucking brave. If they still turn their backs then it's their loss and fuck them forever."

Kacey sniffled and laughed a little. "Promise you won't punch my dad out if he turns out to be a dick."

"I'll do my best."

"I love you, Teddy," she murmured against my chest. "I'll be proud to introduce you to them. I love this baby and this life we're making. I want my parents to be a part of it."

"Me too, Kace," I said, kissing the top of her head. "More than anything, I want that for you."

CHAPTER 43

Theo

We flew to San Diego the following afternoon, rented a car and drove out to Mission Hills where the Dawsons lived.

"That one," she said, releasing the death grip on my hand to point to a blue two-story with white trim. A green Subaru was parked in the drive.

"Déjà vu," Kacey murmured. "This is what Jonah and I did when we came here. We staked out the place from our rental car, watched them leave the house to go out."

"You didn't stop them?"

She shook her head, her eyes on the house. "They looked too happy. I didn't want to ruin it. We stayed in the car and they drove away."

"They never met him," I said.

She shook her head, smiling sadly. "I regretted that," she said. "Now I think it makes sense. I think maybe Jonah and I didn't get of the car that day because he and I…we had a beautiful little pocket of time, a handful of months. And that's all. But you, Teddy. You're the man I'm going to introduce to my parents. You're my forever. That's why we're going to get out of the car today."

I held her gaze a moment, then surged across the seat to hold her face and kiss her.

"I love how brave you are," I whispered against her lips.

"Brave? Look at this." She held up her shaking hands.

"Whenever you're ready. You tell me when."

I felt her body expand and contract in a deep sigh. "It's now or never."

We exited the car, but she got no further than shutting her door. "God," she whispered. "What if they don't accept me?"

My heart cracked a little at that. "Then it's their loss, baby.

Okay?"

She nodded and mustered a smile. We walked to the front door, Kacey holding tight to my hand. She reached out for the doorbell, squinched her eyes shut, and pushed. From inside, the bell rang, and she inched closer to me.

Footsteps, a lock turning, and then a woman in her mid-sixties opened the door. Brown hair, streaked with gray, touched her shoulders and cut across her forehead. Her lips held a polite answering-the-front-door smile for the space of one heartbeat before recognition dawned in her gray eyes.

And her smile fell off like a mask, leaving naked shock and even a twinge of fear. Not joy. Not surprise. Not love.

Damn you, I thought, my heart cracking again. Kacey's hand went slack in mine and I watched my brave girl force a smile through the pain.

"Hi, Mom."

CHAPTER 44

Kacey

I counted the seconds between my "Hi, Mom," and my mother's reply. I got to eight before she blinked as if coming out of a trance. Her hand clutched the buttons on her cardigan. I wanted both of her hands to reach for me and hold me like she did when I was a kid and my dad wasn't around to see. I wanted to fly at her and hug her and breathe her in.

"Cassie," she whispered. For a split second, her eyes filled and a shocked smile tugged at her lips. My hopes soared, and then she gave herself a little shake, composing herself. "What are you doing here?"

"What am I…?" I repeated dumbly, the hope draining out of me.

I'm your daughter. That's what I'm doing here.

I felt Theo's hand give mine a squeeze, and I felt more solid. More present.

Stay here.

"It's been a long time, Mom. I'm here to visit you and Dad. This is my boyfriend, Theo. Theo, this is Linda. My mom."

Mom's eyes darted to Theo beside me in his usual dark T-shirt and jeans. She took in his muscles, his tattoos, the unshaven stubble of his beard, and I saw her hand clench tighter on her sweater.

"Nice to meet you, Mrs. Dawson," Theo said, his tone flat and dry as the desert. He didn't extend his hand to shake, maybe guessing—correctly—my mother wouldn't take it.

"Can we come in?" I asked, hating that I had to ask.

Mom glanced over her shoulder and back. "Now? I don't know…"

I clenched my teeth together so hard I thought they'd shatter, inhaled through my nose to calm myself, to suck courage and steadiness out of the salty air.

"Mom," I said, "I haven't seen you or Daddy in almost seven

years. You stopped returning my calls almost a year ago. I need to see you. You're my parents. And I'm your daughter. I am *your…child.*"

My voice started to crack, and I took a steadying breath. My mom had been doing everything my dad told her to for twenty-four years. Now she was going to listen to me.

"You're going to let me in and we're going to talk for a little bit. You and me and Theo and Daddy. Right now."

My mom stared at me for a moment more, and then, with jerky, nervous movements, opened the door wider and stepped aside to let us in.

Theo gave my hand another squeeze and I glanced up to see pride in his eyes. I felt bolstered by that one look. It gave me the courage to step inside my childhood home for the first time in seven years.

The memories assaulted me from all fronts, carried on currents of smells and sounds. Warm cinnamon, my father's cologne, the little baskets of potpourri my mother kept in every room. The furniture was unchanged. The wallpaper in the front entry was the same white with tiny blue flowers, and I could still see the pencil marks where my mom measured my height as I grew. Late afternoon sunlight streamed in from the large bay window in the dining room to slant across the old walnut dining table.

"I used to do homework there," I murmured. "I was a good student, wasn't I, Mom?"

"Yes, you were," she said in her flighty voice, leading us into the living room. "All A's."

We shared a look and I swear I saw a little crack in whatever armor she thought she needed to wear against me.

"Is Daddy here?" I asked, my throat going dry.

"He's in the den," she said, and glanced at Theo. "Cassie, your—"

"It's Kacey, Mom," I said. "I haven't been Cassie since I was sixteen years old."

She bobbed her head. "Kacey. Your father—"

His voice called behind me. "Who's here?"

I took shelter against Theo's strong body as my heart plummeted to my knees.

Daddy…

Tears sprung to my eyes as I turned around. My father looked much the same as he had when Jonah and I had spied him from across the street. Tall, a little stooped, with a protruding belly on a thin frame and a full head of silver hair. His eyes were the same blue as mine. They fixed on me, then Theo, widening in shock for only a moment. Jim Dawson was never one to get caught off guard. His put his expression in neutral and crossed his arms over his button down shirt.

"Hi, Daddy," I said, my voice a breathy flutter. "It's good to see you."

"Sure," he said, as if I'd asked a question. He turned his icy stare to Theo. "Who's this?"

Again, Theo didn't extend his hand, his stare hard. "Theo Fletcher," he said. "I'm Kacey's boyfriend." He made *boyfriend* sound like a warning.

I mustered my courage again. "Can we sit down, Daddy? There's something we'd like to tell both of you."

"You want money?" my father said. "Because I can tell you right now—"

"We don't want money," I said. "Please, Daddy. It's been seven years. Can we just sit and talk for a minute?"

My father pondered this and I searched his face for any sign of warmth or affection, regret or guilt. But if he felt anything at all besides cold disdain, he kept it locked tight.

"Fine," he said finally. "But it can't be long. I have work to do."

Like a hostess at the world's most awkward dinner party, my mother led us to the living room. My dad took the couch, sitting right in the middle, precluding anyone from sitting beside him. That left only two high-backed chairs for the remaining three of us.

"Oh," Mom said, glancing around, almost panicked. "I'll get a chair from the dining room…"

"I'll stand," Theo said, and took up a position behind my chair, arms crossed, like a sentry or bodyguard. My mother sat down, folding her hands tightly in her lap. My father sat leaning back, his hands resting on his thighs, his chin drawn back and mouth pulled down, waiting.

The moment unfurled before me. Probably my last chance for any hope of reconciliation. Behind me, Theo shifted, reminding me he was there, that he would always be there for me. I sucked in a breath.

"A lot has happened over these last years, since we last saw each other. And I'm not going to lie, I had some really rough times. Times when I needed you. Both of you."

My mother sat perfectly still but her eyes closed for a moment, as if pained.

But my father pursed his lips, seemed to harden further right before my eyes. "You should've thought about that before you broke the rules of the house," he said.

Theo's hand touched my back. I swallowed hard and said, "I think, Daddy, I've paid for that mistake a thousand times over."

Those weeks of being homeless after Chett ditched me came back. The months and years of scraping by with Lola. Then the blurry, alcohol haze of countless small shows we played with Rapid Confession, trying to get a leg up. Throwing all that in his face would get me nowhere. If we had a chance, it was this moment, right now.

"I've moved past all that," I said. "I learned to stand on my own two feet. I have a successful career as a musician. Not with a band, but on my own. And Theo…" I raised my hand and he slipped his into it. "Theo's a tattoo artist and owns his own business. We're going to live in Las Vegas. And we're starting a family."

My mother's head shot up and she gasped. "You're going to have a baby?"

Tears sprung to my eyes at the words. They suffused me with joy every time I heard them spoken aloud. Joy that could spill into this living room, flood this house and break down the walls. It could. It had to. How could there still be animosity or regret in the face of a child on the way?

"Yeah, Mom," I said. My hand tightened around Theo's. "We're going to have a baby, and that's why I'm here. I want… *We* want you to be a part of our lives. And this baby's life. This is your grandchild. I don't care about anything that's come before. I want to start over, okay? A new start as a family."

Tears filled my mother's eyes and she started to nod. Emotion rose up in my chest and throat as she leaned forward in her chair, her hand over her heart. Hope lighting her eyes in a way I'd never seen before.

"Oh, Cassie," she whispered.

Her words floated in the still air, like bubbles.

And my father popped them one by one.

"A musician and a tattooist," he said. "And you think these are good, steady careers by which to raise a child?"

"I'm signed with a label, Daddy," I said slowly, carefully, holding on to the happiness. "I'm not out playing little clubs for $50 a pop. Not anymore. And Teddy is an artist. He's been featured in—"

"The music industry is full of drugs," my father said with a wave of his hand. "And criminals get tattoos. That's a fact. You want to bring those kinds of elements around your child?"

"It's not like that—"

"You know what I see?" My father asked. "I see nothing's changed. Not one damn thing. You've been acting the rebel your whole life. Playing a rock star, fooling around with the same kinds of men."

"That's not true. Teddy is—"

"And now you come here, telling me you got knocked up by a tattooed deviant," he gestured to Theo, "and I'm supposed to be overjoyed about this?"

I reeled as if I'd been slapped. Theo made a low noise in his chest. The heat of his rising anger radiated in the fingers clenching mine. I took hold of it and for the first time in my life, I hit back.

"Apologize," I said in a low voice I hardly recognized.

My father blinked. "Are you speaking to me?"

"You better goddamn apologize," I said, my voice rising. "A *deviant?* He's twice the man you are. You're the deviant. You're a heartless son of a bitch who kicked a seventeen-year girl out of the house because you only see what you want to see. If things don't look right, if people don't look right, you get rid of them. But I'm still here, Dad. I'm right here. I'm *right...here.*"

My father stared a moment, then rose off the couch. "This *visit* is over."

I shot to my feet. "What is *wrong* with you?" I cried. "Why are you like this? What did I ever do to you?" I turned to my mother, crying now. "And you... Why are you just sitting there, Mom? Say something."

She quailed, her eyes darting between my father and me.

"*Say something,*" I cried. Theo move to stand behind me as I looked from one parent to the other.

"Tell me to leave again, Dad," I said. "Go ahead. You'll never see me again, I promise, but I want to hear you say it."

My father held my eyes for a moment and I stared back, unflinching.

Waiting.

Hoping...

Finally, he shook his head, muttered something under his breath and walked out.

I exhaled, staring at the empty space where he'd been.

"All right then," I said. My head swiveled numbly to my mother. "Goodbye, Mom," I said, my voice a whisper.

Calmly, with Theo's arm around me, I walked out of my childhood home for the last time.

CHAPTER 45

Theo

I made it as far as the front porch.

"Fuck this," I muttered, turning back around to push open the front door. Kacey's mother gave a little cry as I stormed past her down the last part of the house I saw Kacey's bastard of a father walk down. I spied him in a chair in what looked like a den. I shoved the door open so hard, it slammed against the wall and bounced back.

Kacey's father sprang out of his chair. "I'll call the police."

"I bet you would," I said. My blood pounded in my ears and adrenaline coursed through my veins like liquid fire. "You would call the cops on your own daughter."

Her father shook his head, as if I were telling him a story he'd heard a hundred times before. "Young man, get out of my house. I don't have the time or inclination for this nonsense."

"Nonsense," I said. "Your only daughter's happiness is nonsense to you." I shook my head. "You have no idea what you're doing. What you're throwing away. And the truly insane part is she *loves you*. She's here. She's trying and you don't give a shit."

Kacey's father stared back, unflinching. "Are you done?"

"No, I'm not," I said. "I'm going to marry her. She'll have a wedding you won't see. Someone else is going to walk her down the aisle because you've got your head shoved too far up your ass to do it yourself. We're going to have a child you'll never meet, and we'll have a life you'll never be a part of because you *chose* not to.

"But fuck it. She doesn't need you. She didn't come here to beg for your shitty kind of love. I'll take care of her. You don't have to do a goddamn thing, not that you ever did. I'll love her enough. I'll love her enough she'll never want for it. I'll spend my entire life loving her and making her happy. And she *will* be happy. Maybe she has to live with the fact you're a cold-blooded son of a bitch, but at least her conscience is clear. Can't say the same for you."

I spun around and nearly bumped into Kacey's mother, her face stricken, her hands at her throat. I wanted to spit fire at her too, but she looked like she would fall over at the slightest push. I shook my head, disgusted at her silence, and strode out.

Kacey was waiting for me on the front stoop.

"I've never heard anyone tell my dad he has his head shoved up his ass before."

I stopped short.

"The den window leads off the side of the house," she said. "I heard everything. But you kept your promise and didn't punch him in the face."

"Barely." I helped her to her feet. "I'm sorry, Kace. It probably won't do any good but I had to tell him."

"Maybe not, but it was everything I needed to hear, or else I was going to lose it, right here on the porch." She ringed her arms around my neck. "Everything I needed to hear."

Oh shit.

She searched my eyes a minute, then tucked her head under my chin as she'd done when we'd danced at Oscar and Dena's wedding. "Are you proposing to me, Teddy?"

My old instincts rose in me, warning me to shut the hell up, to mutter away how I felt. Instead, I told her the truth.

"Not here, not after that. But one day…I will. Because I want nothing more on this fucking earth than for you to be my wife."

"You want to marry me." She sighed, and I felt the tension melt out of her shoulders.

"I want to marry you," I whispered against her head.

"But this isn't a proposal," she said against my chest.

"Definitely not."

"Then I'm not saying yes." She raised her head to look at me, the blue of her eyes shining like the purest glass. "Definitely not…" She brushed her lips to mine. "…Saying yes."

We walked down to the curb, and I opened the passenger door of the rental car for her. As I shut it and turned, my eye caught Kacey's mom standing at the front window. She raised her hand as if to wave, but only rested her fingers on the panes, her gaze trained on the car.

She caught me staring, withdrew her hand as if the glass burned her and let the curtain fall across the glass.

CHAPTER 46

Kacey

"So let me get this straight," Dena said. "We have a wedding *and* a baby shower to plan?"

"Teddy did not propose to me," I said, forking a bite of salad. We sat in the crowded mall, in the food court after an afternoon of house-hunting. "He told my dad he was going to marry me and I overheard."

Dena shot me a sly look. "His version of asking your dad for your hand in marriage."

I nodded, laughter welling up in me. "Exactly. Theo asked for my hand by telling my dad he had his head up his ass."

"He's such a traditionalist."

"Stop," I managed, waving my hands. "My cheeks hurt." I sucked in deep breaths and wiped my eyes. "Oh my God, it was so horrible it's actually funny."

Dena's eyes grew soft. "Are you okay?"

"Not really. But I can laugh about it, anyway." I gave my head a shake. "It's done. They're done with me, but at least I can say I tried."

"You did," Dena said. "You should be proud of yourself."

I felt the laughter bubble up again. "I'm more proud of Teddy for not burning their house down."

Dena bent over her plate as we both dissolved into laughter, the kind that keeps going long after you remember what you were laughing for.

"Oh shit," I said, wiping my eyes. "Okay, belly laughing made me hungry. Either that or my first real craving just hit." I nodded at the storefront at the end of the food court. "If I don't have a Cinnabon right this minute, someone's going to get hurt."

"I don't think that's a pregnancy craving, so much as a mall craving," Dena said. "They pipe the smell of their frosting into the air, I swear."

One sticky, gooey cinnamon roll later, Dena and I returned to her car in the outdoor parking lot.

"Do you want to—" My words choked off in a small cry as a blinding, razor-sharp pain exploded in my lower belly. A stab through my left side, stealing my breath and bending me over. The pain spread like wildfire around my middle, down my thigh, and around my back. I would have screamed at the agony, but I didn't have the air. The ground rose up toward me as I crumpled down, feeling as if I were being ripped in two. A flush of wet warmth spread between my legs, down my jeans.

Oh God, no…

"Kacey? Kacey!" Dena raced toward me. "What's happening?"

I sucked in air, "I can't… I can't…"

Dena and the entire world faded as my vision grayed and then went black.

CHAPTER 47

Theo

I locked up the shop and stared at the front door a moment.

It was mine. I'd been so busy finalizing the details, I hadn't the time to process it. I owned this place. It all belonged to me, including the responsibilities. If a pipe burst, it was my problem. If the electrical blew a fuse, it was my job to fix it. Inventory, advertising, employee payroll, taxes. All of it.

"Holy fucking shit."

This is what you signed up for, I thought and gave a little chuckle. I'd always wanted this, but I always thought I'd be doing it alone. Instead, I had an amazing woman standing beside me, believing in me.

And she's going to have a baby. I'm going to be a father.

"Holy goddamn fucking shit."

I stood there, smiling like a dope on the sidewalk in front of my own place. My entire life was opening up, expanding out. We had baby to prepare for. The grand opening of the shop, Kacey's music career. We were building a life together, and it was fucking better than anything I had ever hoped for myself.

I need to get a ring.

Even though my nervous hands nearly dropped the keys, my dopey grin wouldn't quit.

A ring. What kind of ring? What did she like? What could I afford? And how should I propose. I sucked at romance. Couldn't I just propose in bed? Was that allowed?

My cell rang as I climbed into the truck, Dena's number on the display. She was out with Kacey today, scoping potential houses for rent and hitting the mall for some shopping.

"What's up, Dena?"

"Theo, listen to me," she said. Her tone was calm but her voice trembled at the edges. "I'm at Sunrise Hospital with Kacey."

"What happened?" My blood felt like gasoline someone had set a match to. "What happened? Is she okay? Was there an accident?"

Oh my God, no. This isn't happening. Not again. I can't do this again…

"We were coming out of the parking lot and she doubled over in pain. I don't know what happened, they haven't told me any details yet. You need to come. Just get here quick but drive safely."

I dropped the phone on the passenger seat and threw the truck into drive. It took every bit of my will power to not floor it, to not run red lights, and it felt like I hit every goddamn one.

Hold on, baby, I'm coming.

I screeched into the parking lot in front of the Emergency Room, parked, and ran for the entrance, a refrain in my head pounding along with my steps.

Not again, not again, not again.

I hated Sunrise Hospital. I was here when Jonah was flown in from a hospital in Austin, Texas, after the frantic departure out of Venezuela. I lived here when he was waiting for a transplant. I camped out in his room for the early biopsies. I was on a first-name basis with the staff in the cardiac unit.

The last time I was here was when Jonah slipped away.

I stepped inside the sliding doors and pressed my hand to the wall, suddenly dizzy.

Not again. I can't do this again. I'm tapped out. I'm…

I forced myself to breathe and pushed off the wall. I strode to the front desk reception where a woman sat typing at a computer.

"Kacey Dawson?" I said, my voice sounding strangled. My goddamn heart was pounding my throat. "She came in a little while ago."

The nurse pecked lazily at her keyboard as if the fate of the fucking universe wasn't hanging in the balance.

"Theo."

I whirled around. Dena was there, her dark eyes bright with fear. I got to her in three long steps and she rose to meet me, taking my hands in hers.

"She's in emergency surgery."

I felt light-headed and cold all over. "What for? Is she all right? Tell me she's all right."

Dena shook her head. "I don't know how she is, but sit down, okay? I need you to sit down."

I sank into a chair. "What do you think it is?" I said, my eyes fixed on Dena's, glaring at her hard as if I could will her to say it was nothing, this was only a nightmare and I just needed to wake up.

Not again. God, please, not again. I can't lose her too. I can't…

"She was bleeding in the parking lot," Dena said. "The pain was enough to make her pass out. Theo, I don't…"

"She was bleeding?" I sat in silence for a moment, trying to process this.

Dena gripped my hand harder. "I don't know what to say, Theo. I'm sorry. I'm still…kind of in shock."

I sat back in the seat as if I were being pushed by a huge, heavy weight. It was crushing my chest, crushing the life out of me. Time ticked on and on, with no sign or word from anyone who could tell me what the hell was going on. My parents arrived with Oscar, and I left it to Dena to tell them what she told me. My mother came to sit next to me. She held my hand but I didn't hold back. I sat in the chair, staring at nothing.

If something's happened to her…If I lose her too…

If I lost Kacey, I was going to lay down on the floor and not get up. I was done. Nothing left. I'd finally reconciled losing my brother. I couldn't survive losing her too.

"Are you here for Kacey Dawson?" a voice asked.

A doctor stood there, his face grim. Here it was. The moment. In another ten seconds this man was going to tell me how the rest of my life was going to be.

Stand up for her, I told myself. *Stand up, one last time.*

I found my armor. The old suit of mental chain mail. It was like slipping on an old coat. I stood up and pushed forward on leaden legs, my heart thudding a dull, heavy pang in my chest.

"I'm here for her," I said.

The doctor was young man, early thirties maybe, with sharp blue eyes behind glasses and tanned skin.

A wimp, my tortured brain declared. *No way this guy is going to destroy me. I've faced down doctors before and their bad news. I can take this guy.*

A pathetic bravado but it was all I had to stem the tide of terror ripping through me.

"I'm Dr. Barron. I'm the head of Obstetrics and Gynecology. I was among the surgery team to assist Ms. Dawson."

"And?" I said. "How is she?"

"She's doing well. Stable now. She suffered a ruptured fallopian tube due to an ectopic pregnancy. Are you familiar with the term?"

My brain was hugging *doing well* and *stable* and screaming in relief. I nodded and sucked in a breath, tried to listen over the rush of blood in my ears.

"The embryo never made it to her uterus. It implanted in the left fallopian tube and began to grow. The tube then ruptured, which necessitated surgery to fix the rupture and stop the internal bleeding. She's not out of the woods quite yet, but her prognosis is promising and her vital signs are strong. I see nothing to indicate she wouldn't make a full recovery. We'll keep her here a few days, at minimum, to ensure there are no further complications."

The doctor's face took on a grave expression and he looked at me. "Are you her husband?"

"I'm the father," I said softly. "Was…the father."

"I'm very sorry," Dr. Barron said. "Ectopic never has a happy ending. It's almost unheard of for a fetus to survive tubal implantation. On the other hand, a ruptured fallopian tube is a serious medical emergency. At this time, I'm confident Kacey's going to be fine, and most likely she'll still be able to have children."

She's going to be fine. I clung to those words like a drowning man in a hurricane. My pulse slowed, anchored down now by the other half of his news.

"Can I see her?"

"She's being moved from post-surgery to recovery. I'll have a nurse tell you when she's ready, though she'll likely be quite groggy from the anesthesia."

I sat back down in the chair, my leg jumping.

"I'm so sorry, honey," my mother said.

I didn't look at her or anyone else. I kept my gaze fixed on the nurses' station, following them as they went about their business, inwardly commanding one of them to come and find me and tell me I could see Kacey. So I could tell her the baby was gone.

Goddammit, she's lost enough.

Finally, one nurse separated herself from the desk and came toward me.

"You can see her now."

ALL IN

My beautiful girl looked to be asleep as I pulled a chair beside her. Her face was pale against the white pillow. But her eyes fluttered when I took her hand. My chest was filled with a relief so profound, it made me dizzy, even as my heart broke for her. For both of us.

"Hey, baby," I said, my voice gruff.

Kacey turned her head to me, and smiled a funny, pained smile. I could see the anesthesia was still dragging at her, clouding the usual sharpness in her eyes.

"He says…she's fine," Kacey mumbled. "She's safe. We don't have to worry…"

"Shh," I said. She didn't know. I wouldn't tell her now. Not while she was half asleep. "Just rest," I whispered.

I held her hands as she drifted back into sleep. Staring at the white sheets, listening to the machine that monitored her heart, I felt the weight of it all—the relief, the grief, the guilt she had to suffer another loss. All of it pressed down on me, cracking my armor, stealing my air. I felt dizzy with the tempest of emotions that battered me like a hurricane. I had no Tarot card, no silly toy to shake and give me an answer. It was too much. So much easier to push it down, lock it all back up. I needed help. I needed my brother…

Kacey's head moved weakly against the pillow. "Jonah," she said.

I swallowed hard. "It's Theo, honey."

It's me. Not him. I'm here now. Don't you remember?

She opened her eyes. They were clearer now, and the corners of her mouth lifted in a funny little smile. Not doped-up but patient. "Jonah says she's safe."

Her hand reached up to touch my face.

"Jonah?" I whispered.

"She's safe with him, Teddy…"

The smile still on her face, she fell asleep again.

I fell asleep with my head on the sheet, and woke to Kacey whispering my name. She was fully awake now, the grief shining in her eyes. We held each other, her tears falling to stain the hospital sheets. I felt each one, each shake of her body against mine, like a knife cutting me, leaving scars I'd carry for the rest of my life.

"I'm sorry, Kace," I said. "I'm sorry you had to go through this. I'm so fucking sorry."

"Don't, Teddy. She was ours. Together. Don't try to take it all. Not this time." She clutched my hand in hers. "Stay here with me."

I nodded, let it go on a ragged sigh before it could bury me again. "Okay, baby. I will. I'm here."

She smiled then, the most heartbreaking sight I'd ever seen, as tears spilled down her cheeks. "We can't go back to how it was before. We have to say everything in our hearts." She turned her head to me on the pillow. "I was so happy for this baby. Thinking it could show you how much I love you. I was so afraid you'd never know how much. How deep it runs. Worried some small part of you would always doubt or wonder."

"No," I said. "I don't wonder. Or worry. I love you. You're my fucking world." I started to come undone again. "You're my entire world. My …"

"Universe," Kacey whispered, her fingers brushing my cheek softly. "You're my universe. I love you, Teddy…"

She sighed then, as if content, her eyes closed. "He was right about everything," she said. "We have so much love in us. No end to it."

She slept then, and I held her hand as my tears fell unheeded.

Love had no end. She was infinite. She was a universe, *my* universe, and I was hers.

Love had no boundaries, no rules, no favorites.

And no limits.

CHAPTER 48

Kacey

I stared at the hospital ceiling, my room quiet but for the heart monitor they attached me to. I had forced Theo to go the cafeteria and eat something. He'd left, reluctantly, and Oscar and Dena, Beverly and Henry had taken turns visiting me, offering me sweet words and their love, but was grateful when they left.

My lower abdomen felt heavy from the surgery; a deep ache that protested when I moved.

How can it feel so heavy when there's nothing there?

A pall of sadness hung over me, but it was nebulous and shifting. A shred of a memory from the fog of anesthesia kept trying to find me, but every time I grasped for it, it retreated back. I wanted to remember…because it was good. It brought me a peace, even the whisper of it I managed to catch.

Jonah…

My door opened and a nurse, Carla, peeked her head in. "Are you up for one more visitor? I was going to tell her you needed to rest but she said she's your mother."

I stared, my fingers curling around the sheets. "My…mother?"

Carla pushed open the door. I saw the flowers first, columns of blue bonnets nestled with baby's breath. *My favorite when I was a little girl.*

My mother stepped into the room, holding the bouquet. Her eyes met mine and whatever had happened between us, however many years of separation were all erased. I just wanted her.

I held my arms out to my mom, and she quickly set the flowers down while Carla softly closed the door behind her. My mom bent over me, holding me carefully.

"Oh, my sweet baby," she whispered against my hair. "I'm sorry. I'm so sorry"

I cried against her, inhaled her. She smelled of Shalimar perfume—her favorite. My arms remember what it was like to hold her and be held by her. I was thrust back in time to other moments when I'd been a scared little girl who'd wanted nothing more than to be comforted by her mother. And she'd been there…until she wasn't.

My mom pulled away, and sat in the chair Theo had been living in for the past day and a half. She dabbed her eyes with a tissue from the box beside my bed, and huffed a deep breath.

"I have so much to tell you, to explain," she said in her feathery voice. "You deserve the truth. I wanted to tell you, so badly, when you were there, in our house. I couldn't believe you were really there. The years…." She shook her head. "Once so much time has slipped by, it becomes easier and easier to let it. But when I saw you…I felt every second of those seven years, and it nearly crushed me to know you'd felt them too. I made plans that very day to fly here, to find you. I told your father…" She swallowed hard, her eyes remembering the moment she spoke of, "I told him enough was enough. That I was going with or without him."

Hope flared in my heart. "Is he…?"

She shook her head. "He's walled himself so deep and so thick, I don't know that he'll ever find his way out. "

I nodded. "What happened to us, Mom? What happened with Dad…?"

She cast her gaze down to her hands twisting in her lap. "He never wanted children. We agreed when we got married that we wouldn't. I was a shy young woman, and he was the first man to show me any interest or love. He was my only chance, my father kept telling me, and I knew he was right. But I loved Jim too. I did. I agreed we wouldn't have children but deep down I wanted one. I wanted you."

She shook her head. "But even after five empty years of marriage, I was too weak to say I'd changed my mind. I didn't sabotage him. He thought I did, but it just happened. You happened and I was so happy."

"He acts like he hates me," I whispered.

Tears spilled over her eyes. "He doesn't. I know he doesn't. He's afraid. He married a woman—me—whom he never had to fear would leave him, and he kept you at arm's length your whole life, so he wouldn't have to feel anything real. There is a piece of him that is broken, but I still have hope that it can be repaired. Some day. In the meanwhile…" She smiled at me, brushed the hair from my eyes. "You

have me. I'm sorry. I hope that's enough."
"Yeah, Mom," I whispered, reaching for her. "It's more than enough. It's everything."

CHAPTER 49

Kacey

They released me from the hospital a week later and for the next month, Theo threw himself into his work, remaking the old Vegas Ink into something entirely his. His vision. His legacy. The one he could keep after the other had been lost.

The ache of losing the baby hung between us, and I knew despite what Theo promised, he was retreating into his armor, rebuilding walls.

He loved me. I felt it in every beat of his heart against mine. It kept me warm when I slept wrapped in his arms. His grasp on me never loosened, not even in deep sleep. Always on guard. Always vigilant. He took on everything, shouldering the burden alone so those he loved didn't have to.

Early one morning, I woke and the first feeling that hit me—the one Yvonne said held the truth—settled on the still-bare skin of my shoulder. The space that belonged to Teddy, empty and waiting.

I woke him with a kiss. "The shop is done, isn't it?" I asked.

He nodded. "Finished yesterday."

"I'm going to sing at your reopening," I said. "Grant and Phoebe said the press release was getting a ton of buzz. You'll have a huge crowd."

"Of course," he said. "You're so talented, babe. They'll line up down the block to see you."

"And you," I said. "Your art is astonishing. It's you, your heart and soul." I traced the tense line of his jaw, wishing I could make the hard edges melt away. "I know what tattoo I want."

"You do? What is it?"

I sat up, tugged his hand. "Come on. I'll tell you when we get there."

ALL IN

My heart swelled with pride as Theo unlocked the door of the shop and I stepped inside. Vegas Ink was no more. Theo had knocked down the wall between it and the nail salon, creating a wide entry. The black-and-white checkered tiles and red walls were gone, replaced by gray hardwood. The entry walls were covered with darker gray wallpaper with a repeating fleur de lis pattern. On them were hung large glass displays of tattoo samples, framed in tomato red. An overstuffed vinyl sofa in the same red color sat against the wall beside the reception desk.

I picked up the Magic 8 Ball there gave it a shake. "Has Teddy become a believer in messages from the Other Side?" I watched for the reply and turned it toward him: *It is certain.*

He smirked. "*It is certain* that ball belongs to Vivian."

I smiled, then tugged his hands. "Show me the rest."

He took my hand and led me further into the space. The hardwood floors continued to four tattoo stations, each with a black reclining chairs and smaller, matching chairs for the artist. Prints by Ann Harper and Ted Gahl were interspersed on the dark green walls with more tattoo samples displays.

The entire place was elegant but edgy, masculine to reflect its owner, but not intimidating.

"It's beautiful." I wrapped my arms around his neck. "I'm so proud of you. Have I said that yet?"

"Once or twice."

His tone was teasing but his smile faded quickly. He led me to his station, and readied a paper and blue ink pen, from his desk.

"So," he said. "Do you want…" He cleared his throat. "Something to do with the baby? Or maybe Jo—"

"I want your blue butterfly,"

Theo frowned, and his eyes looked away, toward the past. "You mean the blue butterfly from that old story? When Jonah and I were kids?"

"The imaginary butterfly that got away."

He sat back in his chair. "Why?"

"Because it's everything you are. You're strong and brave, and you'd take all the pain if it meant making those you love feel it less. You shoulder that burden by yourself. You put on armor and put up walls. But inside, you have this gentle, loving soul. A goodness running down the core of you, all along that steel strength. I want that on my body. The essence of you. I love you, Teddy. I want your love with me, imbedded in my skin for all the days of my life."

"Permanent," Theo whispered.

I nodded. "For always."

Before he could say another word, I climbed into his lap and kissed him hard and deep. He responded with a small intake of breath, and I felt the tension coiled in his body fall away. He kissed me with all his fire and the passion. I felt it come roaring back to life, warming the parts of me that had gone cold after what we'd lost.

"Kacey," he breathed. "I love you. God, I love you so much."

"I love you," I said against his mouth, my hands reaching to undo the buttons on my blouse. I stripped off my shirt, then unclasped my bra. I let them both fall to the floor and lay facedown on his tattoo chair.

"I'm ready."

"I have to sketch it out. Show you…"

I shook my head. "I don't want to see it."

Theo's eyes widened. I saw the pulse dance in the hollow of his throat. "You want me to tattoo it on you, sight unseen?"

"Yeah, I do."

"Why?

"I want that butterfly exactly as you imagined it. Nothing from me to alter or change what it was. No sketch. No stencil. I want your art, Teddy. I'm your canvas."

He stared at me a moment more. "No stencil. Freehand?"

I smiled. "Are you this difficult with all your clients?"

"Only the crazy ones," he said, and in his laugh I heard that he was going to be okay.

I waited while he put on his plastic gloves and stack of soft cloths to wipe away excess ink and blood, readied his needles and inks. I turned my head so I wouldn't see the colors he chose. A few minutes later, I heard his chair groan as he stood, and I felt him over me. Soft lips pressed a kiss to my shoulder blade.

"Ready?" he said, his breath hot on my skin.

I turned my head. I wanted to watch him work. "I'm ready."

Theo leaned over me from his chair, the gun buzzed, and I felt his hand rest on my skin a split second before the sharp bite of the needle. It had been years since I'd had a tattoo, but the pain was familiar. A deep, stinging ache. A good tattoo artist new exactly when to relent, to wipe the blood and excess ink and then go again.

Theo was more than good.

I watched him, watched his eyes—intent on my skin—his movements sure and steady, his own tattooed arms holding the gun, muscles tight against the short sleeve of his shirt.

"Is it wrong to say having you tattoo me is turning me on?"

"Yes," he said, not looking up. "As a professional, I find it highly inappropriate."

I smiled, and bit my lip. I hadn't been teasing. I felt the deep bite of Theo's needle on the shallow skin over my shoulder blade all the way down my spine. The vibration settled between my legs. The need grew with the pain, receded when Theo pulled the needle away, to wipe the blood and ink, and again when he changed the needle.

The texture of the pain changed then. The needle's bite was more of a scrape, stinging brush strokes, as if he were coloring my skin with a marker that's tip was made of glass dust.

"You're shading now," I said, feeling the scrape of the tattoo well across my shoulder blade. "That's a big butterfly."

"A butterfly?" Theo said, intent on his work. "I thought you said you wanted a giant happy face with Shit Happens along the bottom."

"Ha ha," I said, only pretending to be annoyed, while inside my heart soared to see my Theo come back.

After three hours he was done. Three hours watching that beautiful man bent over me, creating a work of art on my body, giving me a piece of himself. My shoulder throbbed but the pain was second to the need I had for him.

"You ready to see it?" he asked. His voice was low, gruff, and if he was nervous, he didn't show it. He looked at me with hunger burning in his eyes.

I nodded. "I'm ready."

I moved to stand in front of the mirror he had on the wall of his station, while he took up a hand mirror from his desk. His eyes swept over my naked breasts as I turned to face him. He held the mirror so I could see my back reflected in the larger on the wall.

"Oh my God," I breathed.

A blue butterfly poised on my shoulder, its wings the color of a summer sky when the sun is about to set. Rimmed in sharp, deep black, shining like onyx where the light caught it. It was so real, so perfectly rendered I imagined it would fold and unfold its wings at any moment, fly off my shoulder and into Theo's palm.

But the butterfly remained on its perch. At the end of the universe.

Theo had rendered an arc of Jonah's glass along the right side of my shoulder blade, a dark piece of sky, shining with stars and star dust within. It streaked across my skin before tapering away into forever, beyond what my skin could hold. Unfinished. But unending.

I didn't say a word, but pulled my gaze from the mirror to the eyes drinking me in. He set the mirror down, then his hand was at the back of my head, buried in my hair, the other pulling me close. He kissed me hard, his mouth demanding everything. I parted my mouth, taking him in deep.

"Marry me," he whispered between kisses. "Marry me, Kace. Be my wife…"

"Yes," I breathed. "Yes, God yes."

We gave ourselves up to each other completely, a perfect harmony of love and lust, our bodies striving to show the other what our souls knew. It was in every touch, every kiss; our kisses were words, declarations made with our hands on our bodies. Promises made with every gasping breath we shared. And the joy I felt wasn't only for his proposal, but for what it meant. That despite our losses, we would keep going. Never give in or give up.

Because love always wins. Always.

EPILOGUE

Theo

I shut off the lights over the tattoo stations and grabbed my jacket from the antique coat stand in the waiting area. The appointment book lay closed on the front desk, Vivian's kitschy knick-knacks arrayed around it. The Magic 8-Ball front and center as usual.

I flipped open the appointment book, as I did every night after the other artists went home. The next day's schedule was almost fully booked. I already knew this: Vivian gave me hourly updates about how well we were doing. Still, I had to see it for myself, see it in black ink on white paper, every night before I left.

I'm doing it, Jonah. Building a life. A legacy of my own.

From the front door, the rap of knuckles on glass. By the light of the street lamp, I could see my father shifting from foot to foot, glancing around the empty parking lot. One hand in his jacket pocket, the other running through his silver hair.

I unlocked the deadbolt and opened the door. "Dad, what's wrong? Mom okay?"

"Fine, fine," my dad said rocking back on his heels. "I thought it was time I saw your place."

I stared. "At eleven o'clock at night?"

"I heard you're really busy. Didn't want to interrupt." He met my eye. "Can I come in?"

"Yeah. Sure." I moved aside and watched mutely as my father came inside my shop for the first time. Both hands in his pockets now, he strolled the small entry like a visitor at a museum, taking in the framed tattoo samples. My eyes narrowed, remembering how my father's face had always been wide open with joy at Jonah's exhibitions. Tonight he was closed off, his lips drawn down, his eyes hard.

I crossed my arms, braced myself against his expression. I wanted to ask what the hell he was doing here. What he wanted. To see for himself how I'd squandered Jonah's money? How I'd gotten an advanced degree but chose to use it for a business that polluted bodies with ink?

Fuck that. I wouldn't say a word. If he had something to say, he could say it, but I was done inviting his disapproval.

"Incredible amount of variety," he said, turning to me. "You can do all these?"

"Yes."

He nodded, strolled deeper into the shop, hands clasped behind his back. I followed after, turned the lights back on and watched him take in my place. He went to the nearest station—Edgar's—and tapped his fingers along the reclining chair's brown vinyl.

"Looks like a dentist's chair," he said. "Does it hurt as much?"

I shrugged. "It can."

My dad inspected the art Edgar had on the wall of his station and pursed his lips. Edgar did our more hardcore designs for our more hardcore clients: snarling wolves with blood dripping from their fangs, horned demons, skulls and flames.

"This isn't your station," Dad finally said.

"No, I'm over there." I jerked my head.

"Can I see?"

I tensed. Since I began tattooing six years ago, my dad had never asked to see my work. Not once.

Doesn't matter. You're a success. You don't need anything from him. Not one goddamn thing.

"Sure," I heard myself say, and led him to my area in the back corner.

He stepped inside the low, wooden walls and inspected the art hanging above: prints of my favorite obscure artists, framed sets of client photos, and the Unfinished Series. Kacey had cut out the *Inked* article and framed that, too.

The silence was getting too heavy as I waited for the hammer to fall, for my dad to pass his judgment. I gritted my teeth, determined to not say a word. To not concede ground.

"Okay, I think it's that one," he said, pointed at a sample of a name in sharp, glassy font. "And that one." He swiveled his finger to a boxy, sturdy Old English font. Turning to me, he took off his jacket and set it on the reclining chair, then began rolling up his shirt sleeve.

"Wait. You want a tattoo?" My arms fell to my sides, the shock stealing my strength.

My father nodded. The eyes holding mine were heavy with regret instead of sharp-edged disapproval. "Am I too late?" he asked, his voice fraying at the ends. He cleared his throat. "I mean, it's late at night…"

"No," I said, my heart pounding in my throat, softening my own voice. "No, Dad, you're not too late."

Another silence fell and we stood within it for a moment, then my dad nodded gruffly and looked away. "Good. So… How does this work?"

I moved into my space with him, flipped on the desk lamp. "Uh, well…" My thoughts were scattered over a wave of nerves, as if this were my first tattoo. "You need to tell me what you want and where you want it."

My dad sat on the chair and tapped the inside of his right forearm. "Right here seems appropriate. And what I want is names. Yours and Jonah's."

I stopped, stared.

"Can you do that? In those styles I pointed out?"

I nodded. "Yeah. Yeah, I can."

I grabbed my sketchpad and pen. I envisioned our names in the fonts my dad wanted and quickly mocked up the tattoo: Jonah's name curling over the top of mine, his font more elegant, mine more solid.

"Something like this?" I showed him the sketch.

His downturned lips turned into a smile, and he looked at me in a way I'd never seen him look at me before. "Exactly like that. You're…incredible."

Twenty years leaned on me hard. Two decades of waiting to hear something like that from Dad. The weight pressed, stubborn and mistrustful.

"You didn't come to the grand opening," I said. I tossed the sketch back on the desk and crossed my arms to conceal my shaking hands.

My father didn't flinch or shy from my stare. "No, I didn't. And I regret it. I regret a lot of things. Actions I took. Words I said I can never take back. But even more, I regret the words I never said."

He glanced around my shop, and then back to me. "I always thought Jonah was the glue that held our family together."

"He was," I said.

"Maybe so," my dad said, shaking his head. "When he passed, we all fell apart. We…stopped. Halted in our tracks, helpless and broken. But not you. You kept going. You took care of your mother when I couldn't. You said you were going to buy your own place and you did. You went back to school so you'd know what you're doing. I see it all now, Theo. You take care of yours. You took care of Jonah all the time he was sick. All the way to his last breath, you were there for him."

"Dad, don't…"

He held up his hand. "Let me finish, or I never will." He swallowed hard, but never looked away from me. "You took care of Kacey when she was alone in New Orleans, drinking herself to a slow death. You stepped up when she was pregnant and you stepped up again when she wasn't. You love her."

I nodded, not trusting myself to speak.

He reached out and put his hand on my shoulder, hard but warm. It passed through the wall, melted through layers of armor, sank into my inked skin until I felt my father touch my bones.

"I see you, Theo. I see you. If Jonah was the glue that held us together, you're the rock we set our backs to. I'm proud of you for that." His chin quivered, his voice cracked. "I'm so proud you're my son."

His hand slid around the back of my head and his forehead pressed mine. We didn't cry. We breathed a shared, shaky breath as twenty years let go of my heart like fists unclenching.

Dad clapped my shoulders and cleared his throat. "Talk is cheap," he said. "Let's do this. Get it done before I chicken out, as the kids like to say."

He waited as I sat in my rolling chair at my desk, transferring mine and Jonah's names to the stencil paper. He eyed me as I set a needle in the barrel of my tattoo machine.

"It's going to hurt, isn't it? I might only get through one name tonight."

"You can handle it," I said, grinning and set his elbow on the arm of the chair. "Ready?"

"Ready."

Just as I readied the needle above his skin, he put his hand on my wrist. "Wait."

I looked up. "Yeah?"

He smiled, patted my cheek like he hadn't done since I was a kid. "Do your name first."

"Jesus, Dad, you're killing me." I had to laugh as I sucked in a breath, let it out slowly until my hands were steady. I bent my head over his arm, holding it gently but firmly. The rotor buzzed. The needle went to work. I watched, almost as if from afar as my name appeared on his skin, imbedded there forever in black ink.

Then Jonah's name appeared under my gloved hands, to the side and above mine. When I finished, I held up a mirror to show him. "See. You're tougher than you thought."

He stared at the image of his sons' names in the fonts he'd chosen.

Jonah
Theo

It was one of the best things I'd ever inked. My brother and I on our father's skin.

Forever.

My dad stared too long, his face unreadable.

He hates it. He hates that I did that to him, and it's too fucking late now. Permanent.

I rubbed the back of my neck. "Well?"

"It's perfect," Dad said hoarsely. He caught sight of his reflection, and the tears welling in his eyes. He coughed, shot me a stern look. "Stings like a son of a bitch, though."

I gave him his look right back. "Good."

His eyes widened. For a moment he stared at me, agape. Then a bellowing laugh burst from him, warm and rich, and it filled my shop and every last empty space in it.

EPILOGUE

Kacey

Three years later

The weather in Pittsburgh is hot and sticky at the late end of August. I feel the humidity wrap around me the second I lug my six-month pregnant body out of the rental car and into the parking lot behind Carnegie Mellon's University Center. Theo unstraps our fourteen-month-old daughter from her car seat in the back.

"Stroller?" I ask.

"Nah, I got her."

Theo doesn't like using the stroller. He prefers to hold Frannie as much as possible. He settles her into the crook of his arm, his tattoos stark against the teddy bear pants my mom sent us. She sends Frannie something at least once a month. Through her granddaughter, she's coming back to me, slowly. Little by little, day by day.

We stroll across the Carnegie Mellon campus. The walkways are less crowded in summer. Only a few students cross our path as we make our way to the University Center.

We pass through a little grove of oak trees, their boughs shading little wrought iron tables and chairs. I smile, as I always do, when I see the placard naming the grove: *Legacy Plaza.* Theo meets my eye and smiles too.

Sometimes it's hard to believe in coincidences.

Frannie looks around with mild curiosity. Her light brown eyes—the same as her father's—catch a squirrel spiraling up a tree trunk. She has one pudgy fist crammed against her mouth. Her hair—brown and curling like her uncle's was—falls around her face, rounding it out even more. She's a calm, happy baby. She hardly ever fusses and I can count on one hand the meltdowns she's had since officially becoming a toddler. I wonder if she remembers the trip we made here last year.

She was only a few months old, still part of me likes to think she was aware of everything.

Immediately inside the University Center, the atrium opens up and out, revealing the installation. A riot of color and light in the sunlight streaming in from the windows. Every piece of glass illuminated: the waterfall, the sea life and the blazing sun hanging above.

"Your Uncle Jonah made that," I tell Frannie.

"Pretty! Pretty!" she says, her eyes lighting up.

As we do every year, Theo and I move to the small stand to the right of the installation. On it, a smiling picture of Jonah next to a short—too short—biography. I touch the letters of his name. Theo stares at his brother's face. A moment of silence. The sun outside slips respectfully behind the clouds. Even Frannie is quiet. A shared inhale and exhale, then we smile at each other.

Frannie reaches for the colorful glass and Theo brings her closer to look it. He shows our daughter the exhibit, helping her name the turtles (*turls*) and the octopus (*ock-a-push*).

I ease myself onto a bench and run my hand over my bulging belly. The baby within—also a girl—kicks and turns and pushes against my hand as if she's trying to break out. She never stops. Often times I'm up in the middle of the night, walking back and forth in our living room, singing lullabies to her until she falls asleep. She's going to be a handful, I can tell already.

Like her daddy... I think. I look to Theo holding Frannie, and my heart feels like it's too big for my chest.

The sun emerges again, slicing rays through the installation. I lean back and watch the glowing light play off the colors. The pearly sea foam, the flowing cerulean water, the violets and pinks of the coral reef.

But it's the sun—Jonah's sun—that always draws and holds my eye the longest. It's a tangle of orange, yellow, and red curls. Chaotic, yet perfect, every piece as it should be. Except...

My eyes are drawn to the left side of the sun. A gap in the tangle where one ray of orange light is missing. The curl that smashed to bits when the installation was hastily removed from the Vegas gallery three years ago. It hit the floor, scattering into a thousand shards that were then crunched underfoot to dust. Only a few slivers remained for Theo and I to find.

Theo comes to sit beside me. He settles back on the bench and

Frannie slumps against his chest, her eyes drooping. I reach along the back of the bench to rest my hand on my husband's shoulders. I kiss him lightly, then our baby's chubby cheek. We sit for a minute in silence as Frannie falls asleep.

I see Theo's eyes drink in the installation. He smiles as he finds the gap in the sun.

"It's still my favorite piece," I say.

Theo takes my hand, kisses my fingers. "Mine too."

I feel the warmth from the red and gold curls of glass. My love for Jonah a warm glow in my heart, like a sun that never sets. And deeper within, a fiery core—my love for Theo burning with powerful, unending intensity.

"Love again," I murmur. "He told me to love again, and I do. So much."

"He told me to love you." Theo's warm, soft eyes meet mine. "But I already did. So much."

Only the tiniest wave of shock courses through me, followed by understanding. "I knew," I say. "Somehow…I think I've always known." I touch his cheek. "Why tell me now?"

Theo shrugs, making Frannie rise and fall with him. "Felt like the right time. And the right place."

I smile and turn my gaze back to the glass. "Yes, it is."

We sit a little while longer, and when we rise to leave, Theo takes my hand, our daughter tucked securely in his other arm. I recall when he and I got up off our knees in the Wynn Gallery. Shedding tears and love amidst the shattered remains of Jonah's glass. We stood up together, emerged from the barren space together, bonded not in shared grief, but in shared love.

Theo and I, a treasure out of the ruin.

THE END

ALL IN

DISCLAIMER

This is a work of fiction in which a character, after months of steady intoxication, chooses to quit drinking alcohol cold turkey without medical intervention. The side effects she suffers are very serious, and in real life, could pose life-threatening consequences. It is advised that anyone in a similar situation who wishes to quit heavy drinking *not* do as she did, but seek professional, medical assistance.

Substance Abuse and Mental Health Services Administration (SAMHSA) hotline:
1-800-662-HELP (4357)

Alcoholics Anonymous
http://www.aa.org/

SNEAK PEEK

Ava Lake is married to her job. As assistant managing editor for the *World Voice,* a London-based activist magazine and growing political news organization, she spends her every waking minute exposing injustice and acts of terror across the globe. It is a tough, and often dangerous job, and she is relentless at it, leaving little time for anything or anyone else.

Keaton Stafford is a freelance photo-journalist and award-winning documentarian, who has stumbled across the biggest story of his life. He's on the verge of exposing a multi-national group of arms dealers who are providing weapons to terrorist cells. He wants to take down its leaders—many of whom aren't living in the caves of Afghanistan, but the penthouses of the world's cities—and cut off the flood of weapons to those who seek only to sow fear and terror.

Keaton brings his story to the *World Voice,* where he clashes with its ice queen, Ava. Both stubborn, both fiercely dedicated to their work, Keaton and Ava must come together to uncover the story of a century while they struggle to keep their relationship professional. Ava fights to protect her heart that she's never entrusted to anyone, even as Keaton, with his easy charm and wit, seems to be stealing it right out from under her.

But when events take a deadly turn, Ava is faced with her hardest test: to keep her perfect, if lonely orderly world…or let love in, no matter the risk. No matter if it costs her everything.

Add to your Goodreads TBR: http://bit.ly/2bMK82e

Printed in Great Britain
by Amazon